THE CREW

NAMED

DARLEEN URBANEK

ISBN 979-8-35097-239-9 eBook 979-8-35097-240-5

*This book is dedicated to those who seek
God's face. May they find Him as I did.*

*I am deeply grateful to God for the inspiration for this
story, my dear friend Linda for her unwavering support
and encouragement throughout the book-writing process,
and my husband for his unshakeable belief in me.*

*I thank my dear friends who have stood
by me with patience and love.*

*If just one sees Jesus for the first time or understands
Him on a deeper level because of any of these words,
my heart will be full and purpose accomplished.*

WHO WE ARE

We are **The Crew**, as we call ourselves. How we met, well, that's quite an exciting story.

But before we get into that, let me tell you a little about myself; the others can introduce themselves, too.

I am Zoe. Some would call me brave; some would call me tough, smart, or crazy. Others would say I'm a 16-year-old who has worked through her less-than-favorable upbringing. You see, my father left when I was maybe two years old. I never saw him again. I don't remember him, probably a mental safeguard, so don't feel sorry for me. I don't. Without going into too many details, my mother should never have had children, but, alas, here I am. She remarried when I was four. My step-father's name is Charlie. He is a nice enough guy with the patience of a saint, so he lets my mother boss him around. He's a truck driver, so he is gone a lot. But, when he was around when I was young, he took me places. Places like Karate, baseball practice, and gymnastics. I think mainly this was to get away from my mother and her complaining. We were friends more than father-daughter. We still are.

I got a job last year at a restaurant in an area they updated to look like an old, quaint village.

After a particularly difficult argument with my mother, I made the decision to leave home. I sought refuge with friends, passing off my stays as innocent sleepovers. Unbeknownst to my mother, Charlie, in a gesture of support, bought me a small, weathered car as soon as I was old enough to drive. Despite its humble appearance, it was a symbol of my newfound independence and resilience.

When it became springtime, I started sleeping in the car on pleasant nights. Again, I don't feel sorry for myself; it was more enjoyable to sleep in the car than being around my mother. I would go to school at Winston High during the day, shower in the gym or at the restaurant where I worked after school, and do homework at the library or a friend's house.

The owner of the restaurant was a nice lady who knew my situation. She lives upstairs over the restaurant, lets me use her facilities whenever I want, and lets me eat there for free. Charlie would come to the restaurant often and bring me money or things from the house I wanted or to see how I was doing. I assume he told my mother where I was, but she never reached out to me. With his help, I earned enough to get by, plus I knew he had my back. The restaurant owner will let me rent a small apartment over the garage behind the restaurant as soon as the current renters move out. With all this, it was still a relief not to argue with my mother or constantly hear criticisms. Life was good.

Alex

Hi. My name is Alex. I go to school at Winston High, too. I guess you could call me a jock. I play sports and am pretty good at them. Most of the kids seem to look up to me, literally, as I have grown a lot in the last year. I'm 6'2 now. Even taller than my dad.

My Dad is a good father. He is the CEO at the biggest company here and travels – a lot, like at least a couple weeks every month. He goes all over the world. He's a pretty important guy…I guess.

He always asks about my games and school and what's going on in my life - but when I answer, it's like he is only listening to be polite while thinking about his next project at work. He means well. He and my mother wanted me to go to Winston High, not in the fancy neighborhood where we live, to get a taste of the 'real world,' different kinds of people, and life outside of excess before they send me to college. The Winston people seem pretty nice to me. Often nicer than the kids in my neighborhood.

My mother is a high-level defense attorney. She is usually in meetings with clients, at court, or doing whatever she does to prepare for cases. I typically get to talk to her at least once a day, sometimes more.

I watch her, surrounded by papers and documents and pacing on the phone, and actually feel sorry for her…and me sometimes. But she means well, too. She will ruffle my hair and kiss my forehead as she rushes to her next meeting.

They love me.

They have always bought me anything I needed or wanted, sent me to bodybuilding training, entered me into sports leagues, or got me the best equipment for my sports activities. I don't brag or anything to the Winston kids. I don't want them to feel bad. I often give them my "old" equipment and stuff. It's better than anything they could have gotten on their own, and I like the smiles on their faces when I ask them if they want these things that "I was going to get rid of." Or say, "Would you take this off my hands so I don't have to take it to the resale shop?"

They are good people.

My biggest confidant, and the one who is around the most, is our housekeeper, Mrs. Griffin. She has been living with us since I was a baby. She used to take care of me and drive me around before I got my license. She does the housekeeping, shopping, and cooking and helps me with my homework. She's more like an aunt to me. We talk a lot.

Bridgett

Hello there. It's Bridgett. You will notice me. I'm the tall, thin girl with long, shiny blonde hair whose clothes are on-trend and whose makeup is applied perfectly. *Blah!* I hate my "image!" Yes, I'm all those things, and most would call me beautiful, but I want to wear jeans with holes in them, no makeup, and scuffed-up tennis shoes.

But my parents were so proud from the start to have a little girl who was so pretty. Neither of them was more than average in the looks department, so they were surprised at their good fortune. Even as a baby in the carriage, strangers would tell them how beautiful I was and how they should get me into commercials or something. They went out of their way to promote me and did get me into commercials. Eventually, they were told I should be a model. They sent me to modeling school. I was taught how to apply makeup, what kinds of clothes to wear, how to style my hair, how to walk, how to stand up straight and give myself an 'air of importance'. My parents were delighted.

But what about me? What about what "I" wanted? I would rather be comfortable in sweats, live off the grid in the mountains somewhere, and be an artist. I always have drawing paper and pencils in my room, and you will find me drawing animals, people, or happy scenes. Drawing is my place of peace. I can get away from the life that, somehow, I had fallen into. My parents adore me. They are so happy with my 'progress' and how I will move into professional modeling when I graduate from Winston High. I dread it.

Henry

Henry is my American name. My real name is Asim, but my mother changed it when we came here. We are refugees from Sudan. I was very young, but I remember a hard life there. We had very little food, mostly a millet porridge, and I remember the water tasted like mud. It was dry and hot. I remember being afraid most of the time. There was war in our country. My father originally got us all to Ethiopia. Many of us were in camps, mostly women and children like me. There was a lot of sadness and abuse. I don't remember what happened exactly, me being only maybe three or four, but my mother and I somehow got to America. My father was not able to travel with us. He was a brave man who fought for us and loved us. I have asked my mother many times what happened to my father, but she won't speak of it. She says he will join us someday. I miss him.

I know it was a long process coming here. My mother was helped with the language, but it is still difficult for her. I was seven years old when we came, so I still have a bit of an accent, I am told, but it was easier for me to learn English than for her. They helped us find an apartment and helped my mother find a job. There is a Middle Eastern community in this area, and the manager at the supermarket hired her despite her language challenges. She doesn't make a lot, but we have all our needs met. We have clean water, food – much better food than I'd ever tasted before - and a place of our own that is more than a tent. Her favorite saying is "Inskla Allah," which means 'if Allah wills.' A lot of the anxiety from my life still exists in me. I still have a fear that appears for random reasons. I find my solace in food. So, not only do I look different with my dark skin and sound different with my accent, but now, being plump has caused me to be the point of many jokes from my fellow students at Winston High School. But to be able to go to a school and learn is a privilege, so I am thankful for that.

Max

Yo! Max here. I'm the last of "The Crew." I find myself here now because I went on a joy ride with my low-life buddies one Friday after skipping school. I was probably going to get kicked out anyway for missing most of the semester, so who cared? After my parents got divorced, I didn't care about much anymore.

My buddies and I wound up drinking too much, driving way farther than we had planned (like two days, I think; I was drunk most of the time) until we ran out of money. My friends decided to rob a little store to get gas money to go home, more liquor, and some food. I wasn't into it, but I figured if I was going to eat the food and drink the booze, I'd better participate. I didn't figure anyone was going to get hurt. I was wrong. Three of us went in. Only two came back out. I didn't know Jake had taken his father's gun. It was smaller than the shopkeeper's gun. The story didn't end well.

I wound up in juvenile prison for a time. Luckily, I was sent there because I didn't have a record and was only an accessory to the crime. The bail was not much, but my dear, sweet mother wouldn't bail me out. She said I was going to be a loser like my dead-beat father and good riddance. Her new boyfriend would be happy I am gone anyway. He and I hated each other.

After her accident, my mother started drinking even heavier than she did before, add in prescription pain medications and some surgeries to try to fix her back, and she just got mean. I remember my father having to work three jobs to try to pay the bills. He was gone a lot. We had to move because we couldn't pay the house payments. She blamed my father for everything. He couldn't take it anymore. The day he left, he knelt in front of me, holding both my shoulders in his big, rough hands, and looked me square in the eyes. He said he couldn't afford to keep both my sister and me. He said I would need to take care of myself, that I was a tough kid, and to be strong. He had tears in his eyes. So did I.

After that, I caught the brunt of her anger. I had to help her do everything that a young boy shouldn't be expected to do. I had to cook, clean, get groceries, help her dress, and…. well, everything.

Then she met Barry. He moved in. It got worse. I reminded her of my father, she said.

When they were drunk, which was pretty much all the time, Barry would hit me, or take the food off of my plate and throw it in the trash because "I hadn't been a good boy that day," or break my school pencils when I was trying to do my homework. She would laugh.

That seems like a long time ago now.

When I was let out of jail, they gave me my paltry belongings, and I walked out of the front door of the building into a city I didn't know, had no idea where I even was, no money, and just the clothes on my back. There were people everywhere, rushing off to … somewhere. I looked around and had nowhere to go, no one to turn to. That's how I wound up sleeping on the streets and begging for money. I tried to get a job, but no one would hire a dirty, smelly kid who had no address. I walked and walked and finally found this little old-fashioned-looking town and this park.

CHAPTER ONE

N ow that you've met all of us, I'll tell you how we came to be "The Crew."

Zoe - It was an evening in June. The night was calm and quiet. A gentle breeze rustled the leaves in the big trees here in the park in the middle of town. Most people were off the streets by now as the shops were closing. The old-fashioned street lights came on. The park was supposed to look like a Victorian-era one with a gazebo and benches around the circular area. Water fountains, bushes, and beautiful, brilliant flowers were planted all around—a very pleasing place to be, especially at night.

I sat on one of the benches across from my workplace restaurant. Mr. Cznarki was turning off the lights in the drugstore on the corner. I could see Myla, my boss at the restaurant, back upstairs in the apartment she had above it. My car was parked across the street, where I would sleep for the night. That car might be old, but it still ran and was pretty comfortable with pillows and blankets; at least it was my home for now. I almost have enough saved for the security deposit on the apartment above the garage behind the restaurant. Myla had talked to the building owner, and he was okay with me moving in. It won't be long. I'll figure out what to do after that. I always do. I am self-sufficient and can figure things out on my own; thank you very much!

As I sat there, I turned my head too quickly and felt the pain in my shoulder, and the swelling around my eye began to throb. I rubbed my shoulder. I'm sure I had a black eye by now with how it felt. But that young guy who had come into the restaurant and followed me out into the alley when I closed for the night probably felt worse. Who did he think he was anyway? Just because he had heard I was on my own, he thought he could try to push himself on me. The slap to my face and his big hands on my shoulders didn't stop me. I pushed back and went into my Karate training moves. Then, I brought my knee up - hard! And when the pain finally subsides, he will think better of trying that again! If Myla had seen what happened, she would have called the cops on him, but I didn't want to get sent back to my mother's house. So, I'll be fine. My mother said she wanted to raise me to be tough. Well, I guess it worked, especially with all the Karate training Charlie had taken me to. I'll have to thank him for that when I see him next.

Alex - After the game, I walked slowly back to my car after stopping in town for something to drink to replace my electrolytes. "I sure sound like Ms. Griffin now," he chuckled to himself. "And boy," I thought, as I stood gazing at nothing in particular before getting into my Jeep, "it sure was a good game. We had won by a landslide! I thought we had an excellent chance to go on to win this year's championships. The crowd in the stands had gone wild."

I broke out of my reverie and noticed a girl on a bench in the park across the street. It was getting dark, and the street lights were coming on, but I could tell all the way from where I was that she looked like she was in some kind of distress as she rubbed her shoulder. "Hey," I thought, "it looks like Zoe from school. I've heard she's a tough little cookie. She is about 5'2" tall, but you don't want to mess with her. She's one of the top students in her classes, though. I wonder if she needs help. I'll brave it and go ask.

Zoe looked up and saw that jock from school, Alex, coming her way." He'd better not try anything," she thought, "or he'll get it too!"

Alex walked cautiously up to the girl sitting on the bench. "Hi. Are you Zoe from Winston?"

"Yes. What do you want?!" She replied gruffly, sitting up straighter and pointing her face toward him defiantly, ready for a fight if necessary.

"Ah…nothing, really," he said sheepishly, "I just wondered if you …. Well, you looked like you might…. oh, anyway, mind if I sit down?" Alex answered.

Zoe looked at him with narrowed, mean-looking eyes, telling him he better not try anything. "Sure, go ahead," she said.

He looked like he had been in a fight himself.

Alex plopped down on the far side of the bench. He suddenly felt pretty tired. He leaned forward, put his elbows on his knees and his head in his hands, and rubbed his head, trying to rub the tired-ness away. He sat up, pushed his thick hair back that had fallen into his face, and looked at Zoe briefly.

Neither said anything. They just sat, looking out over the quaint downtown setting before them. It was on the outskirts of the high-rise urban area to the east and had brick-paved streets and brightly colored storefronts. The night was quiet in this part of town.

Zoe still watched him out of the corner of her eyes, ready to spring into action if necessary. She rubbed at her sore shoulder again.

Alex just sat quietly, winding down after his strenuous game.

The street lights came on, and the few other people in the area got in their cars and left.

Soon, it was deserted except for these two. It was very peaceful.

This area had been renovated and restored a few years back to look like the original town before all the high-rises and businesses had been built further uptown. A little piece of 'pretty' before you got to the less-than-desirable neighborhood beyond it toward the west, what people called the slums.

The slums were where the original town had been before all the jobs had left. It was pretty much deserted now except for stray cats, dogs, and the occasional homeless person. It looked like the set of an old, deserted town in the west, except with trash cans and junk cars instead of bramble wood and horses.

The city officials had wanted to get tourists back into this area as they came through off the interstate, so they had built up the shoreline, created cabins for vacationers, put in docks and restaurants, restored the few buildings that had originally been here in the park area, and built others to look old and quaint. It had worked. Marketing and revitalization had brought many visitors in the summers. The once empty small stores had become little shops where you could find anything from hand-made items to beautiful art to mugs with the town name on them. The buildings were painted bright, happy colors. There were flower pots with beautiful plants all over town hanging from the street lights that had been made to look like old gas lanterns. The signs above the stores looked old-fashioned, and there were a-frame ones on the sidewalks, highlighting sales and food items, which were then folded up at night to be brought back into the stores.

Most of the more expensive homes were toward Lake Lesure'. The docks there were brightly lit with string lights, and there were many drinking and eating establishments.

Summer was good. Winter, it died.

Many shop owners went to warmer climates in the winter, so the town became half of what it was in the summer. But it was home.

Finally, being brave enough to look over at Zoe, Alex asked, "So what happened to you?" He nodded his head toward her eye.

"Some guy, "she answered, giving him her tough look again. "He thought he could take me on. He quickly found out differently". She put her good arm defiantly across the back of the bench and stared at him, not even trying to hide her puffy eye.

Alex did his best not to smile at her bravado. "Yep, she definitely was a tough cookie," he thought.

He relaxed back on the bench. "Well, I'm sorry you had to put up with that," he said. Although he meant it, he looked away before she saw him smiling at her tough attitude.

Changing the subject, he looked around and commented, "Nice night, eh?"

Zoe relaxed a little, seeing he meant no harm, and took her arm down from the back of the bench. Even though he was a big guy, he didn't seem to be a threat.

"Yeah, nice," she answered as she looked at the peaceful scene and relaxed her sore body.

It was such a calm, quiet night that they both just sat there enjoying it.

Alex realized how physically tired he was, so he didn't move to get up to leave right away, and Zoe just sat as well, not anxious to go to her car to sleep just yet. It was pretty dark by now. The streetlights sparkled at night, and the shops turned off their lights, making the scene even more picture-like.

Zoe noticed the tall blonde everyone was so taken with at school walking out of one of the shops and locking the door – her name was Bridgett. Zoe had one class with her, but she never talked with anyone and always had her head up high like she had smelled something yucky. Yes, she was beautiful, but Zoe considered her a snob.

Alex had never felt she was very approachable—she was pretty, yes, but he had never tried striking up a conversation with her—he didn't like rejection.

They watched Bridgett walk across the street toward the sidewalk at the park's edge, obviously headed home. Maybe she had an after-school job at that small store that sold candles and beauty products, Zoe thought. She never seemed to talk or look at any-one at school, and when she did, it was just curt, short answers or head nods. Zoe didn't think she had many friends.

You couldn't help but watch this tall, blonde beauty stride con-fidently across the street. But as Bridgett walked with her head held high as she usually did, like an Egyptian princess or some-thing, she tripped on the curb, falling abruptly to her knees on the street in front of her. Her backpack and purse flew out from her arms, spilling everywhere. Zoe and Alex shot up to help her as they were only about 20 feet away.

When they got to her, she was getting up, looking at her bloody, scrapped knees, sobbing quietly.

"Hey. You, okay?" Alex blurted as he reached out with his hand to help her up.

"Oh yes, just lovely!" she shouted as she took his hand to stand up, straightening her short, designer skirt as she did," Of course I'm not okay! Look at my knees!" She dramatically pointed to her knees. "I've got a photo shoot this week! My parents are going to have a fit!"

Zoe and Alex looked at each other at her outburst, not knowing how to respond.

Zoe shrugged at Alex as Bridgett stood staring at her knees. Then she started to move around to collect the items that had fallen out of Bridget's purse and backpack, wondering at all the makeup and beauty paraphernalia she carried and at Bridgett's anger about her knees, which didn't look that bad.

Alex helped Bridgett hobble the 20 feet to the bench, walking as if she had a broken leg, as Zoe stooped, trying to get all the items back in her purse, which was proving difficult. Why would anyone need to carry all this stuff with them anyway, she wondered. She stuffed things back into the backpack and huge purse and took them to the bench where Bridgett was sobbing.

Alex stood there, wondering what he should be doing.

"Let me have that!" Bridget snapped at Zoe as she snatched her items out of Zoe's hands, dropping half of them out again. "Everything was all sorted and stored in specific areas," she blurted out, and she started sobbing again. "Now look at them! And my makeup bottle is broken, and the brushes will need to be washed, and…look at this mess!" She forlornly laid the purse on the bench and looked at it miserably.

Zoe and Alex looked uncomfortably at each other again. Zoe shrugged her shoulders when Bridgett began looking into her backpack. She could see why she didn't have any friends, Zoe thought!

"Here's some tissue that fell out of your…." Zoe tried to say as she handed her the small pack of tissues.

"Give me that!" Bridget snarled as she grabbed the tissue, pulled one out, and loudly and grossly blew her nose in one, and then grabbed another and tried dabbing at her bloody knees.

"Hey! I'm just trying to help you!" Zoe bristled. She was not good at hiding her feelings, and she started to get miffed by Bridgett's dramatic attitude.

Alex looked like he wanted to sneak off into the sunset. He didn't want to get involved in the middle of an argument between one beautiful blonde who was very ticked off and acting like it was the end of the world over a scraped knee that anyone else would have just blown off - except maybe a three-year-old, and another, soon to be angry, short spit-fire. But he stayed. "Your knees don't look too bad," he said, trying to make her feel better.

She started sobbing again. She cried for a few minutes and then dabbed her eyes, as you could see the anger diffuse. Her tall, beautiful stature slumped. She now actually looked at them. "I'm sorry, you guys, it's just…. it's just…" she said, blowing her nose into the tissue and looking up at them—black makeup now running down her cheeks. " Oh, you wouldn't understand," she said.

"No, I guess us mere mortals don't understand how a couple scuffed up knees could be the end of the world," snorted Zoe as she plopped down on the other side of the extended bench.

Alex rolled his eyes as he moved behind the bench, anticipating the fight between them to start, but surprisingly, Bridgett just sat there and looked dejectedly down at her knees, dabbing at the blood with another tissue.

There was silence in the park except for Bridgett's quiet sniffling. Finally, Alex walked around the front and sat down in the large gap between them, thinking it was a dangerous place to sit, but he was tired and hoped perhaps his presence would diffuse any further drama.

They all sat for a few minutes. He offered sheepishly, "They've stopped bleeding."

Zoe glanced at him, rolled her eyes, and looked away.

"Yes, they have," Bridgett said as she slumped farther and looked sideways at him. She looked neither tall nor beautiful then, just like a normal kid.

"Look, I don't much care about this," she pointed to her knees, "other than the stinging that is. And I don't care much about any of this either," she pointed to all the beauty paraphernalia, "or this," she stood up and motioned up and down her body.

She picked up a few stray items and placed them into her back-pack. "I don't want to be… all this! I just want to be a regular kid, like you guys".

Alex and Zoe looked at her, then each other yet again. "Then why don't you be?" Zoe said a bit briskly.

Bridgett shot Zoe an angry look like she was going to get into it with her, but then sat back down on the bench, looking straight ahead, "Because my parents have spent a lot of money and effort trying to give me this 'image.' They want me to become a famous model or get into acting or something." She turned to look back at the two, abruptly slumping back onto the bench.

Zoe had never seen her slouch.

"But I don't want any of that. I never have. But how can I disap-point them?" she said, almost to herself.

There was an uncomfortable silence.

"Yeah, parents can be a challenge," Alex offered. Mine say they will stand behind whatever I want to do with my life…as long as it's being a CEO, lawyer, doctor, or something. They don't say that out loud, but I know that's what they expect." He paused. "I don't have a clue what I want to be."

He sank back against the bench as well.

"Oh, but I do know what I want to be!" Bridget perked up and turned to look at Alex." I want to be an artist! I love drawing and painting. I've loved it since I was a kid – it's not just a hobby; it's my passion. It makes me feel at peace and ...... I think I'm pretty good at it, too. But every time I show my parents one of my pictures, they brush it off and say, "That's nice, honey. Now, let's practice walking again like the teacher showed you."

Zoe sat forward a little to look around Alex at her. "You are kinda stuck there, aren't you? Maybe you could have Mrs. Clawson, the art teacher, talk to them? Maybe…."

"I've thought of that," Bridgett responded, cutting her off. "But they have spent a lot of money sending me to these modeling schools, buying me all the most fashionable clothes, and teaching me how to walk like a model… Well, they aren't exactly wealthy people. I know they've sacrificed for me. I would feel bad."

All three sat back now and said nothing for a while. They looked out at the now empty town square, deep in their own thoughts.

Zoe broke the silence. "I got a scholarship into Thompson Academy to become a law enforcement officer. I'm going to take classes now at Winston that will help me: criminology, forensic science, US Government." She spoke more gently. "I'll start the academy after graduation."

"Wow, that's great," said Alex.

"Yes, that's wonderful," Bridgett responded half-heartedly as she looked over at her – finally really looking at her. "Hey, you are Zoe from school, right?" Bridgett asked.

"Yes, I am Zoe," she answered, "and I've had parent problems just the opposite of you. I'm mostly on my own now, but I'm very happy about that".

And Bridgett looked at Alex now, "And you are the guy who plays in all the games."

"Yes," he answered, looking at her, realizing she was very beautiful even with raccoon eyes and slouching. "My name is Alex."

Bridgett nodded at both of them.

Alex noticed both girls' temperaments had softened. He didn't have to sit on the edge of his seat anymore.

They heard movement behind them. Alex, Bridgett, and Zoe turned to see someone standing by the big tree in the middle of the park.

"Hey, isn't that that Henry kid?" Alex asked.

"Yep, that's him," said Zoe, and she waved at him.

"He seems like a nice kid," said Alex. "I hate it when the kids pick on him like they do, just because of the way he talks with his broken English, his dark skin, and because he's a big guy who obviously likes food the way he does. I think I'll go talk to him. Be right back." Alex got up and walked toward him, waving hello as he went.

Henry had by then sat down at the base of the tree and was opening a bag with a large submarine sandwich in it. As Alex approached, they spoke briefly, exchanging names and confirming that they both went to Winston High. Henry reached up to offer some of the sandwich to him, but Alex waved him off. They talked for a minute more about school before Alex strolled back to the bench, sitting down heavily. "He says he likes it outside on a night like this instead of being in the small apartment where they live. Besides, his mother is still at work," he said. "He's a nice kid."

"I have a hard time understanding him sometimes. He's from Africa somewhere, isn't he?" asked Bridgett.

"Yes – he's told me, Sudan. And, yes, he is a good guy," Zoe said as she waved back at him again. "He's had experiences that have shaped him in ways we can't even begin to understand. We talk sometimes when he comes into the restaurant when there aren't any customers. He sure likes food, maybe because he didn't have much before they came to America. He smiles and closes his eyes when he tastes new things that I give him that will be thrown out – especially sweets. He has helped me with some of my history classes. He's pretty smart, considering his language barrier and the fact that he started school later than most kids his age. His resilience and determination are truly inspiring.

"Wish I could eat sweets," Bridgett said dejectedly, "or even a sub!"

Zoe and Alex turned and looked at her.

She saw them wonder at her statement. "Oh, they monitor my calories....to help me," she explained. Then, smiling at them, she said, "I'm so sick of vegetables!"

They all chuckled.

"At least you got some food!" It seemed a voice came at them from nowhere. They all jumped. Then, a figure of a ragged, dirty, small-framed kid rose slowly from behind a bush near the bench. Alex jumped up and looked like he was ready to punch whoever it was. Bridgett stood behind Alex as she peeked around his shoulder. She was almost as tall as him.

Zoe turned quickly at the voice. She, too, looked ready for a fight if need be but then relaxed when she saw who it was.

"Oh Gosh, Max! You scared the daylights out of me!" Zoe said. Alex and Bridgett turned to her incredulously, wondering how she knew this kid.

Zoe turned to Bridgett and Alex. "This is Max, you guys. He's a runaway street kid I encountered just a few weeks ago. He was wandering up and down the main street one night. I asked him who he was, and he told me his story. He said he was hungry and had nowhere to go. He asked me to please not call the police." She smiled down at Max, who was listening to her talk about him with a grin on his face. "I could see he was just a scared kid," she reached over to where he had plopped down on the grass and gave him a tender punch on the arm. "So, I gave him a sandwich from the restaurant, which he devoured in two bites, and then drove him to the homeless shelter I knew about on the other side of town. It isn't too far away, so he occasionally shows up here in the park or in front of the restaurant."

Max finished, "The shelter gives me a place to sleep and food once a day, but I can only stay three days in a row. Then, I have to fend for myself before I can go back." He smiled at Zoe, "I kinda lied about my age, being officially a minor, but I guess they knew Zoe from her volunteering there a few times and trusted she wouldn't bring any trouble to them."

Bridgett wrinkled her nose at the smell of him. His clothes were pretty dirty and very much in need of repair and a shower would be in order. She moved back away from him as he moved closer toward them.

Max noticed and said defensively, "Oh, excuse me for offending Ms. Beauty Queen here." He moved back to the grass a few feet from the bench.

The rest of them saw he was safe, even though ragged and smelly, and sat down as well.

"How is it going at the shelter, Max?" Zoe asked.

"Well, they try. I seem to be a problem because of my age, even though I told them I was 18. The beds have bedbugs, and I'm kinda afraid to use the showers…. there are…well, not nice things can happen to you when you are in there." He looked sheepishly at them, then lowered his eyes. "They have a laundry, but what would I wear while my clothes are getting washed? The food is okay, but you don't get much if the cafeteria lady isn't happy with you. She has her favorites. But it's better than nothing, for sure," he said and smiled at Zoe.

"You know, my parents are both gone for the week." Alex ventured enthusiastically. "Mom is in New York consulting some high-level case, and my dad is in Singapore…I think. Why don't you come home with me, just for the night, and you could get cleaned up? I think I have some old clothes I was going to get rid of that might fit you. They will be way too big, but better than …. Well, better. That is, if you want. You don't have to." Alex offered, not wanting to sound like he thought he was better than him.

Max looked at Zoe, who nodded her approval; after all, he didn't know Alex at all, and he had had some bad experiences with men who 'wanted to help him.'

"That would be, well…awesome," said Max softly.

"I'll go get my car…." Alex stood excitedly.

Before he could take two steps, **BAM!** A loud boom shook the night air, and it sounded like a bomb had exploded! All the lights in the park and down the streets went out. They all jumped to their feet. Then, out of nowhere, in the middle of the intersection in front of the park, a glowing white horse and rider–both of immense size—appeared out of nowhere! They all backed up and held onto each other or the back of the bench out of fear.

This immense figure, who was almost iridescently glowing, looked like a Viking or some warrior from the old days. He was about nine feet tall and built like a wrestler. He wore some kind of shiny metal armor. There was a dense, blueish-white cloud around him and the horse. The horse reared up and snorted. The rider's helmet covered most of his face, but his long, thick, white hair looked like it flamed out from underneath it. The horse was bigger and more muscled than any horse they had ever seen, even in the movies. And, as it reared up as high as the trees as the rider spoke. His voice was like that on a loudspeaker in a stadium and boomed, making the ground quiver. It was so loud, he didn't have to shout, but he said to them, *"**YOU HAVE BEEN NAMED!**"* And - **CRACK** - he disappeared! He was gone!

The streetlights all came back on in an instant. The park was once again quiet, eerily quiet.

They all started talking at once! Henry ran over to where the others were, looking dumbfounded and scared, too. His ordinarily dark skin was pale, and he was shaking. Max, who had fallen back to the ground after trying to stand, stayed there, looking scared to death.

"Did you see that?! What was that!?" Henry shouted, his hands shaking.

Bridgett's eyes were as big as saucers. She kept mumbling, "That couldn't have just happened. Did it really just happen?"

Alex's eyes darted around, his heart pounding in his chest, as he braced himself for the unknown: "What…. Who…. Ah, where did he vanish to?! What was he?!"

Max's body jolted upright, his eyes wide with disbelief. "My God, if you guys hadn't witnessed it, too, I would have questioned my sanity! That was beyond bizarre!"

Zoe's gaze lingered on the spot where the horse and rider had materialized. She sprinted to the intersection, her heart racing, in a desperate search for any trace the rider might have left behind: a scorch mark, a hoof print, a whisper of his presence...nothing. A frown etched on her face, she returned to the group, who were still in a state of shock.

"And what did he say?" She asked. "You have been named? What did that mean?" She stood thinking pensively as the others continued to freak out.

When they settled enough to let her question sink in, everyone looked at her and each other, shaking their heads, visibly shaken by the experience, the bright light, the booming sound, the .... what was he, a 9-foot rider on an immense horse!?

"I have no idea," Alex said as if to himself, shaking his head and looking back at the intersection.

"Wait a minute!" shouted Henry, "Look at this! Was this here before?" He stooped to pick up an oddly colored, almost sea green but luminescent, scroll-like piece of paper from the grass beside the bench. He hesitated a minute, looking at it as if it were a slimy slug, but he picked it up, holding it by its edge.

Zoe walked over and took it from his willing hand. She looked at each of the others before unrolling the scroll. She slowly unrolled the heavy paper, which seemed to be losing its luminescence as the seconds passed. In the center, there was simply an address—11444 Mound Road.

She looked at it for a moment, and then the others gathered around to see what it said. They all stared at the writing, then at each other.

Bridgett broke the silence. "So, what does this mean?"

"Is there something there that we are supposed to see?" Max wondered.

Zoe noticed Henry shaking and put her hand on his shoulder–"Hey Henry, it's all right." He was still shaking, possibly remembering the war-torn place he had come from because of this noise, the suddenness, the lights, and the trauma.

He just looked at her and nodded his head. He took a bite of his foot-long sub as his hand shook.

Alex said, "Hey, I wonder if we should call the cops or something and report this?"

Max started to back away. "The cops"?

"And who is going to believe a bunch of kids that claim to have seen a glowing giant on a horse the size of an elephant who appeared out of nowhere, boomed a message, and then disappeared all within 10 seconds?" Zoe said as she plopped down on the bench, obviously in deep thought. "And, this paper certainly wasn't here before the rider appeared," she said, looking at the small scroll. "It's got to have something to do with him. And still, what did he mean 'you have been named' – by who, for what, what kinda name?"

"Yes, that's the big question. Well, one of the big questions," said Bridgett as she plopped down on the bench, visibly shaken. "This has been a strange evening, very strange indeed."

Alex started pacing. "Well, it's got to mean something. When was the last time you saw anything like that? Like *never*, maybe in a science fiction movie, but never in real life!" he answered his own question. "And what does this scroll and address mean? And why were we in this park, at this time, all together, on this night?" He stopped and looked at them as if they were going to chime in an answer, but all he saw were blank looks.

"Okay!" Zoe stood up, "Just sitting here rehashing it isn't going to help us figure it out. The most logical thing to do is to get back together, say this weekend, and go to this address and see what is there. Maybe we will know what he meant and what we have been 'named' for?"

Henry looked around anxiously, hoping someone would say this was a bad idea, but no one did.

"I do not have a vehicle," he said.

"That's not a problem," Alex said, "I can borrow my Dad's Van. He will still be gone next week, and he said I could use it any time I wanted. It will fit all of us."

Bridgett said, "I can be here. I will just tell my parents I'm going to a friend's house to practice my model walk or something."

"Your model walk?" Max chimed in sarcastically as he started strutting around, making fun of her.

"Stop it, Max. We all have our stories; let it alone," Zoe said as she rolled up the little scroll and put it in the pocket of her hoodie.

Bridgett looked thankfully at her as Max snorted a little.

"I don't know, I'll have to check my calendar," Max said sarcastically and laughed.

They all laughed except Henry, who was still shaking.

Henry stood behind the bench, eating his sub as if it were protecting him. "Do I need to be there?" he asked.

"Yes, Henry, you are part of this," Alex said. "We'll all be together; it will be okay".

A car rolled into view. The headlights hit the group, blinding them. They put their arms up in front of their eyes. Then, a car horn sounded, and a woman's voice called. "Bridgett! Bridgett!" and a rather short, plump woman opened the car door. She ran around toward Bridgett with her arms outstretched. "There you are! We were so worried, Bridgett! You were supposed to be home long ago, sweetheart! Oh my!" She shrieked as she looked down. "Look at your beautiful knees! What happened, my little darling?" Bridgett's mom asked as she fussed over her daughter's scrapped knees.

"It's okay, Mom. I fell. We can cover them with makeup or something. My friends here were helping me, and…"

Her mother cut her off. "Well, come on, my precious." She ushered her daughter to the car while nodding briefly to the group, gathering her purse and backpack on the way.

Bridgett looked back and nodded goodbye over her mother's head as they walked. Her father had remained in the vehicle, but he could be heard exclaiming over his 'poor daughters' knees,' He asked, "Should we take her to the emergency room or something?"

"No, Dad, I'm fine, really, just fine…."

"Wow," Max said as they drove away, "I think I'd rather be homeless."

Alex and Zoe smiled at each other.

"Hey, come on, Max. We gotta get you cleaned up and fed. Mrs. Griffin makes great food and loves to see me bring home friends." Alex started to walk to his car with Max in tow, then, thinking about it, stopped and looked back at Zoe. "Hey, do you need anything? Do you have someplace to go? You, okay? You can come too. There are plenty of extra bedrooms." "Thanks," Zoe replied. "I eat well at the restaurant, and it's a great night to sleep in the fresh night air while I think about tonight's events. Anyway, it will only be a couple more weeks before I get my apartment. Thanks for asking, though."

Alex turned back to Max, and they walked down the main street to where Alex's car was parked.

Zoe turned to gather her things and noticed Henry still standing, looking very sad.

"You okay?" she asked.

Henry looked at her, "No, not really. I get very nervous inside. I don't know how to control it sometimes. Sometimes, I think of the fighting and bad people we had to run away from, especially that night. Sometimes, I feel like running away from myself. Then, I get depressed because I don't seem to have any control over my own feelings. It gets confusing." He looked at her. "I'm sorry, Zoe, I shouldn't have made you listen to all that. I feel like such a failure. I have been given a new life here in this wonderful country of America, and I should be happy all the time." He looked at her again with a little tear in his eye. "And yet I am not."

"Henry, it's all right," Zoe's voice was gentle, her touch comforting as she patted him on the back. "You're not alone in this. Many people, including me, have felt this way. You're not a failure, Henry. Remember, I'm here for you, always ready to listen."

Henry shoved the last of his sandwich in his mouth as he walked with her to the edge of the park. "I wish I could be like you," he said, "so brave and always knowing what to do."

"You are brave, too, Henry. Look at all you've been through, and yet you are doing well in school; you have overcome learning a new language and coming to a new country with many different ways. You are very brave!"

Henry looked at Zoe and smiled. "When you say it that way, perhaps there is a little bravery in me. Thank you. I will try to be part of this adventure with all of you".

Zoe smiled at him as they parted ways.

CHAPTER 2

THE QUEST BEGINS

I t was Saturday afternoon, and they all gathered back at the park as they had agreed the week before. Alex pulled up in his dad's van. Max was sitting in the passenger seat, waving and looking very happy. He was clean, his hair had been cut, and he wore nice, clean clothing. He had a smile on his face from ear to ear. When Alex had taken him home last week, Mrs. Griffin, the Housekeeper (alias Alex's friend and confidant), had insisted Max stay the week since Alex's parents were gone. She had arranged for a haircut, she 'found' some clothing that was Max's size, he had eaten very well all week and slept in the spare bedroom - on sheets that smelled like flowers! During the day, when Alex was at school, she talked to Max and listened to him as no one in his life had ever done. She called the shelter and spoke with the people in charge, asking for Max's consideration in explaining his situation. He had appreciated that so much. Then she had called different places to find out what training programs she could get him into for job placement/apprenticeships. And as soon as he passed his GED test, he was going to be able to begin! He had never had anyone treat him like this. He didn't know if loving someone in a week was possible, but he sure loved Mrs. Griffin.

Zoe had just gotten off work from the breakfast crowd at the restaurant, so she still had her apron on as she strode over to the van. She untied it and threw it on the seat as she got in, still thinking about the odd strangers who had been in the restaurant that morning. They hadn't acted like most tourists. They hadn't talked to each other or smiled or anything. They just sat there looking around solemnly. Strange. But she shook it off, remembering they had more important things to think about today.

Henry followed Zoe after he had stopped at the corner drugstore to pick up some chips and soda pop. He did not look too excited about going, but he got in the back of the van, smiling sheepishly at them as he did.

Bridgett, the last to appear, had just finished her shift at the boutique down the street. Her long legs carried her swiftly to the van. Her mind was filled with curiosity and apprehension. "Was this really the best idea?" she wondered. But she pushed those thoughts aside, smiling as she sat next to Zoe.

"Hey," Zoe said to her, her voice filled with determination. Bridgett half-smiled back, her eyes betraying a hint of worry. "Hey back," she replied, her voice soft but filled with excitement and nervousness.

Alex turned and asked if everyone was ready. He was the most excited to see what they would find.

The four had stopped in the halls during the week at school when they saw each other. Again, they wondered what the sight they saw could have been but did not want to talk about it much in public.

They had agreed on the meeting time and that they needed to figure it out. The sight had stayed with each of them.

"Yep, we can go now," Zoe said, "we're all here. I've got GPS going on my phone, and here is the address." She pulled out the small scroll on the piece of parchment paper, but it was no longer luminescent. The numbers on the paper were starting to fade.

Alex put it in gear, and they headed out. The address was in the 'not so great' part of the old town, a place that seemed to have been forgotten by time. They drove, mostly in silence, each in their own thoughts, looking out of the windows as the surroundings transformed into an almost post-apocalyptic scene. The houses were mainly boarded up or falling down; their once vibrant colors now faded. Broken bicycles, trash cans, rusting cars, and wandering dogs littered the streets. Some houses looked like they had been on fire but had just been left in rubble. The old commercial buildings were mostly concrete, run-down, graffiti-covered, empty factories. Some looked like stores, but they had long since been looted, and the windows were broken.

"I've never been out this far," Alex broke the silence.

"It kind of looks like my old country," said Henry solemnly, "except the buildings were blown up from the war there."

Zoe looked at the GPS. "We only have two miles to go," she said.

The buildings were getting farther and farther apart as they were getting into open country.

"This must be where they did the manufacturing in the 30's that we learned about in class," Zoe said aloud. "Good thing the tourists came, and we were able to build a new community."

They were coming to where the valley began. The hills had been mined and depleted long ago. "This is depressing, eh?" she commented.

They all mumbled agreement.

The GPS indicated the destination was the next driveway on the right. They pulled into a large lot with dead trees. There were no other buildings around it. It looked like the last commercial building past the end of the old town. Beyond it was farmland, broken-down barns, and old mines.

The GPS said they had arrived at their destination. It was an old factory with windows broken out and doors partially open. Alex put the van in park, turned it off, and they all sat silently for a moment, looking at the building. "Well, I guess this is it," he said.

"Now, what do we do?" asked Max, looking a bit nervous.

"We get out, go in, and see what we need to see," Zoe responded. She shoved Bridgett to move out of her seat since she was closest to the door. Bridgett was startled at that but opened the door and got out. The rest piled out of the van.

 Zoe took the parchment scroll out of her pocket, but as soon as she did, the paper crumbled like powder in her hand and blew away. The others looked at her and each other wide eyed. Henry, especially, had gone a little ashen at the sight of that, and his eyes were as big as saucers. Bridgett clutched at his arm, then realizing what she had done, pulled her hand away quickly, looking a bit embarrassed.

Zoe broke out of her startled moment. She looked at the others, and you could see the resolve come across her face. She strode forward and determinedly set off briskly toward the building, "Come on. Let's go."

Everyone looked at each other, and then Alex strode off following Zoe. Max quickly leapt behind him. Bridgett and Henry looked at each other like - okay, if we have to…. and reluctantly brought up the rear.

Zoe and Alex got to the building first. Alex was tall enough to wipe the grime off the glass window and try to look inside. "Looks pretty empty," he said.

Zoe pushed at the heavy metal door that was coming off its hinges. It creaked and moved a little but then fell more sideways with a heavy clunk.

Max had walked around the side of the building. "Hey guys!" he yelled. "There's another door over here, and it's open."

They rushed around to the side and found him peering into the building. "It's pretty dark in there," he said.

"Wait, I'll pull up my flashlight on my phone," said Alex.

Alex walked through the open door with the flashlight on, Zoe right behind him, turning hers on as well, and Max right behind her. Henry and Bridgett stood at the door and peered in.

The flashlight showed rubble, turned-over tables, debris falling from the ceiling, old machinery, and lots of graffiti. Alex and Zoe walked slowly forward. Max dug around in the trash behind one desk and yelled, "Hey, I found a cool, old cowboy hat!" He brushed it off.

"Don't you dare put that on! It's filthy!" yelled Zoe.

Max looked at it and tried brushing some of the dust off but said, "Okay, but I'm taking it back with me!" He held the trophy hat in his hand.

"Whatever," said Zoe as they kept walking.

Bridget and Henry looked at each other outside the building and at their surroundings. There was nothing around but brush shrubs, old bottles and trash, and a considerable drop-off down the valley. You could see they unanimously decided it would be safer with the others and hurriedly joined them, stepping gingerly over piles of trash and who knows what else. Bridgett pulled up her flashlight, too. Henry didn't own a phone because of the cost.

It looked like there was another room ahead, so they all headed there, almost moving as one. When they pushed open the door, they found themselves in the middle of a large, empty area. It looked like it might have been where the large machines once stood. The ceiling was 30 feet tall, and the broken windows at the top let in enough light they could see, so they turned off their flashlights. Birds flew overhead, and they all jumped at the sound. There were also sounds of rustling in the corners, probably rats. They all stopped and looked around at the vastness of the room. The building didn't look that big from the outside, but here they were.

Zoe pointed toward the middle of the room toward the back. "Look at that," she said. Their eyes followed her point, and there was a sunbeam streaming in from one of the high windows, and it lit up a small table with something on it. They looked at each other again, a bit of fear showing on each of their faces, but Zoe moved toward the table in the cavernous room. Her steps kicked up dust as she walked. They all slowly followed, coughing through the dust.

When she approached the table, she found a round, black object on it. It was about the size of a kid's Frisbee but shiny, smooth, and thick like a stone. Strangely, it didn't look dusty or old like every-thing else in the building.

She looked at Alex as he approached.

"What do you think that is?" he asked quietly.

"Don't know," she offered but stepped slowly closer to it. She circled the table to see if it was hooked up to anything and was maybe a booby trap or something. She looked back at the others. Some debris fell from the ceiling on the other side of the room, and they all jumped. "Well, this is ridiculous," said Alex, "we won't know what it is unless we look at it," so he moved forward and hesitatingly put his hand toward the object.

"Be careful," said Henry in a quivering voice.

"Yes, be careful," chimed in Bridgett softly.

"Oh, just pick the stupid thing up already!" shot Zoe.

Alex slowly picked up the round object. Zoe and the others came closer to see. It was about six inches round and an inch thick. There were five smaller round indentations around the top and one larger one in the middle. He turned the disk over in his hands, and there was nothing to see on the back or the sides. They could see no openings or seams.

"What is that thing?" Bridgett questioned aloud.

"I don't know," said Zoe as she took the disk out of Alex's hands, gave it a quick once over, and handed it back to him. There didn't seem to be much to see.

She walked around the area and looked up and down the empty room. A variety of old tables and chairs were strewn about. There was some old machinery and tools but nothing else to look at in the dim light.

Then she spotted the heavy metal door at the far end of the room they had tried to open to get in. It was ajar enough to let light in. "It doesn't look like there's anything else here for us to see," she said as she started to walk toward the door. I think we can push that door back from this side and get out. The van should be right on the other side."

Alex put the disk in his jean jacket pocket, and he and Max followed with the others close behind.

The old door was thick, with big metal rivets around the edges. Alex first, then the others put their weight into an area of the door and pushed as hard as they could. It completely fell off the hinges with a **crash** and lots more dust. When the dust cleared enough so that they could see, they climbed over it into the sunlight, coughing and waving the dust clouds away from themselves. They walked out into the brightness of the day.

Bridgett pulled the designer scarf off her neck and wiped at her face to get the dusty grime off.

After coming out of the darkened building, they had to squint for a minute at the sunlight.

Near the door, there was an old picnic bench. Bridgett, Max, and Henry walked over and sat on it.

"Let's check this thing out," Alex said. He pulled the round object out of his pocket and put it on the bench.

Bridgett wiped it with her scarf, then jumped back, falling off the bench as she moved backward so fast! Zoe caught her by the arm so she wouldn't fall to the ground.

"What is it?" Zoe asked, looking at the frightened girl.

Bridgett couldn't speak; she just pointed at the disk and kept moving back away from it.

Zoe and the rest moved to look closer at the object. Underneath each of the smaller circles on it were their names—chiseled into the hard metal of the disk! This freaked them all out.

"How" … "Who?" …. Bridgett exclaimed as she backed away and stopped, reaching behind her and touching the front of the van.

"Why would our names be on this!" Max said with a catch in his voice.

"How could *our* names be on this, even my native name of Asim…?" Henry asked quietly, his voice shaking.

Then, they all went silent, standing away from the bench that held the mysterious disk.

Then Henry said, "That big, white, powerful guy on the horse in the park said 'we were all named'…."

The rest looked at him wide-eyed, remembering.

"Yes, and we were given this exact address to find this…whatever it is," said Zoe. "But what does it mean?" She moved back toward the picnic table and straddled the seat to look more closely at the disk in front of her.

No one offered an answer.

"I don't know, but this isn't the safest place to be," said Alex. "We probably need to get out of here. It will be dark soon".

"I'll second that," said Max.

"What are we going to do with this thing?" asked Alex as he picked it up and looked at it more closely, then put it back down like it was a hot potato.

"I guess we have to take it with us and try to figure it out. It's got our names on it, after all," Zoe said.

She slowly picked up the shiny metal disk and started moving back toward the van, turning it over and over in her hand. The others also walked toward the van but gave Zoe and the disk a wide berth. When she got back to the van, Zoe grabbed the apron she had thrown on the seat, wrapped the disk in it, and slid it under the seat. They drove in silence for some time.

Bridgett broke the silence, startling them all.

She yelled, "We have to turn around! I left my scarf back on the bench, and it's a very expensive one my mother gave me." She had panic in her voice.

"Okay, okay," Alex grumbled as he made a U-turn in the old town, trying not to get a flat tire on any street debris.

They drove, and when they turned into the driveway where the building had been, they all stared in disbelief! The building was …. ***gone***…!

But that was impossible.

Zoe checked her GPS, which gave this empty lot as the address where they had been.

Now they were all really freaked out.

Alex pulled forward in the driveway, and there, blowing in the wind, caught on the side of the picnic table, was Bridgett's scarf.

No one uttered a word. He put the van in park, slowly got out, and walked over to the picnic table. He looked around, seeing nothing but the drop-off on the other side of where the building would have been. He pulled the brightly colored scarf off the side of the bench it had wrapped itself around. He looked around again as if hoping the building would reappear, then walked back to the van, shut the door, and just sat there for a minute. He turned to look at everyone else, and they had the same look of disbelief on their faces. Zoe felt under the seat and pulled out her apron. The disk was still there and still had all their names on it. She wrapped it back up slowly and put it in her lap. Alex handed Bridgett back her scarf, who hesitatingly took it. Everyone looked at it as she held it out away from her, their minds filled with unanswered questions.

Alex slowly backed the van out of the long driveway and drove the long distance back to the park. No one said anything.

As the van pulled up to the park, it was getting dark.

"So now what," Alex asked no one in particular as he put the van into park.

"We all need to get together again to figure this out. There have been too many weird things happening," Zoe said, her voice filled with a sense of urgency. "I'd better keep the disk because if your parents find it, it will bring up a lot of questions we can't answer yet, and you can't take it to the shelter, Max."

They agreed, looking at it like they didn't want it anywhere near them anyway.

"I will have enough money to begin renting the apartment above the garage behind the restaurant this week," Zoe said. "How about we meet there next Saturday?"

They all agreed that would be the best, and each went off to their own thoughts for the week.

CHAPTER 3

AMAZING MAX

The following weekend, they all found their way to Zoe's new apartment. There was an alley behind the restaurant in between where the two-story garage was located along a long row of storage garages for the other businesses on that block. The alley provided room for delivery trucks to bring items to the stores and restaurants. It was relatively clean, though. To get to her apartment, a metal stairway was attached to the side of the garage to get to the second story. The usual trash bins lined the alley that the garbage trucks would empty once a week. It wasn't the most glamorous place to live, but it was heaven on earth to Zoe. It meant freedom, no more verbal abuse, and peace and quiet, a fresh start that filled her with hope.

The first to arrive was Henry. He looked like he hadn't slept well all week but commented how lovely her apartment was as he pulled some licorice from his pocket. Alex came next, immediately followed by Bridgett.

Alex and Bridgett were used to nice homes, in Alex's case, big, fancy ones, but were very gracious, commenting on her place. She had painted everything a nice bright color and had made curtains for the windows using her boss's sewing machine and scrap fabric from the fabric store down the street. They were lively and cheerful. She had scrubbed and polished everything and made things pleasant. The kitchen only had a propane cooktop, but she was okay with that. Myla, her boss and friend from the restaurant, gave her a couple of pots and pans, a few dishes, cups and silverware, and some old sheets. The refrigerator was ancient and had one of those old freezers on top that you had to scrape the ice out of occasionally, but it worked, so it was just fine with her. The small couch there had seen better days, but Zoe had gotten an old, brightly colored bedspread from the resale shop and covered it, and it looked cute. The small bedroom had a twin bed, a windup alarm clock, and an old dresser that she had painted a cheerful color as well. The old kitchen table was metal and had four mismatched chairs, but Zoe thought they were beautiful. Overall, she had made the place look bohemian and cheerful. She smiled from ear to ear as each one came in. She had put in a lot of work over the week and was very pleased with her handiwork. She had plans to keep shopping the resale stores for other items she needed as time passed, but it was perfect for now. It's much better than sleeping in the car and showering at the gym or Myla's.

As they came in, Zoe offered them soda from the two bottles she had gotten and poured the liquid into paper cups. This was the first time she had ever had 'company,' never at her mother's house. No one ever came there. She sat on the floor as they talked.

All her work over the week had kept her mind off last week's strange events. The others hadn't had the same luxury of forgetting about it.

Alex said he hadn't been able to sleep very well at the beginning of the week, and Henry and Bridgett agreed.

Henry said he still could not sleep as the anxiety had gotten worse than he had ever had it before. He could not tell his mother why he was so distraught, "She would have prayed to Allah to heal

34

me as she has in the past. But he has not." He said forlornly as he looked down dejectedly.

Bridgett said she told her parents she was acting nervous because she was just worried about her upcoming tryout for the modeling gig they wanted her to get. They said they understood and comforted her.

Alex said he had not told Mrs. Griffin, who was usually his confidant, simply because the whole thing was so…. unbelievable, even to him. His parents had come home on Monday, but as usual, they superficially asked what was new and how he was, but then immersed themselves in their work issues. Sometimes, he felt sorry for them. This last week, he felt sorry for himself, too, because of all his wondering. Besides, they would probably have made him see an expensive psychiatrist if he told them what he saw and what happened. "We did see all that, didn't we?" He wondered out loud.

The others just shook their heads in the affirmative.

Zoe went to her bedroom and pulled the disk from her small dresser. She now had it wrapped in a small orange towel. She placed it in the middle of the small dining room table and then pulled up a folding chair to the table. They all stared at the orange towel.

Just then, Max knocked on the door, and Zoe yelled, "Come in, it's open!" Not that she had to yell too loud; the place wasn't that big.

Max busted in, grinning from ear to ear, happy to see his new friends. Then he looked at all their sleep-deprived faces and the orange towel on the table with the disk in it, and he sat crossed-legged on the floor.

Zoe began, "We have to try to figure out what to do with this thing and what all this means. I mean, we all saw the same things

– the horse and rider, the note, the disappearing building. We all heard his words, 'You have been named.' Why us? What kind of name…...? Then our names being on this thing…" She unwrapped the towel from around the disk, and they all glared at it. Then she noticed the small circle above Max's name lit up!

They all saw it and looked at Max, who was still on the floor, grinning from ear to ear. He hadn't seen the light on the disk from his location yet.

Since they had all slowly turned to him, staring at him with weird looks on their faces, he said, "What…...?"

Zoe held up the disk and showed him the light above his name. His face dropped, and his jaw fell open. Then, he quickly looked back and forth between the rest with a scared look.

"Why is your name lit up, Max?" Alex asked. "Did something happen this week to you? Do you have any idea why this might be?"

Max sat for a minute, and then a light bulb went off on his face. He jumped up, becoming very excited and animated. He talked with his hands, walking around the room as he spoke, looking at no one in particular, talking as if to himself… "Did something happen to me? Wow! How can I explain it? Well, I will start from the beginning…

After Saturday and the crazy disappearing building and finding this disk thing, our names, the horse and rider and all… I went back to the shelter, kind of freaked out. Sunday, I was sitting in the cafeteria staring into my cup of soup, trying to figure things out, when this guy came up and asked if I would mind if he sat at my table. I waved him to sit, although I watched him as some folks at the shelter can be weird. He didn't say much as he ate; he just kept watching me out of the corner of his eye. Most everyone cleared out of the cafeteria, and it was just him and me sitting in the corner. He was an older guy with a white beard and those big eyebrows that almost covered your eyes. His hair was white too and long but pulled back in a ponytail, but that wasn't unusual to see at the shelter. He was kind of a teacher-looking kind of guy.

"My name is James; what's yours?" he asked me with a gentle-sounding voice.

He seemed like a nice guy, so I told him my name.

He just sat there for a while, looking out the window next to our table as I continued to look for answers at the bottom of my now-cold soup bowl.

Then he asked, "Is something troubling, you kid?" He asked it in such a kind, gentle way; I thought, 'Hey, I have to tell someone what happened, and I will probably never see this guy again, so if he thinks I'm crazy, what's the difference?" So, I told him everything! From me getting into trouble with the law, my home life, my jail time, the horse and rider in the park, the note, our names on a black disk, the crazy disappearing building – all of it. He just listened patiently with no judgments and no comments. Then I said, "And I'm trying to figure out what all this means. I mean, what are we supposed to do? How did I get involved in all this? What's supposed to happen? It's all so confusing! I don't know what to think!"

James waited for a minute, then said, "It's a 'God thing,' kid."

I told him I didn't know what that meant. He said, "You will."

"I looked at him and told him I got the same feeling of peace from him that I got from Mrs. Griffin, that nice lady at your house, Alex." He pointed toward Alex as he walked by on his trip around the tiny living room.

He said, "I know Mrs. Griffin very well." That made me sit up straight.

"You do?" I asked.

"Oh yes," James said. "She sent me here to talk to you."

"She did?" I asked again.

"Let's go out in the garden and talk," James said.

In the garden, James told me how he used to be a Pastor in a small church in old town and how, after the factories closed and they quit mining, all the people moved out. He said he had moved across the country to a big church out there. Eventually, he longed for his family and moved back. His family had all moved or died in the meantime, and he was between jobs right now, so that is why he was here at the shelter. Mrs. Griffin was a distant cousin, and when they had spoken, she told him she would have taken him in if she had her own home, but she could not since she lived with some rich folks uptown. He said, and she asked if I could look you up. Max, she cares a great deal about you."

"She's the nicest, kindest, most gentle person I have ever met," I told him. "I wish she was my mother. Things could've been so different."

"Things can still be different, Max," he told me, pulling an old, ragged Bible from his duffle bag. He read some of it to me.

It sounded nice, but I told him I didn't really believe in God, but he said that didn't matter because God believed in me.

After about an hour of listening to him, something inside changed. Something inside me wanted what he was talking about, and somehow, I knew what he said was true. I asked him how I could ever be good enough to go to Heaven. He said I couldn't. But he told me how a way had been made. That very hour, he asked me if I believed. I told him I did; he asked me if I trusted. I told him I absolutely did. We prayed together, and I felt free!"

Max looked everyone in the eye! "I feel freer now still. I can't explain what happened, but my whole life and mind have changed on the inside! I don't hate everyone anymore! I don't feel sorry for myself. I don't care what happened to me in the past. I don't know what all this means, but the future is beautiful. God will show me - us, what to do! He gave me this little bible, and I read it every day!" Max pulled a small, black bible out of his shirt pocket and showed it to everyone. "There's some good stuff in here!"

He stopped and looked excitedly at everyone, waiting for them to reply happily. It seemed no one knew quite what to say.

"That's great, Max," Zoe finally said. "I'm glad you had such a good talk with your new friend."

Max said, "Well, James never came back to the shelter after that day, but do you want to see....?" He started to show Zoe the little Bible, but she put her hand up quickly.

"I'm good, Max, I'm good," Zoe said.

Max looked disappointed.

"What about you, Alex? Want to see?"

"No, thanks. I have one of those myself that Mrs. Griffin gave it to me. But we have to figure out this disk thing…" He turned back to the table, as did the others.

Max looked at all of them, and you could see him deflate. He had thought they would share his joy and want to know all about it…. He went and sat down on the couch. He had thought his new friends would… well, he didn't know what he had thought. He put his little Bible back in his shirt pocket.

CHAPTER 4

NoT FIGURING IT OUT

As they turned back to the table, they looked at each other, slightly shrugging their shoulders without Max seeing and wondering if they should react in some way. Then, they looked back to Max sitting dejectedly on the couch. Since they didn't know what else to say to him, they turned to the disk.

Bridgett said, "So why do you think Max's light came on this week? Do they come on when we are happy or learn something new? And if yes, what does that mean?"

Everyone shook their heads with no answer to give to her and looked down at the disk.

"My mother would say 'it's a sign from Allah' of some sort," Henry offered. "Want me to ask her?"

Everyone shouted, "***No!***"

Henry got wide-eyed at their response and sat back in his chair.

"We don't need anyone else involved right now," Alex said, "Especially an adult."

"We need to figure this out better before we tell more people, especially adults, about it. Max's friend James was understanding. Most won't be." Zoe said. She got up and started pacing, silently thinking, stopping at the sink and looking out the window.

"Well, it must have something to do with what happened to Max," said Alex. "I have no clue what that something was, but it was something."

Max looked up and nodded at that but said nothing.

They spent a couple of hours trying to put the puzzle pieces of their experiences together but just got more and more frustrated.

"I guess we just meet every week and see what happens," said Zoe. "We can meet here. It's the safest place. And let's set up an emergency contact phone group. If you get a message that says…ah… how about, 'disk now,' it means we need to meet up right away, no matter what you are doing. If you get in trouble and need help - send a cell message to the group and put in 'disk now' and where you need us to go - like 'disk now Winston High' or 'disk now - my house.' How does that sound?"

Everyone agreed and set up a group text.

"For some reason, we are all in this together," Alex said. "We need to trust each other and agree to help each other with whatever this thing turns out to be. We were told we were 'named.'" He thought for a minute. "We will call ourselves…. The Crew! Yeah, that's us! We don't know exactly what that means yet, but we'll go with it. The Crew! Kinda catchy, don't you think? A team name, just like in sports! Do we all agree?" Alex said.

Each one nodded in agreement, even Max from the couch.

"Next week, then," Zoe said.

And they all left, Zoe, smiling at Max and patting him on the back as he left. He stopped for a moment as he walked past. He looked at her as if he wanted to say something, but then he just kept going with his head down.

CHAPTER 5

RESOLVE REOPENED

As planned, they met weekly for a while. They talked about what they had seen and experienced—the disk, the disappearing building, all of it—over and over and over again. They came up with numerous crazy possibilities but just as quickly discarded them as not fitting the scenario.

Classes ended, summer was here, and they would be approaching another year at Winston High.

Zoe was pretty excited about the scholarship to the police academy if she passed the special curriculum they asked for.

Bridgett's parents had gotten more photos taken for her portfolio – they were excited, Bridgett, not so much.

Max had passed his GED with flying colors and had gotten into a computer tech apprenticeship program at the local community college. He went to school and then to work. He was going to program robotics and was pretty good at it. He had applied to a government-funded apartment complex that Mrs. Griffin had found for him and would be moving there from the shelter as soon as they started paying him in the apprenticeship program. Max would stay with Alex when his parents were both out of town, at least every couple weeks, so he was well taken care of in the meantime.

Alex's parents had taken him to a few colleges on free weekends to check them out. He enjoyed the time with his parents but not the colleges they wanted him to attend. He just didn't feel it. He still didn't know what he wanted to do.

Although Henry was extremely smart, he couldn't afford college. He didn't have plans for after he graduated. His mother assumed he would start working and provide money for their daily lives. He seemed more and more depressed about it as the spring and summer wore on.

Amidst the ebb and flow of their lives, The Crew's weekly meetings became less frequent. The once-regular gatherings, where they would share their experiences and theories, were now scattered and sporadic. Sometimes, when Zoe was held up at the restaurant, the others would convene in the park. Other times, it would be just a few of them, as the rest were preoccupied with their own commitments. The dynamics of their group, once tightly knit, were shifting, mirroring the changes in their individual lives.

The disk hadn't changed. Answers had not been found. The next year at Winston High was looming on the horizon.

Zoe called a meeting asking everyone to attend.

It was the Saturday afternoon two months before school was going to start. Everyone came to Zoe's apartment just like they had in the beginning, but now it had become quite a cozy little place. Zoe had purchased, been given, or found secondhand treasures that filled her little place with comfort and cheer. There was a comfy blue chair and a small, round, wooden, antique-looking coffee table that Alex had given her from his parent's basement, which 'no one was using.' She had found some cute lamps at the thrift store; one, she painted all different colors in the grooves at the bottom, and the other, she had painted the shade with a vibrant pink. She had also found a couple more mismatched dining room chairs that fit in nicely after she painted them with black and white checks and different colors at the balls of each spindle. She had found a rug in the trash that someone was throwing away when she drove past an uptown home. There was nothing wrong with it. It had an oriental design with pretty colors everywhere. After she had washed it, it was perfect in her living room. Her bedroom had a colorful bedspread with flowers all over it, another thrift store find, and a small dresser that she painted to match the other one. She had accomplished quite a boho, colorful, pleasing, and comfortable look in her short time there. Everyone smiled as they entered. When you walked in, it was like putting on an old, comfortable pair of slippers.

They all sat at the kitchen table (Zoe had also painted the legs black-and-white checks and hot pink, teal, and green designs), which now had enough chairs for everyone.

Bridgett had brought soda pop for everyone and a special present for Zoe—a picture she had painted just for her! It was a lovely landscape with cheerful colors and a serene, still lake. Zoe was delighted and showed her the perfect spot on the wall where it would hang.

Zoe had some day-old donuts from the restaurant that Myla was going to throw away, and Mrs. Griffin had sent some chips and snacks when Alex said he was meeting with his friends.

Some of them hadn't seen each other in a month or more, so they enthusiastically greeted each other and shared what had been going on in their lives. Their kinship was quickly reestablished. After they talked and ate for a time, and the conversation was dying down, Zoe went to her bedroom, pulled out the orange towel, and brought it to the table. She placed it in the middle and slowly unwrapped the disk. They all stopped talking and looked at the disk. It hadn't changed. They looked at each other.

Alex broke the silence. "Okay, so now what do we do?"

"Yeah," Max said, "we've hashed and rehashed about this forever now, and nothing has changed …except me (and he smiled sheepishly at them all)."

It was true. He had changed quite a bit. The straggly, angry, smart-mouthed kid had begun to take care of how he looked, didn't cuss anymore - well, except once in a while, a few choice words would slip out - and he now smiled a lot. He always had his nose in a book, learning programming that he found he was really good at, and sometimes they caught him in that little bible he carried around with him everywhere. They smiled at him. What a transformation.

Bridgett said, sounding flustered, "We can't just quit though. I know we haven't figured it out yet, but there has to be something we've missed, or…. Oh, I don't know".

"She's right," responded Zoe as she picked up the disk and turned it over and around in her hands. It felt like a smooth stone but was very light, like metal. And those circles over their names seemed chiseled out without any mechanical workings. And the writing - the letters their names were written in - it was so…different, almost like a foreign language script. It's recognizable but different somehow. "This thing alone isn't anything we can just forget," she said, her voice filled with a mix of curiosity and concern as if she was on the brink of a discovery.

Henry leaned forward and took the disk out of Zoe's hands. He was not usually one to talk much, but after looking at the disk for a few seconds, he said, "My new friends. This disk and our experiences will grow dim over time, just like my experiences from my old country, but they will never go away. I think we must pursue other avenues to determine what our experiences have meant. Perhaps what happened is common to people in your ...well, our country, but in my mind, the questions need to be answered still. We have this time at school together before we all start to go our separate ways. We must use it to see what the disk is trying to tell us."

Everyone looked at him in silence for a moment.

"He's right!" confirmed Alex, pounding his fist on the table, startling everyone. They laughed at their response. "Sorry," he said, laughing as well. "Instead of trying to forget what happened, we need to embrace it and look for the meaning. We have to go about it differently. Pick it apart. The answer is there! We just need to find it! It could be really important. After all, like Henry said, when was the last time you heard of anyone seeing an Olympic-sized, glowing, thunder-sounding rider on a horse the size of an elephant or an entire building disappear!"

"And, if we needed proof of what we saw, here it is," said Zoe as she held up the disk.

Everyone nodded.

With a determined look, Zoe began assigning tasks based on each person's unique skills.

"OK, so who's good at research? Henry, your knack for it is unmatched! How about you delve into other sightings of horses and riders who mysteriously vanish after delivering messages? And Max, your extensive knowledge of computers and engineering could be useful. See if you can find anything that might resemble the disk. As for me, I'll dig into any documentation on the rider's term 'you have been named.' And Alex....," she paused, thinking for a moment... "see if you can find any historical references in the park itself. Any history. Anything to do with the location itself." Zoe looked around – "anything I've missed?"

Bridgett said, "What about me?"

Zoe quickly looked at her, feeling bad she had forgotten her, "What about if you help Henry? His research could be a big task, and the two of you could find out more if you worked together."

Henry looked at Zoe wide-eyed, and the color drained from his dark skin. He found Bridgett quite intimidating because of her beauty and aristocratic confidence....

"Sure!" said Bridgett quickly and smiled at Henry, who forced a half smile back at her.

Max said softly, "I will pray God will give us wisdom."

No one knew what to say to that. To hear that come from the kid who had been a young alcoholic, jail time juvenile only a few months ago, was.... well, shocking.

Henry offered, "Thank you for your prayer, Max. I will ask Allah to do the same."

Now, everyone else was quite uncomfortable, so the group broke up. They all agreed to meet back in two weeks to report their findings.

Zoe's attention was drawn to the window as they left, each going in different directions except Bridgett and Henry, who were obviously discussing when to meet for their task. Her eyes caught three figures walking down the alley behind them, their slow pace and lack of interaction with each other raising her curiosity. There were tourists everywhere this time of year, but these figures seemed out of place. She watched for a moment, then saw them turn down a side street, leaving her with a lingering sense of unrest.

CHAPTER 6

DISK NOW! HOSPITAL!

It was the following day after their meeting.

Suddenly, they all received the emergency message: **"Disk now! Hospital - Henry"!**

Although it was pretty early in the morning, they all jumped up, dressed, and rushed off to the hospital in town, knowing it had to be critical. Their friend Henry was in trouble!

Max was the first one there since his shelter was near the hospital. He had run all the way! After finding out where he was, he slowly opened the door to Henry's room. Henry was lying in the hospital bed with his mother sitting by his side, holding his hand. Henry quickly introduced Max to his mother, said something to her in their language, and then his mother leaned in and kissed his forehead. She smiled and nodded at Max as she left the room. He didn't know her, but she looked exhausted. She pulled the head covering back up over her dark hair as she left.

"Max," Henry called to him gently. Max walked hesitantly toward the bed. He had many bedside visits with his mother in the past, none of which were pleasant, so he didn't know what to expect. This brought back many negative memories.

49

"Henry," Max almost whispered, "What happened to you? Are you all right?"

"Max, thank you for coming. I needed my friends around me. This has been very scary for me."

"But what happened? Why are you here?" Max sat on the chair near the bed, looking up intently at his friend's face.

"I have been told I had a panic attack. I always knew I was nervous inside much of the time, but last night and this morning, it got really bad, Max …. I thought I was having a heart attack. I almost passed out this morning. My mother was still home before going to work, so she got the neighbor in the apartment next to ours. He agreed it appeared that I was having a heart attack. He had a car, so they drove me here. My blood pressure was very high, they told me. I was sweating, it was hard to breathe, my heart was pounding, I was shaking even harder than I usually do, I couldn't think. It was terrible, Max. I was really scared."

"A panic attack, Henry? I've never heard of that before." Max replied, "So, what do they do for that? What does that mean?"

"Well, they want to keep me long enough to make sure my blood pressure goes down, and they gave me something to calm me. They ran a bunch of tests to make sure my heart was okay, but I guess I'll be here the rest of the day, anyway. They want me to lose weight to help with the blood pressure and to read these papers about how to deal with things better. They suggested I talk to someone, but my mother couldn't afford that. Luckily, this hospital will take people without insurance. My mother was relieved to find that out."

The door to the room opened again, and Zoe, Alex, and Bridgett walked in quickly. They were panting and looked at Henry and Max anxiously.

Alex said as he walked toward the bed, "Henry, are you okay? What's going on? We came as quickly as we could. I drove around and picked everyone up, and then we had to sneak up the stairs because they didn't want so many of us coming to see you at once."

Zoe went around the other side of the bed and put her hand on Henry's shoulder. "You okay, buddy?"

Bridgett silently stood at the end of the bed, looking a bit fearful herself.

Henry proceeded to tell the rest of them what had happened.

Just then, a nurse came into the room. She looked like an army soldier. "Hey! How did you all get in here? One or two at a time is all that is allowed. There is a waiting room at the end of the hall if you want to take turns, but Henry here needs to relax."

She held the door open until Bridgett and Alex moved to leave. She looked over the top of her glasses at Max, who got the message and followed the others out. "We'll be back in a minute, Henry," Alex called over his shoulder. The nurse took Henry's blood pressure and left them. "Looks like you will be able to go home in a few hours …. IF you can keep yourself stable." She looked at Zoe and nodded as she left the room.

"So, Henry, whenever you need to talk or something, please call one of us. We will support you in any way. You know, we are your friends," said Zoe gently.

Henry looked at her with such a wave of release you could see his body relax. He began crying silently. "My friend, Zoe. You and the others have no idea what it means to me to have you as friends. I have had no friends all my life before now. I have always been afraid of losing people like I did my father. I have been afraid of strangers who my mother always said could hurt us. The stress of the war, of the refugee camp, coming to a new country and not knowing anything about it, the bad eating habits I created for myself to comfort myself, the stress of this new 'situation' that we experienced, doubting my sanity sometimes, the fear that never leaves me. What if they decide to send us back? What if I never see my father again? What will I do after high school? The dreams I have of the gun fighting and bombs and bad men in the camps, my mother crying. I am not a strong person – not inside. Now this new project," he looked at Zoe sheepishly, "the thought of having to work with Bridgett, being alone with her, having to talk to her.... I got myself all worked up, I guess." He wiped his eyes and looked down at the bright, white sheets, "I've never told anyone any of this, my strong friend, Zoe," he looked at her again with his red eyes.

Zoe sat down on the chair next to the bed. "Henry, all those things would have made anyone fearful. You are a very brave and strong person! Many would have taken much different routes, like drinking or worse. You are smart. You're a…. you're a good guy, Henry. People think I'm tough and brave, but there have been many times I've cried myself to sleep. You just have to understand that the past is done, and there's nothing you can do about it. It's over. You have a new life here, and it will be a good one. You must find your strength, use your intelligence, and move on. I can help you figure out if you can get a grant to go to school somewhere, maybe even something like Max is doing, so you could get paid while you are learning. School ending in a couple of years will not be the end of anything – it will be the beginning for you."

Henry reached out, put his hand on the back of her hand, and smiled at her. She looked around and saw a box of tissues on the nightstand. Standing, she handed it to him.

"And," Zoe said, "As far as working with Bridgett, she's a kid, just like you and me. We all have our challenges. She's a nice person, Henry. It will be good for you. Good for you both to work together."

I will learn to be brave - like you, my friend," he said as he looked at her, pulled a tissue out of the box next to him, and blew his nose.

Zoe smiled at him as the door opened, and the three came back in.

"Hey buddy, you will be all right," Max said softly. "I'll let you visit with these two. Maybe when you go home later, we can get together for a burger and fries or something.

"Oh no, Max," said Henry. I'm going to start taking better care of myself. I never want to feel like this again! I will learn to find comfort in other ways. Maybe we could even go for a walk, or you could teach me to play one of your American games, like basketball."

Max smiled at him and backed out of the door with a wave.

I'll go wait in the waiting room with Max before we get yelled at again, said Zoe. She patted Henry's arm as she left. "You got this, buddy, you got this…" she said as she winked at him.

Alex moved to the side of the bed. Bridgett stood at the end again, still looking scared.

Alex and Henry talked a bit. Alex offered to help Henry learn to exercise like he did for his sports and offered to pick him up once in a while to show him how to use his home gym equipment to relieve his stress. He offered to show him the YMCA, which was not too far from his apartment. Henry perked up quite a bit when they spoke of these things.

Zoe poked her head into the room and called to Alex to come out for a minute.

"Hey, when you need a ride home later - just call me," Alex told him and left with Zoe pulling him by the arm.

Bridgett stood looking at Alex leave and then back at Henry, and you could tell she didn't know what to say. Henry was silent and looked like he was going to have another panic attack again.

Bridgett stammered "Hhhenrry. I'm so sssorry this had to happen to yyyou."

Her stammering seemed to calm Henry down to realize this beautiful blonde was nervous, too.

Bridgett walked slowly to the side of the bed and plopped down onto the chair. Looking around the room as if looking for something to talk about.

Henry didn't know what to say to her either, so there was a brief, uncomfortable silence.

Finally, Bridgett faced him and blurted out, "I have anxiety, too!" And she sat forward and watched to see his reaction.

"YOU have anxiety?" he asked incredulously as he looked at her.

"Yes, me. Sometimes, I just shut down and don't look at people. That's when my thoughts are going quickly inside me, my heart starts pounding, and I feel panicked. I get completely quiet and am incapable of making eye contact. People think I'm just being stuck up, but that's not it at all." Bridgett stared into his face as she rapidly spoke, getting it all out. "I've never told anyone about this, Henry, not even my parents."

Henry looked at her and saw the 'curtain' of aloofness come down. She looked like a fragile little girl to him all of a sudden. His heart went out to her. "I would have never thought this to be true…" he said softly.

"I know," she responded. She looked away, "I get really irritable until I can get away from what's stressing me out, or I tap on the back of my hand or leg to try to calm myself if I'm in class or something. The tightness in my chest, tingling, and nausea that followed closely behind. The irritability is another reason they think I'm a ...., well, they don't think I'm a very nice person, but inside I'm freaking out!"

Henry sat forward, "But, but you are so ... I mean, you don't look like you have any problems...or, well, I'm very surprised, is all."

Bridgett stood, walking around the bed to look out of the window. "Looks can be deceiving, can't they? It all started when I was very young; my parents constantly doted on me and watched my every move to make sure I wouldn't hurt myself. They took me to photo shoots where I had to act like I didn't want to act. 'Smile,' they would say, 'don't you dare cry in front of the camera; don't mess up your hair that I just spent two hours fixing up; sit up pretty....' I just wanted to go out and play in the dirt!" She turned to him and leaned back on the window ledge. He could see a tear in her eye. Then, turning again to the window, "When I was nine, they took me to this grimy model studio for a photo shoot. My father had to go to work, so my mother drove him and said she would come back and get me. The photographer was an old, hunch-backed man who smelled bad but was cheaper than the other photographers. I had to wear a costume for the shoot, and when I was changing, he came into the dressing room and .... well." She turned back to him with tears in her eyes. She grabbed some tissue from the box on the bed, dabbed her eyes, and continued. "My mother never knew. I couldn't tell her. I felt so ... dirty." She looked down. "I don't know why I'm telling you all this, Henry," she said as she sat back down in the chair, "I'm sorry. I'm supposed to be here to cheer you up."

Henry didn't quite know what to say. He just looked at her with a tear in his eye as well. "I guess it is good we both face ourselves today. Perhaps it is the beginning of healing for us? Yes?"

"Yes," she said as she looked at him softly.

The door abruptly opened, and it was Alex with Zoe behind him. "Hey, you guys. Are you doing okay in here? We're trying to stay away from the 'general' out there," implying the nurse. He smiled at Henry and Bridgett clueless at the energy in the room.

Seeing the two of them looking at each other, Zoe quietly elbowed Alex in the side.

Zoe said, "Henry, we've got to get going. I have to get to work, and Bridgett's parents wanted her back in a couple of hours. They thought we were just going out to breakfast. We have to make sure they know she didn't eat many carbs, as they called after you," she smiled at Bridgett.

"Don't forget to call me when you need a ride home later," Alex called back to Henry, "Your mom has gone to work, too. She took the bus even though I offered to take her. She was happy we had come to see you. She said to tell you she would be back later."

Bridgett stood. She and Henry looked at each other for an embarrassed minute, smiling gently. "We'll get together for our project this week. Maybe we could meet at the library or something." Bridgett offered as she dabbed at her eyes once more.

"That would be great," he said.

When the nurse came back a few minutes later, she smiled as she pulled Henry's blanket over his relaxed arms. He slept soundly, with a slight smile on his face.

CHAPTER 7

WHAT THEY FOUND

Two weeks had gone by. Henry was out of the hospital and was eating more "mindfully" as the doctors had coached him to do, along with practicing some breathing techniques, finding distractions to get himself thinking about other things when he started to get anxious, and some of the other suggestions on the papers they had given him, which he had shared with Bridgett when they met. They agreed it was such a coincidence that they had met and shared the same problem of anxiety and how they could now help each other without anyone else knowing anything about it. (Was it a coincidence, hmmmm.)

On the agreed-upon day, they all piled into Zoe's apartment. Alex had picked up a couple of pizzas so they could eat while they talked. Everyone commented on how good Henry looked since they had seen him last. He looked less worried, stood taller, and seemed perhaps happier. Henry smiled self-consciously and gave a sideways look to Bridgett, who smiled back at him. The others all caught their exchange and glanced at each other with brief smiles on their faces as well. Little did they know the real excitement would begin in the next chapter. Their shared mission, their camaraderie, and the unspoken understanding between them created a bond that was unbreakable, a bond that would carry them through the mysteries and challenges that lay ahead.

Zoe broke the moment before someone said something stupid. "Okay, everyone. Did we find anything out? Who wants to go first?"

"I'll go," Max said, pulling his chair closer to the table and pulling out some books from the backpack Alex had given him. Alex handed him some papers. "Here's the stuff you wanted me to print for you," Alex said.

"Thanks." Max stretched out his arm to take the papers and pushed the pizza boxes back so he could spread everything out in front of him. Everyone gathered closer as he opened the biggest book first. "So, look here," he said as he looked around the table at the others, just like a detective reviewing a case. "I searched for anything that looked like the disk, and one of the things I found was Meteorite. It looks like the disk in color, but the description says they look more like rock and would be heavy for their size – which the disk isn't at all. These pictures show small round structures on them or layers of minerals." He turned the books so the rest could see the pages he had marked, turning the pages slowly for the group. "The biggest reason I chucked that idea was the weight issue. The disk feels like a feather. The room was filled with anticipation as they all leaned in to get a better look at the evidence, their eyes wide with curiosity and a hint of fear, as if they were on the brink of uncovering something truly extraordinary.

Everyone nodded in agreement.

"Then I found these other various minerals, some of which are black like the disk." He showed the group the lists with various columns with the color " black." Pointing again to another rock on one of the papers that Alex had printed for him, "See, like this thing called Pyrolusite here. It is listed as black, but the pictures show radiating fibers or a spikey appearance. I don't think you could grind down those spikes to be as smooth as our disk." He

58

showed them another page of pictures. "There is also something called Magnetite, which is black, but they say it's magnetic. I came over last week, and Zoe and I tested it. Our disk is not magnetic at all." He showed them in another book, along with other rocks and minerals, but none were black, and they all had unique character-istics that eliminated them. "The closest I could come to anything that remotely looked like the disk was black obsidian or black onyx. We did the tests this paper said to do for Onyx, and that's what I believe it could be made from." He kept looking from one to the other as he spoke. "It doesn't scratch. If you heat it and drop it in water, it doesn't crack, and the surface appears well-polished and reflective with a waxy luster. Any engraving on Onyx - like what I assume our names are on the disk - in these books turned this light grey color." And he showed them the picture. He picked up the disk Zoe had placed on the table before they arrived and looked at it. "But assuming it is Onyx, how did our specific names get engraved on it and stay black? And then there are the lights that seem to be embedded without surface holes or hardware..." They all silently looked at the disk for a moment as Max turned it over and over in his hands, almost stroking the smooth, cool object. "He looked at everyone and, with an odd look on his face, said, "Then when I was reading the little bible last night..."

The others sat back and glanced at each other.

Alex stopped him before he continued, "Is this really something we need to hear right now, Max?"

"Yes, I think it is guys. Listen." And he opened his little bible and read, *'And they wrought the onyx stones, inclosed in settings of gold, graven with the engravings of a signet, according to the names of the children of Israel.'* He sat with the little bible still open and looked around. "Onyx... names engraved.... Don't you find that, well, kinda interesting?" he asked.

They looked at him and then at each other. Henry said, "Yes, Max, it is very interesting, and it is interesting that you should have read that just last night."

Bridgett nodded in agreement at Henry's statement but didn't say anything.

Zoe quickly changed the subject. "Ok, it's interesting, but I don't know how it ties in with what we are trying to do right now. Let's see what else we found." She looked around. "Henry and Bridgett, what did you find out?"

Henry and Bridgett looked at each other, and she nodded at him to start the discussion.

"We did as everyone else does now, searched the internet at the library for any horse and riders giving messages." Henry began. "We came up with things like Paul Revere's ride, but he was a real person with a real message of imminent danger. There is a horse and rider motif common in Jihadi visual propaganda. It is," he continued as Bridgett handed him printouts they had brought to show what he was discussing, "a joint symbol of vengeance and revolt that traces its roots to prophetic times. I don't believe our horse and rider was giving a call to revolt, do you?"

Bridgett nodded 'no,' as did the others.

"We found these articles about messengers on horses, but this one, for example, was a human on horseback in George Washington's day carrying significant news to waiting crowds. Not applicable in our time, news travels through TV or social media. There is a David Wynne sculpture (he showed the article) of a young man bareback on a horse. The article said it was a tall, wise horse that had never known a bridle. They called it a magical horse. The boy was calling out to his friends, who had forgotten that they, too, were heirs to his kingdom. The description says.' The rider is giving his message to his audience and seems to be saying that there is another world that all should know about.' But the horse is just as important as the man. The horse is more austere and has his feet firmly planted on the ground, one hoof pointing to the Centre of the earth. They are a team where 'the man needs the horse, and the horse needs the man,' it is written. Reed Business Information Company commissioned it to capture the idea of communication. This is interesting," Henry continued, "but where does this fit with our horse and rider?" He nodded at Bridgett so she could proceed with the rest of the information.

She swallowed and fidgeted a bit, then showed them other pictures. "These are other statues, such as the Horse and Rider by either Leonardo da Vinci or Carlo Pedretti. It was to portray the Governor of Milan parting from his loved ones." She showed them other statues and pictures. "But none of these fit with a glowing, speaking, disappearing, 15-foot-tall horse and 9-foot-tall rider like we saw." She looked around sheepishly, then back to Henry, who nodded at her to continue. "Our search did find mention of a bible figure…" Seeing the looks on their faces, she continued quickly. "But wait, it read, 'Then I saw Heaven open wide – and oh! A white horse and its Rider. The Rider, named Faithful and True,' and it goes on," she said. She put the printout on the table. Max grabbed it and continued to read silently.

"I'll go next," said Alex as he grabbed another piece of now-cold pizza. Amid chewing, he said, "Okay, well, I don't have any bible things to talk about, but I did find some interesting facts. I wondered if the rider could have come from underground somehow. So, I searched that topic and found some of the least likely cities have hidden catacombs under them." He pulled his cell phone out to read the articles. "There is one in Indianapolis, an abandoned city under Seattle; Dallas has underground tunnels. Here, look at this one," he showed his cell around to the others, "– prohibition tunnels under Los Angeles, and tunnels under the Colorado State Capitol." He rattled off other cities: "Houston has seven miles of tunnels, and New York has a subterranean world, they called it.

Pretty interesting stuff," he went on. "Then, I found articles about mysterious underground cities in Italy, Britain, Turkey, France, Poland, Ethiopia, and Beijing. One they called the cameo for the movie 'Indiana Jones.' They all had different hypothetical reasons for being there. This was quite an interesting subject."

Then he sat up taller and nearer to the table, making himself look more dramatic. "Then, I thought, "He said with a glint in his eye, "Wouldn't it be cool if there was something underground here in our town? So, I went to the city and, after talking to a ton of people, found some old surveys that – guess what – showed there were some tunnels! And guess where they are?" He looked around and paused for effect. "They happen to be under the park!"

Everyone exclaimed in surprise.

"Wow," said Max. "That's an amazing find!"

"Good job, Alex!" Zoe said.

Henry looked puzzled, "But what are they there for? Who created them? How could the rider and a big horse get in and out of one so quickly?"

"That's what I wondered, Henry," Alex said. He got up and paced as he talked. "I could only find a bit of information about the park from old times. But there happened to be a historian at the library when I was there. He had gone to get books for the class he teaches at the University. He saw me looking around for tunnel information, trying to figure out where to look next. When I told him what I was researching, not saying anything about the horse and rider, he said he could help me. He was pretty old and said that he remembered hearing about this from Grandparents and older family members. It seems there was a cheese factory where the park is today in the 1800s. They dug a tunnel to store things in the cooler temperatures before there were large refrigeration units like we have today. In the 1920s, when prohibition hit the country, some creative minds extended the tunnel to a few speak-easies. 'You won't find any of this in any history book, young man,' the old guy told me, "But I can tell you the tunnel was a very popular place.' He said. 'Eventually, prohibition ended, and the cheese factory burned down; the fishing industry took a downturn, and the factories in the old town location closed due to the coal mines running out, so the Governor decided to bring in tourists or watch the city die. They created the park and the rows of the little stores you all know of there now, and the tunnel was blocked off. But," Alex said dramatically as he turned back to them, "I did some snooping around the park the last couple of weeks, and I think I've found a way to get down there!" He said excitedly. "There is an old, I mean really old, grate behind that big rock at the back of the park. It's under the trees and pretty much covered by bushes and stuff. But when I threw a stone into the grate, it sounded like it went a ways back before it hit the ground! I'll bet a couple of us could move that grate. It's heavy metal and into the side of the hill that separates the park from the fancy houses behind it." He sat down again, looking excited. "Maybe the horse and rider were projected somehow from down there or something? What do you think? Are we up for an adventure?"

Max said, "I'm in, but it sounds pretty dangerous."

Henry looked very nervous about this. "I don't know if we should do this. What if there are snakes or other animals? What if it caves in? What if…."

"If we all go together, we can watch each other's back, and if it gets too dangerous, we can always back out," said Alex excitedly, trying to calm Henry. "This is the only grain of a clue we've had so far. We have to try to see if 'he' came from the tunnel somehow. What do you think, Zoe?"

Being the logical, steady one, Zoe thought about it for a minute, everyone's eyes on her.

"It wouldn't hurt to try and see what's down there. Like you said, Alex, we could find out if this is all a big hoax. Although, on the other hand, I don't know how you make a building disappear, but then, we have to start somewhere. We all have to be on board, though." She looked at Henry and Bridgett. "Are you willing to try? I know this will be outside anything you would do on your own, but we would be there with you, and we might need your knowledge at some point. What do you say?"

Henry's hand had started shaking on his knee under the table, but Bridgett put her hand on his arm to steady him. No one saw this.

Bridgett piped up first, "I will go. I always wanted to play in the mud when I was a kid," she smiled at the others and Henry.

Henry looked at her and nodded. "Okay, I will go as well," he said with a little tremble in his voice.

"Okay, then," Zoe said, "we meet at the boulder next week. There is a festival downtown, and everyone will be going to the pier, so there shouldn't be too many people around."

"Hey, Zoe," Max shouted, "What about your assignment? What did you find out about what the rider said? About being 'named'?"

"Well, strangely enough," Zoe responded, not very enthusiastically, "I did the same as you guys and did an internet search. The only thing I could find with those words specifically *'have been named'* was in a bible verse. I'm not really into the bible, but it said, *'Whatever one is, he has been named already.'* Then another one, *'Fear not, for I have redeemed you; I have called you by your name; You are Mine. ...'* There were also things about an 'Angel of the Lord' appearing and giving messages, but I didn't see any wings on our guy. So, I guess you could say I wasn't able to find anything helpful."

She changed the subject quickly, and they talked about what they might need to bring to their tunnel excursion: flashlights, gloves, rope, a shovel, and old clothes. Bridgett said she didn't have any, and Zoe's would be too short for her, so Alex offered to bring her some of his old coveralls.

They broke up, and Zoe watched them walk down the staircase outside her apartment.

There were some more of those strangers walking in the alley. If they were tourists, she wondered again, why would they be in the alley, and why don't they talk to each other or act like tourists? She had a perplexed look on her face as she closed the door slowly.

CHAPTER 8

UNDERGRoUND

It was the day.

Zoe was the first one to the park since she lived so close. She walked to the back of the park and saw the boulder Alex had talked about. She went around the back but didn't see any grate. She was walking around the boulder, looking into the high-weeded areas, when Max showed up silently behind her.

"Boo!" Max shouted from behind her.

"Don't do that!" Zoe shouted back as she jumped and clutched at her chest. "You scared me!"

Max chuckled as Alex came around the boulder, looking ready for the adventure.

The boulder was about 15 feet tall and 20 feet long, so one could easily not see someone approaching. This immense rock must have been there for thousands of years. Just think of the things it had seen, Zoe thought as she looked at it with her hands on her hips.

"I wonder how this even got here," she said almost to herself. "It's huge!"

There were other smaller boulders within that 40-foot area, but nothing as big as this one. It was pretty secluded back there and private once you got in between the rocks.

"Don't know," Alex said as he leaned against it to change his tennis shoes to hiking boots. He had a rope around his shoulder and had set down a backpack with a small shovel attached. He wore rugged-looking clothing that looked like he could go hiking in the Himalayas. He saw Zoe looking comically at him with raised eyebrows and commented, "My Dad has taken me on hiking trips occasionally. I figured we didn't know what was down there, so I came prepared." The excitement in his voice was contagious, making the others even more eager for the adventure.

"You sure did," Zoe responded. She had on old, torn jeans, tennis shoes, and an old plaid shirt she had gotten from her favorite resale store.

Max didn't look much different in his jeans and blue T-shirt, except for the old shirt Alex had just tossed at him. He was buttoning it up over his T-shirt as Henry approached from around the corner of the boulder.

"Here, try this on," Alex said to Henry, his tone filled with camaraderie. "You're almost as tall as I am now. It might fit and keep you cleaner." Alex playfully tossed him a shirt, adding, "Gotta outfit my "Crew!" with a mischievous grin that spread from ear to ear.

When Henry turned, he saw Bridgett walking around the corner of the boulder. She was wearing the clothes Alex had lent her during the week. She, too, was almost as tall as Alex. She was wearing one of his old T-shirts that was four sizes too big, with a tank underneath, his old coveralls, and a baseball cap. She also had a broad smile on her face. Henry had never seen anything so beautiful in his life.

"I changed at the store downtown," she said. "My parents would be appalled at the way I look," she said as she twirled around, "but I LOVE it! She stopped mid-twirl as she looked at Henry, "Hey, you are buttoned up crooked, Henry." She smiled, walked to him, undid his buttons, and grinned at him as she did them correctly.

Everyone chucked to themselves, seeing Henry's dark face flush at being so close to the beautiful blonde.

"Well, I'm glad everyone is in such good spirits," Zoe said, smiling as she looked around. This could be a less-than-exciting adventure."

"Oh, come on, Zoe," Alex said as he gathered himself together with his gear. "We could find out what this whole thing is about already. And when was the last time you went on an adventure like this? Huh?" He kiddingly poked her arm a couple of times.

"Stop!" Zoe said, trying to look mad at her tall friend. "So where is this grate you told us about? I haven't seen anything, and I've been looking."

"Ok," he said as he pointed toward the old shed about 15 feet away between another set of smaller boulders. "See those bushes and weeds right next to it? That's where it is." And he strode that way. Everyone followed.

They peered into the bushes and weeds but didn't see anything.

"Where?" asked Max as he pushed at the brush and weeds, "I don't see anything either."

Alex stooped and started pulling thick ivy and heavy weeds back, and you could see the top of something metal. "Here," he said. He took out a long hunting knife and started cutting at the brush like someone in an Indiana Jones movie.

Max stepped in and started pulling back what he had cut. Zoe and the rest of them pulled and helped cut with the extra knife and shovel that Alex handed them, and before long, they could see the top of a large grate. It was on an angle on the side of a small hill that went down from the shed. There was some writing on it. Alex brushed away the mud and scraped it with his knife, and when it was finally legible, he read, "Smith's Cheese Factory." He tried to pull the grate up, but it was heavier than expected. "Come on, guys, I can't move this myself. It's really heavy." He started digging around the edges buried in the hill's brush and soil. They all started digging out the grate's edges, which was more like a metal door, now that they could see it more clearly. It took some time, but they could finally pry the door away from what they could now see was a doorframe in the hill. Alex tied the rope to the handle side of the grate where there was an opening, and they all dug in and pulled, and pulled, and pulled – looking like one side of a rope-pulling contest, and finally, the grate, with a loud creek opened a bit. They all fell on their butts with the rope in their hands.

"Whew!" said Max.

"Yes, whew!" mimicked Henry. "But it feels good to be doing some physical labor now that I am stronger." He had been jogging and lifting the hand weights Alex had lent him.

Bridgett smiled at him. His heart melted.

"Okay, guys…I mean, 'Crew,'" Alex said, looking at them all as he rolled up the rope, "this is it. Let's get to the bottom of this…literally". He chuckled.

Alex, Max, and Henry pulled on the edge of the iron door as Zoe and Bridgett held back the bigger branches of the bushes that had been hiding it for many years. The door opened enough for them to get in. Alex wedged a large branch at the bottom so it wouldn't close before they got out.

Alex pulled out his military flashlight and showed it into the darkness. He saw ancient timbers holding up the rock and dirt roof and a long corridor that seemed to go downward. It was very dark in there.

The five stood and peered into the tunnel as much as they could see, standing next to each other and looking in.

All of a sudden, loud - '**Bang! Bang! Pop**!'. They all jumped back but soon realized it was the fireworks from the festival at the Pier. It had gotten dusk while they had been working.

"Oh my gosh," said Henry as he sat down. "I thought it was…." He clutched at his chest.

Bridgett moved toward him and sat on the grass near him, "Remember what they said…take long, slow breaths, focus on your chest rising and falling…."

Henry nodded and, after taking a few deep breaths, nodded at Bridgett and stood up, although he was still shaking.

"Thank you, my friend," he said to her, his voice quivering.

"You're welcome." She smiled gently at him and stood, brushing the grass off of her. She touched his arm to help him walk more steadily.

Zoe took a deep breath and said, "Are we ready?"

Everyone nodded and started moving forward, the flashlights Alex had brought in hand.

The tunnel was only about four feet wide, not wide enough for two people to walk side by side. It wasn't smooth on the sides, and those who had carved it out of the rock and dirt must have used pick axes and shovels. The timbers holding the roof up were very old but very thick. The top of the ceiling was just tall enough for most of them to stand up in; Zoe, being short, had no problem. They saw two passages about twenty feet in as they moved farther into the tunnel. One went toward the park's center, where they had seen the rider, and the other went behind the shed.

"Looks like we'll have to split up," Alex said, guiding the group. "Max, you, Henry, and Bridgett take the one that goes toward the park, and me and Zoe can check out this one in the back of the shed. Max, you will be the one to understand any technology you find, and Henry, you will understand any machinery that might be there. Bridgett, keep an eye on those two." He winked, "Zoe and I will join you as soon as we scope out this back tunnel, but it just looks like a bunch of old barrels and storage containers," he said as he showed his flashlight into the area. "Here," he said, handing Max one of his knives and an extra flashlight. He handed Bridgett the small shovel he had on his belt. "Are your cell phones working?"

They all looked, and the reception wasn't great, but they seemed to be working for now. "So, if you need anything, try texting, but we probably won't be long." He nodded to Zoe, and they both went into the right tunnel.

Henry gave Bridgett a worried look. She put her chin up with resolve and nodded at him.

"Come on, guys," Max said as he moved slowly forward. Bridgett purposely stood taller, although she couldn't stand too tall with the height of the tunnel, and quickly moved forward. Henry stared at her abrupt manner, then followed, not wanting to be left alone.

71

The tunnel grew narrower as they moved along. There was some water on the rocks underneath their feet every once in a while. Max moved slower the farther they went. It seemed like they had been walking for hours, but they had not. They were probably only in the middle of the park now.

"Hey, look at this," Bridgett said as she pointed her flashlight at some writing on the wall. It was someone's name: "Peter Adams 1846, " it says. I wonder what these tunnels were used for back then and why Peter wrote his name here?" They found an old metal cup and things that looked like someone had been living down there.

Henry looked around and froze as he pointed to the ceiling just ahead of them. "It's…. it's a ssssnnnake…." he pointed toward one of the timbers toward the ceiling. Max pointed his flashlight toward where Henry was pointing his shaking finger.

There, with his head pointed down toward them, was a large, copper-headed snake.

In the next instant, Bridgett rushed forward, pushing Max and Henry aside, and with a stronger blow than they could have imagined, cut the head off the snake with one mighty whack of the shovel!

"Wow, girl! Where did that superpower come from? Good job!" Max congratulated her as he picked himself up from where she had knocked him down.

"I…I don't know," Bridgett said. "I just….it was going to hurt us…. and I just…". She looked as surprised as the rest of them that she had done that.

"My hero," said Henry with a smile on his face. "He looked rather pale even in the darkness but relieved."

They moved forward in silence. Max shined the flashlight up the walls and floor to check for other snakes.

"Listen…," Max said as he stopped for a minute, holding his arms out to hold the others back. They could hear faint music in the silence. "I can hear the band from down by the pier. We must be near the park's center where we saw the rider."

They examined the walls as they moved but saw no technology whatsoever, nothing but rock and old timbers.

"Hey, wait a minute! I dropped the shovel back there. I'd better go get it; we might run into more…ah, of those things, "Bridgett said as she turned her flashlight back and moved quickly back to retrieve the shovel.

Just then, the walls started shaking. One of the timbers behind Max and Henry cracked right up the middle with a loud "**crack"** and rocks fell around them. Both Henry and Max were knocked off their feet. When the dust settled, they could see they were trapped. The way back had rubble almost to the ceiling, and fallen timbers and rocks all around blocked the way forward. They were in an area of about ten feet, and small stones and dirt kept dropping as they sat where they had fallen.

Max got up quickly and started trying to pull rocks out of the tunnel behind them. They were too big, and as he did, more fell. He rushed to the tunnel in front of them, and a pile of rocks closed the opening, with a large timber blocking the way.

Henry stood and brushed himself off. He found the flashlight he had dropped when they fell, but it was broken. Max's flashlight was a few feet away, but it still worked.

Henry was shaking as he knelt on the cold, wet dirt. "Max…. what are we going to do now? Did Bridgett get buried? Oh my, oh my… Are we going to die?"

"I don't know yet what we are going to do, and no, we are not going to die," Max said unconvincingly. He tried his cell, but there was no reception.

Suddenly, they could hear Bridgett and see her flashlight over the top of the rocks behind them.

"Are you guys all right?! Say something!" She yelled.

Max yelled back. "We are okay but can't go forward or back toward you."

"Oh no! What should I do?! I'll go get the others! The way back from here seems clear," she yelled. "Deep breaths, Henry, take deep breaths. You'll be okay!"

Henry started trying to take deep breaths but was unsuccessful at staying calm.

Max stood looking at the situation, trying to figure out what to do.

"Oh my, we are going to die, aren't we? We are going to die!" Henry started wailing.

Max just kept looking up and around, trying to figure out what to do. After a few minutes of Henry's wailing, Max shouted, "Stop it! That isn't helping! Do some of that meditation stuff or something like they told you to do at the hospital so I can think."

There wasn't much room in the tunnel, especially with so many fallen rocks, but as Henry knelt, he began chanting something in his native language in a shaking voice. All Max could understand was 'Allah.'

After what seemed like forever, they could hear Alex.

"You guys, okay?" he yelled over the top of the debris behind them. As he spoke, more rocks fell. He must have been trying to dig them out.

"Not really," Max said. "I don't know if trying to move those rocks is a good idea. More keep falling in here."

"I think if I can get some 4x4s, I can shore up this part of the roof timbers long enough to get you out. My dad has some in the garage. Can you hold out long enough?"

"Don't have much choice, do we?" Max said.

Henry kept chanting.

Bridgett yelled, "I'm so sorry! I must've loosened the timbers when I hit the snake. I'm so sorry!"

Henry yelled, "You did not mean harm, but good. Do not be sad."

Zoe yelled, "We better hurry and get those 4x4s. It's supposed to rain tonight, and I don't know how waterproof these tunnels are. I'm going to guard the entrance to make sure no one closes it, and Bridgett and Alex will get the wood. Hang tight, guys. If nothing else, we'll call the cops, and they will have to dig up Central Park!"

"Ok, hurry," said Max. He was getting nervous, too.

Henry kept chanting and chanting.

"Henry, whatever you are saying, it doesn't sound like it's working. Could you just do the deep breathing thing again?"

"I am asking Allah to save us from this trouble, Max," Henry said as he took short breaths, "Perhaps he is asleep." And he sat back against the rubble, shaking and looking like he was ready to cry.

"It's okay, Henry," Max said, "You tried."

Henry looked at Max, "Perhaps you could pray to your God and ask for help? Maybe He is awake?"

"I'm kinda new at this God stuff. I've never talked out loud to Him." Max looked at Henry, who had a pleading look on his face. "But ok." Max stood as much as he could in that small area, closed his eyes, and looked up. "Hi, God. I don't know if you remember me, I'm Max. I just met you not too long ago…and you somehow changed me…from the inside out. Thanks for that, by the way. I'm…we're in kind of a pickle here, God. I know it says to ask you things, and you will hear us. Well, if you could, of course, you could, but if you would – would you make a way…somehow for us to get out of this without …" he looked at Henry and changed his mind on what he was going to say, "well, as soon as you can. If you wouldn't mind…please. Amen."

Max looked around, expecting something drastic to happen, but nothing did. He sat down next to the other side of the narrow wall.

They sat for a moment in silence. Then Henry startled with a gasp and quickly moved back against the fallen debris. He shouted as he pointed, "What's that!?"

Max turned to look up, startled, too. It looked like two burning eyes in the darkness.

Max quickly pointed the flashlight toward the burning orbs, and it displayed a cat! A black cat with bright yellow-green eyes, sitting on top of the rubble ahead of them, purring!

"What the heck!?" shouted Max. "How did he get in here!?"

Henry grabbed Max's shoulder. "The cat has come into the tunnel from somewhere! There must be an opening to the outside somewhere up there!"

As if on cue, the cat turned and climbed a few big rocks and disappeared.

"Oh my gosh, Max! Your God has answered us and shown a way for us to get out. We must follow that cat somehow!" Henry was up in a flash and climbing up the steep pile of fallen rocks in front of them. "Here, Max! There's the moon! I can see it!"

Surprised at Henry's quick action, Max said, "Be careful, Henry! We don't want all these rocks to cave in and bury us!"

But Henry was already at the top and was pushing at something. You could hear metal scraping and debris of some kind, and soon, the top of his body was out of sight!

Seeing this, Max followed, pushing Henry from behind into the hole he had found, then crawled out himself as gingerly as possible.

When they were out of the hole, they looked around and found they were in the alley behind Zoe's apartment. There was an area where the cement driveway had collapsed, but this hole was where the cement had pushed itself up, looking like tectonic plates colliding. The metal they heard was one of the trash bins and some of the trash cans that had collided as the street buckled. And there sat that black cat on top of one of the trash cans that was still upright, just looking at them and wagging his tail.

"Oh my God!" Max exclaimed as he breathed deeply of the fresh night air.

"Yes, your God!" Henry replied calmly.

Max nodded in understanding. He then jumped up from the ground, where he sat after climbing out of the tunnel. "I've got to go tell the others we're okay!" he shouted as he began running toward the park, pulling out his cell phone.

Just then, Alex drove up with Bridgett in the van; they jumped out, leaving the doors open when they saw Max running toward them. Henry could see the welcome exchange from where he was in the alley. He saw Max point back toward him. He moved to sit on top of an overturned trash can. He saw Alex texting, probably to Zoe. They all turned toward him and started running toward him. The black cat came and stood beside him, rubbing against his leg and purring loudly.

"Thank you, Mr. Cat," Henry said as he picked him up and stroked the black, shiny animal. "You, Mr. Cat, we must give you a name. How about savior? No! Our Savior was Max's God! He prayed, and his God sent you to us! I don't understand him, but I believe in him...now. He was not asleep." Henry's voice was filled with a newfound faith, a glimmer of hope in the darkness that had surrounded him.

Henry looked up at the stars. Just then, there were fireworks again. From where he was sitting, he could see them clearly. Beautiful, he thought. "That is how my heart feels right now," Henry said to the God he had just encountered. "I don't know you, but I will learn. And thank you.... thank you so much." He sat there amid the trash and broken concrete, calmly stroking the black cat, and felt peace for the first time in his life.

CHAPTER 9

THE WRATH OF ZOE!

It was the day they had agreed to regroup after the tunnel experience. The city had put up caution tape all over the alley near the garage where Zoe's apartment was, and they had begun to dig up the collapsed cement. They attributed it to soil erosion underneath the street and were going to bring in bulldozers full of dirt to fill in the rather large hole. Either they didn't know about the tunnels, or they didn't want others to know about them, but in any case, this would be the end of the tunnel they had escaped from. The other tunnel Alex and Zoe had gone into contained storage barrels and crates, some rather interesting, very old cash journals, and letters about the Cheese Factory, but it ended about 20 yards in.

After the accident, They shut the heavy door to the tunnels in the back of the park by the giant boulders. They had piled lots of heavy stones up against it, along with brush and branches, so it was almost invisible again. They didn't want other crazy kids to go in there and get into trouble like they had.

The cat had begun to hang around, and although she said she wasn't a 'cat' person, Zoe started giving him scraps from the restaurant. Henry had named him Sparkles because he said that was what his eyes did to show them the way out of the tunnel that night. The others thought it was a dorky name, but they let Henry go with it since he seemed to love that cat.

As they climbed the stairs to Zoe's apartment, they saw her standing at the top with her hands on her hips and a scowl on her face. As she let everyone in, she briskly motioned them to sit at the table. She did not sit, and the scowl did not leave her face. When she got angry, she had 'that look' on her face that could take paint off a wall. She was obviously furious now.

"What's up?" asked Max cautiously as he sat cross-legged on the floor. He, like the others, was rather intimidated by her fierce look.

She didn't say anything but picked up the orange towel they knew the disc was in, walked over to the kitchen table where they were sitting, and opened it to show them the disk, which now had three lights lit up! They were Max, who was first to light in the beginning, but now Henry and Alex were lit up too!

Max, who had hurriedly gotten up from the floor and joined them at the table. He, Alex, and Henry now sat with mouths open, staring at the disc.

"Wow…." Alex said quietly, taking the disk from Zoe's hand. He turned to Max and Henry. "You know what this must mean, don't you?"

They each nodded, looking from him to the disk.

"Well, you want to clue **me** in on this!?" Zoe's words seethed out. "You guys have been doing something behind my back! I thought we were a team – The Crew (she made air quotation marks), and we were all in this together! Now, I see that was just a joke! You all turned your backs on me, didn't you? You had better have a good explanation, or this will be our last meeting. I will put all the weird things behind me like I've put other things behind me all my life. I can move on, and we can all go off and do whatever we were going to do with our lives before all this started." She stood with her arms crossed, waiting for an answer.

Bridgett shrugged her shoulders and raised her hands at Zoe in an 'I don't know what's going on either' motion.

Alex looked at the disk and back at the other guys. "It's nothing like that, Zoe. We haven't been researching or doing anything behind your back. It's…. I think it's…." he stopped, and you could tell he was trying to sort it out himself and find words.

Max piped up. "Here, just sit down for a minute while I try to explain what I, what we, think happened." He got off his chair, pulled it over to where she was standing, and pushed it into the back of her knees so she had to plop down. Her scowl did not leave her face as she raised her eyebrows at him.

"I want to hear this too," Bridgett said quietly. "Henry?" She and Henry looked at each other.

"I think Max will be best at explaining this…" Henry nodded at Bridgett with a slight smile on his face. "I don't know if I fully understand it all myself yet."

"But…" Bridgett started.

"Just let me talk for a minute," Max cut her off.

"Yeah, let him talk for a minute. Maybe I'll fully understand, too," said Alex as he kept looking at the disk and the lights above their names, which seemed to be glowing from some unknown power source.

Max started walking around the small apartment, collecting his thoughts. "What I, what we think it means is that the three of us have…. changed." He looked at Zoe, who raised her eyebrows at that. She also looked at Henry and Alex, who just returned her stare.

"And how have you changed exactly?" Zoe said with short, brisk words.

"This will be hard to explain..." Max said. He saw Zoe roll her eyes, and then he continued quickly: "Okay, I'll just tell you what happened and why we think this is it. After Henry and I escaped the tunnel, Henry felt a strong need to understand the God who had changed me and saved us."

Zoe just groaned. "Here we go, more religious stuff," she said as she folded her arms across her chest and sat back in the chair.

"It's true, my friend," interjected Henry to Zoe. "Something happened to me: my mind, my emotions, my body. After I heard Max pray and saw what his God did, and the cat appearing just then, and how we escaped .... it was like I should have been terrified, and nervous, and all like the feelings I used to experience, but it was like a light switch had turned on, and I felt at peace and was totally calm. I had never felt those things before! Ever! I had to understand Max's God because He had touched me somehow." Henry was sitting forward as he spoke, with a look of calm on his face the others had never seen. You could see it in his eyes.

Max, standing with his back to the kitchen sink, continued. "So, he asked me to explain God to him. I'm new at this, so I didn't know what to tell him other than how I felt changed from the inside out too, so I called Alex, and we went to Mrs. Griffin. Mrs. Griffin explained that the Holy Spirit - not like a scary ghost spirit or anything - but the Holy Spirit, who is God, had touched our hearts and opened our eyes. She opened her bible and took us on what she called a 'Romans Road,' where she read a bunch of scriptures to us, mostly the same ones that guy, James, had read to me. The scriptures talked about how we can't get to heaven on our own and how Jesus, who is really God, had died for us, but then he came back to life! And how God loves us even when we are jerks. And she said that anyone who calls on His name will be saved. However, we need to surrender our old lives to Him and admit we were jerks. I had done that. That's when my light was turned on. She explained that the Holy Spirit had touched Henry's heart when he had turned toward 'our' God in the tunnel."

"Yea, yea, blah, blah, blah, so Henry heard about Jesus. But what about you, Alex? Why did your light come on?" Asked Zoe agitatedly.

Alex looked at her and the guys. "Well, Zoe." He said, "It's kind of a long story. This information she gave Henry has been seeping into my mind since I was a kid. Ever since Mrs. Griffin has been in our house, which is as long as I can remember, she has always prayed over our meals when we ate alone when my parents were gone, and when she tucked me in at night when I was a kid, she would pray over me. Nice prayers, I remember. She might even read scriptures to me, like bedtime stories. I never thought much about it because my parents said that it was nice that she believed in that stuff, but it wasn't for us. My folks didn't have time to go to church except maybe on Christmas or Easter, and they never prayed or read the bible. So, I just always thought it was something Mrs. Griffin needed, and I loved her like family, so I just accepted it as her thing. Then, when Max started coming over after his 'experience, ' I overheard what she told him and what she read to him from her bible. Some of it spoke to me somehow, but I blew it off, thinking I'm a jock, I believe in God, I'm a pretty good guy and do lots of nice things for people, so I'm okay - right God?"

Zoe nodded, "...that's more like it, Alex! That's how I feel! I believe in God, and I'm a good person! That's good enough. But get to the explanation about your light."

"BUT," Alex continued, speaking more excitedly, "When we brought Henry into the mix, I heard the questions he asked about

God, like why couldn't he worship Allah and God too. Mrs. Griffin read to him about how God is a jealous God and all the reasons why He didn't want us to worship another – mainly because He loves us. Like if you marry someone, you don't want them intimate with other people because you love them. And she read, *'not everyone who says to me 'Lord, Lord' will enter the kingdom of heaven…'.* That made me nervous a little. I heard her say how people are saved by faith – that's what happened to Max and Henry, and how we couldn't earn it by doing good things – ouch!" he mimed stabbing a fictitious knife into his chest, signifying he was cut to the heart by that. "Mrs. Griffin then said how this Nicodemus guy asked Jesus how he could get saved, and Jesus said, you had to be born again of the Spirit…"

"Ok, stop! I've heard enough!" Zoe rose from her chair, walked over toward the sink making Max move, and looked out the window. She was looking even more angry than before when she turned back to them. "I've heard all this before when my 'sweet-in-front-of-others' mother would periodically drag me to church on Sundays, then act like a devil when we got home!"

"But wait! You have to hear this part," Alex said as he moved toward her." You wanted to know what happened, right? Well, when she read about how **Jesus said He was the way, the truth, and the life and how no one would go to the Father except through him** – I wanted that more than anything I've ever wanted in my life, Zoe! More than winning a big game, more than a new car, more than…. well, more than anything! I told Mrs. Griffin how these words had gotten to me. She prayed with me and Henry both, and I know something happened…inside. I can't explain it. I just know it's real."

Henry added, "Mrs. Griffin gave me a little bible, too, and I have read it every night since last week. There is so much to learn! I can't get enough of it!"

Zoe stood staring at them and fumed, "So you three think that this thing lights up when you have some kind of religious experience? Are you nuts? What would that have to do with anything? And what about the rider and the building and….".

Just then, Sparkles jumped up on the counter next to where Zoe was ranting and began rubbing against her and purring.

"Oh, get away from me, you stupid cat!" Zoe put the cat on the floor, but Sparkles rubbed against her legs. "Ugh!" So, Zoe abruptly sat down in the chair by Bridgett to get away from the cat, who calmly followed her and kept rubbing against her and purring as she sat there angrily. No one said anything, each in their thoughts. You could see Zoe start to calm down and finally pet the cat.

"You three have exhausted me!" Zoe put her head onto her folded arms on the table as she breathed heavily.

Bridgett patted Zoe on the shoulder. "I don't get it either, Zoe, but the lights are on, and they seem to have had some similar experience. It seems like the most logical explanation."

Zoe picked her head up from the table and rested it on her hands across her forehead. Max sat back down, and they were all silent for a moment as if trying to sort it all out themselves.

Zoe sat back and looked at them. Sparkles jumped up into her lap and curled up for a nap. Zoe started stroking him. "I'm sorry I flew off the handle. I thought you were all off doing things without me, and it made me mad."

"Really?" Max said sarcastically with a little grin on his face.

Zoe narrowed her eyes at him, then continued. "You see, I have this anger problem. It started when I was very young. I don't remember exactly what happened between them since I was only like two, but my dad left. I never saw him again. Then, my mother turned mean and took out her anger on me."

"I can relate," said Max.

Zoe nodded at him but continued. "I did see a picture of him once, and I look like him, so maybe that's why she was mad at me. I don't know. I do know she would tease and frustrate me to the point of exasperation, even as a toddler. She found it amusing when I got furious or if she made me cry. She always made hateful comments to me, like 'she could be out having fun if it wasn't for being tied down with a kid.' Or, 'You aren't like other kids; don't ask me for things – you won't get them.' Or, if I started to cry after falling or scraping my knees, she said she would give me something to cry about if I started. Or tell me when I was even younger – people don't like kids who talk, so just be quiet."

Zoe paused but uncharacteristically began talking about her past again, remembering. "Once, when I was sick, my grandmother brought me soup. My mother got really mad and took the soup away, saying I should be serving my grandmother, not my grandmother serving me. I was just a kid! My grandmother loved me, but she died." Zoe wiped a tear from her cheek as she looked down at the table.

"She did get remarried - to Charlie. My Aunt introduced them." She turned to Henry, "You've met him once at the restaurant, remember?"

Henry nodded.

"He's a nice guy. He always took me to baseball practice or Karate when I was a kid. We were, and still are, more friends than stepfather/daughter. When Charlie wasn't around," she looked at them, "he's a long-distance truck driver, she told them, then continued, "My mother would make me do things like cut the lawn with a rusty, old push mower, and if there was one ridge in the grass, she would make me cut it over again. Or, I would have to pull a stupid wire cart - you know, the old lady kind with the wheels on it - the mile home when she bought groceries. I remember she would often go to two different grocery stores and make me stand outside the second one, sometimes in the driving rain or snow, waiting for her to get things from the other store – and she took her good old, sweet time. People would walk by and ask why I was outside - picture this shivering, snow-covered kid standing in the snow outside the grocery store door. They would ask why I couldn't wait in the vestibule. But she wouldn't let me and would get very angry if I did. Sometimes, my feet would feel frozen when I got home."

Zoe looked at them and continued to speak as if to herself. "On the rare occasion anyone came to our house, she would make comments like, 'She was so ugly when she was a baby, I was going to leave her at the hospital!' and laugh and laugh. I heard her tell people that she would just let me cry as a baby; she didn't have time to pick me up and just left me in the crib all day. She would purposely frustrate me to make me mad or cry and think it was hilarious. When I got older, people would tell me she had been sitting there acting and talking normally until I arrived, then her voice changed, and she got mean and spoke harshly to me."

Zoe looked at the others; they weren't used to her telling them personal things, so they just sat and listened.

Zoe went on quietly, "I remember one time there were bad winds and tornado warnings, and a picture of Jesus fell off the wall. I was scared, being just a kid. She said, 'God is mad at you, so you had better get on your knees and pray you don't get blown away by this tornado!' It didn't get any better as I got older; I just got angrier. I thought rage was normal. As soon as I was old enough, I determined to get a job and buy a car. I always hated buses. When I traveled by myself on them, there were always men smell-ing of booze who wanted to put their hands where they shouldn't be or women with strong perfume sitting next to me!" Zoe looked up at everyone, then down at Sparkles, sleeping soundly on her lap. She paused and spoke again as if to herself. "She has never once said she loved me, or held me, even as a child, or comforted me when I cried."

She looked at them with anger coming back onto her face and continued, "Yeah, so you talk about religion. When I was maybe eight, the neighbors would take me to church with them. They would ask me a bunch of questions beforehand about what it was like at home, then say, 'Oh, you poor thing.' I think they were just being nosey instead of wanting me to know God, but they took me anyway. That was my first inclination that my home life wasn't normal. I prayed and yearned for God to help me and show Himself to me. I looked for something Holy when I went to church. I was in awe of the beautiful building and the ceremonies. But then I would hear men yelling at their wives and kids in the parking lot after service, and no one would smile at me. No one was nice at all. When going to confession, I always got what seemed like a million prayers to say so that God would forgive me. I didn't feel forgiven. When I was 13, I stopped going. It didn't seem God was there." They could see another small tear form in the corner of her eye. She looked up and brushed the tear away quickly. "So, when you talk about having a wonderful experience and how you've found God, it turns me off. It's all hogwash. Manufactured garbage."

"But..." Henry started to speak.

Zoe stood and held up her hand for him to stop, "If you guys feel you experienced something, that's great; just don't talk about it around me. Okay? And let's not assume this whole thing is a 'God thing' because if it was, I would be out." She looked around the table. Henry had a look of sorrow on his face. Alex shrugged in compliance, and Max looked back at her with sadness.

"So," Zoe went on, "now that we've cleared all that up and you've heard my sad story, which I **do not** want any sympathy for." She glared at them," Where do we go from here? We're mostly back at square one, and other than three lights on the disk and the supposition it is made of Onyx, we still don't have a clue about the rider or the message. And don't even start to think it's some religious message. Okay?"

After hearing Zoe's story, they looked sad and uncomfortable, but it helped them better understand her.

Bridgett broke the silence that followed, "We are a team all right, a team of misfits, aren't we?" She looked at Zoe next to her and the rest of them around the table. "But we're in this together."

Sparkles jumped down from Zoe, moved over to Henry, and jumped up into his lap. Henry got a big smile on his face as he made 'baby talk' to the cat. "How's my Mr. Sparkles today? You are so handsome and sleek. And I love those big eyes that sparkle," and he scratched and petted the cat, who started to purr loudly and snuggle against Henry.

Zoe couldn't help but smile at his evident love for the cat, as did the rest. It broke the heavy tension in the room.

"We are kinda running out of time to figure this out. School will be starting again." Alex said. "What if we go back to where we found the disk? Do you think we might get another clue there?"

"Wonder if it will be a vacant lot this time or a deserted building?" Max questioned.

"Who knows," said Zoe, "but it's worth a try. Tomorrow?"

Everyone agreed since the next day was a Saturday.

"Let's go get a pizza and go to the park where we all met!" Henry piped up. Everyone looked at him with wide eyes. "It's okay," he chuckled. "I haven't had pizza since the hospital, but I will have some slices and not the whole thing. Then, I will run around the block two extra times tonight. I need to stay healthy for our adventures."

They all laughed and made their way downstairs.

Sparkles followed them out but waited at the top of the stairs, flicking his tail back and forth.

CHAPTER 10

REMINISCENCE

The pizza was good. They all sat at the picnic table near the gazebo. These strangers, now calling themselves 'The Crew' had become fast friends in this short time.

"That was certainly wonderful," Henry said as he closed his eyes and smacked his lips. "Before, I would have had three more pieces!" He paused and looked at the pizza still left. "It is still tempting, though, so let me get it away from where I can reach it!" He laughed as he pushed the pizza box down the table away from him.

Bridgett looked at Henry from across the table and smiled. Henry returned the smile.

Zoe caught their exchanged looks and half smiled to herself. They seemed to be getting along quite well ever since the hospital, she thought to herself,

"Good job, Henry!" Alex encouraged him and patted him on the back. We all loved you the way you were, but you now seem to have much more energy and a better attitude about yourself.

Henry nodded in agreement.

"Just think!" Max piped up. "It wasn't that long ago that we all met! Right there by that bench by the sidewalk. And I was a homeless street bum."

"Yes, and I was sitting over there by that big tree eating as I always did when I was nervous. A really big submarine sandwich if I remember correctly, and I wasn't even hungry," said Henry.

"And I was afraid to approach you to ask if you needed help with that puffy, almost black-eye you were nursing," laughed Alex toward Zoe. "I think you were ready to punch me out too."

"And I would have too if you were like that other guy!" Zoe laughed back, squinting a feigned mean look. She was still sad at recounting her story to her friends but determined to get it out of her head. They didn't seem to feel any less friendly toward her now than before, so she guessed it was okay.

"And I was in such a hurry to get away from 'people' because they were making me feel nervous, looking at me all the time like so many did, that I tripped on that curb and gave myself bloody knees," Bridgett recounted. "And I gave you guys a hard time when you tried to help…. sorry," Bridgett said sheepishly to Zoe and Alex.

"That you did," Zoe smiled at her. "Then that … whatever that mysterious guy was, appeared and his voice that sounded like thunder told us 'We were named' …."

They all sat there for a minute, remembering.

Bridgett caught Henry looking at the pizza box again. "Hey, Zoe," how about I take this back up to your apartment and put it in your refrigerator?"

"Sure," said Zoe as she tossed her the apartment keys.

"I'll be right back," said Bridgett as she grabbed the pizza box and hopped off the picnic bench.

The rest turned to talk about the week and what they had planned for the end of summer. Zoe happened to look at Henry watching Bridgett walk down the street.

"Hey, Henry, I left my phone upstairs. Would you go get it for me?" she asked.

Henry looked quickly away from staring at Bridgett and over to Zoe. "Sure! I will go catch up with Bridgett."

She had just turned the corner of the building where the restaurant was. Henry jumped up and started running to catch up. He could run now, thanks to Alex.

Alex and Max smiled at Zoe.

"Nice move," Max said. Then, the three continued small talk.

As Bridgett rounded the back of the restaurant, she almost ran into three men hanging around in the alley behind the building. She didn't recognize them as town people. They were leaning on motorcycles, drinking beer and smoking…something. They must be tourists, she thought. She had seen many strange-looking tourists around lately.

"Oh, sorry… excuse me," she said as she almost knocked one of them over as she ran into him.

"My, my," said the one she had bumped into. "What is a pretty thing like you doing in an alley all by herself?" The three turned to her. She tried to go around them, but the other two blocked her way. "What's your hurry?" one of the others said. "And look, she brought us pizza too!" he laughed as he grabbed the pizza box.

"Hey! Give that back!" She said as she tried to grab it back.

"Feisty, too! I'll tell you what I can give you, little lady, and it will be better than pizza." The tall, older man laughed and grabbed her arm roughly.

Bridgett tried to get away, but the three backed her up against the building.

"Hey, what are you doing!?" Henry yelled as he rounded the corner and saw what was happening. "Leave her alone!"

They let go of her arm long enough for her to rush away from them toward Henry.

"Oh, Miss Pretty has a boyfriend, does she?" the other biker with the leather vest said as he stepped back and laughed. And, what do you think you are going to do, buddy?" he asked as he pulled a switchblade out of his vest pocket, and you heard the click as it opened.

Bridgett and Henry backed up as the three men stood and started menacingly toward them.

Just then, the strangers stopped. They all got wide-eyed as they looked toward Henry and Bridgett and started backing up slowly. Henry and Bridgett heard a low, deep growl from somewhere behind them. They didn't want to take their eyes off the three, so they didn't turn to look at what was making the rather frightening sound.

The bikers slowly backed up, jumped on their bikes, sped off down the alley toward the main street, and headed out of town.

"What the…." Bridgett mumbled.

Henry quickly turned to see a huge black panther behind them with fangs bared. "Oh my God!" he yelled. As he did, he tripped over a rock on the pavement and almost fell backward as he grabbed Bridgett's arm to steady himself. When he turned back around, all he saw behind them was Sparkles.

"Sparkles?" he said.

"They were afraid of Sparkles?" Bridgett asked as she turned as well.

"No, Sparkles was.... he had changed into... oh, let me sit down for a minute," Henry said as he sat on the steps in the alley that went up to Zoe's apartment. Sparkles strolled over and rubbed against his legs, purring loudly.

Bridgett came and sat next to Henry. "Thank you for saving me, Henry."

"But I did not save you," Henry replied. He turned to look at her. "It was Sparkles...you aren't going to believe this, but Sparkles was a big, really big, black panther - that's what scared them." He looked at her and raised both hands in a motion that told him he didn't believe it either.

"Huh?" Bridgett said.

Henry tried to explain what he had seen but didn't understand himself. They both looked at Sparkles, who was now sitting in front of them, calmly looking at them and flicking his tail.

After they picked up the strewn pizza and threw it and the box away in one of the trash bins, they started walking back to the park.

"Will anyone believe us?" Henry said as they walked.

"With everything we have been through before, I think they will," Bridgett said as they approached the group.

They just stood there when they got back to the others, who were still talking and laughing about school and Alex's last game. Alex was facing them and did a double-take when he saw their faces. The others saw Alex's face and turned to look as well.

Henry and Bridgett told them what had happened: the men, the knife, the .... panther, and as if on cue, Sparkles jumped up on the table and sat, purring loudly.

Sparkles cocked his head as everyone looked at him.

CHAPTER 11

GOING BACK

The following weekend, they again met at the park.

Bridgett now had a small old car her parents had bought her since she passed her driver's license test, but it wasn't big enough for all of them.

Zoe's car was too old to trust on long ventures, so they agreed that Alex should bring his dad's van again. Alex pulled up and opened the doors so they could all pile in.

"I wouldn't think your dad would drive a van," Max commented. He had briefly met his dad as he was leaving Alex's house one weekend, and his dad was coming home from one of his trips. He was a very distinguished, good-looking, gentlemanly-looking guy. "It's nice, but I figured him to be a fancy sports car kind of man."

Alex chuckled. "He only uses the van when everyone goes some-where together, which isn't often anymore. He used it when he would take me and my buddies to practice, but it has just sat in the back of the driveway after he started traveling so much for his work. I usually drive the yellow Jeep he bought me, but this is perfect for our trips, don't you think?" Alex buckled up as Max sidled up into the seat behind him.

Zoe got into the passenger seat, and Henry and Bridgett sat in the back.

Before he closed the side door, Sparkles jumped in.

"A cat that likes car rides?" Max chuckled. "Let me put him out," he said as he turned to grab Sparkles, who had jumped onto the back seat with Henry and Bridgett.

"No! "Henry said as he sat forward in the seat, "He has been sent to help and protect me twice now. He needs to come if that is what he wishes!"

Zoe rolled her eyes so Henry couldn't see, but she said, "Oh, let the cat come then! Let's get going!" She had a hard time believing Henry's story that Sparkles had turned into a big black panther, but she didn't exclude anything anymore.

The others smiled at her comment, and the door was closed. Sparkles curled up on the empty seat next to Henry and went to sleep. They drove out of town toward the address they had initially been directed to on the little luminescent scroll that had burned up and the mysterious disappearing building where they had found the disk.

They were mostly silent as they drove, and the only sound was Max's music playing softly. Max, lost in his own world, was listening to music on the cell phone he could purchase with the money he was earning as an apprentice. Henry and Bridgett, sitting in the back, made occasional small talk. Zoe and Alex, in the front, just watched the road and the deteriorating scenery, the same as they had seen before.

Henry couldn't contain his excitement as he shared with Bridgett how Zoe had told him about videography and how fascinating it sounded. This career also offered apprenticeships, which made it even more appealing. He had found this one company while researching online at the library. It was a local company, and he couldn't wait to call them on Monday! He turned and asked Bridgett if maybe she could be an actor if he wrote a little play or something - as soon as he could afford the equipment, that is.

"I would love to, Henry!" She also responded excitedly.

Alex heard and piped up from the front as he drove. "Hey, Henry! I happen to have an old camera and tripod at home, which you can have! If you want it. It's not the best, but it's just sitting there."

Zoe smiled as she looked forward because she knew Alex was probably giving away an expensive piece of equipment. He was good at humbly helping people like that.

"Oh, I would love that, my friend, Alex! If you are sure that you don't need it anymore. I would be most appreciative!" Henry responded excitedly. He turned to look at Bridgett with the biggest smile on his face.

Bridgett smiled back at this guy who had become her best friend and confidant. She watched him as he talked about the videography. She had never had anyone like her just for being herself as he does, even with no makeup, wearing what her parents would call ragged clothes, and if she was in a cranky mood. Of course, her parents loved and doted on her, but they always tried to make her into something she wasn't. She thought of the coming fall months and how they would try to get her involved in this big-time modeling agency so that she would be 'discovered' once she graduated. Ugh! She slumped into the seat at the thought of it, still trying to look interested in Henry's newfound interest as he talked.

Henry finally stopped talking, still with a smile on his face, with newfound hope for his future. He wasn't much of a talker normally, so he was glad Bridgett was such a good listener. He looked out of the window, thinking of the possibilities. He never knew he had a creative side to his mind; he had always been busy being afraid of everything. Ever since he had found peace through God, he had so many more ideas about how his life could be different, like writing and creating pictures through photography that people could relate to. He could tell a story about things like the war in his homeland in this way so that people would understand things outside their own worlds.

He had started working for the summer at the fast-food place not far from his house so that he could help his mother pay bills. He hated it. He tried to smile at people, but they were all in a hurry and not very friendly. They sometimes had difficulty with his slight accent and perhaps his dark skin. Maybe they were going through something inside as he and his dear friend had experienced and still do on occasion, but not so much as before, so he smiled at them anyway. He looked over at Bridgett, who had gone silent and looked gloomily out of the other window as if deep in thought. She had become much more relaxed since he had shared what the doctors at the hospital had told him about dealing with anxiety, but she still held a lot inside. He could tell. He would listen to her, no matter what she needed to say to him. That seemed to help her, too, to be able to talk to someone who understood. He wished she could find the peace he had found. He had feelings for her that he didn't even know how to articulate. She was …well, he cared very deeply for her.

Bridgett turned and saw Henry looking at her. She smiled at him, not wanting him to see her bummed out, and asked him what he might write about. That brought a big smile to his face as he went on about pictures that could make people relate better to the world and their feelings and ….," he kept talking quietly.

In the front seat, Alex turned to Zoe as they drove farther into the old town and saw, again, the deserted buildings. "So, what do you think we will find this time?" he asked.

"I don't know," she answered as she rested her head against the back of the seat. "Nothing is going to surprise me anymore."

"I wouldn't say that!" Alex chuckled as he drove.

The ride was long. The empty, run-down town was still as depressing with the half-broken signs hanging, the broken windows, the trash, and the building with doors standing open. Zoe wondered what had happened to all these people after they left.

The GPS said, "Your destination will be on the right…". They all looked past the stand of trees to see what was there this time. It was the building! It was back! Alex pulled into the gravel parking lot. The picnic table was still there. The windows were still broken. It still looked creepy. But it was there. He put the van into the park, but no one moved to get out.

"We're here, kids!" Zoe spoke up quietly. Still, no one made a move to get out. "Come on. Let's see what we can find this time," she said a little louder, opening her door, and getting out.

Max opened the side door, and Sparkles jumped out. "Hey!" he yelled at the cat, but the cat bolted toward the side of the building where they knew there was an open door.

"Oh, I hope he doesn't get lost!" Henry said as he quickly climbed out.

"If a cat can turn into a panther and back again, I don't think you have to worry about him too much," said Zoe.

No one spoke as they exited the van and looked at the building. Henry was in a hurry to find Sparkles, though.

"Just to confirm, this building wasn't here the last time we pulled up, right?" Max asked as he looked around.

"Correct," Zoe said. "But, it's here now, so let's see what it has to offer this time, if anything."

Alex, Zoe, and Max moved toward the side of the building where the door was that they had entered the last time. Henry and Bridgett looked at each other. Henry looked apprehensive for a moment, then stood up straighter and smiled confidently at Bridgett. "I need to find Sparkles," he said. "Let us go!" And he moved determinedly forward. After a few long strides, he realized Bridgett was not beside him. He turned to see her still by the van. He walked back and took her hand, "You…we can do this. God is with us!" He slowly moved forward, and Bridgett hesitantly moved on with him. He smiled broadly at her, and you could see the resolve on her face begin.

"Okay, Henry. I trust you and your God. Let's do this!" She stood straight and passed him by quickly.

Henry smiled at her as he walked fast to catch up.

They got inside and turned on their cell flashlights. They remembered traveling through the small, dark rooms before they got to the big, open area. Everything looked the same.

"I think it was this way," Max said as he moved through the small rooms and hallways.

Henry began calling for Sparkles. "Sparkles! Sparkles! Where are you?"

Zoe and Alex kept moving as well, but they showed their flashlights on the walls and tables, overturned chairs, and debris as they moved. Zoe saw the old, dusty hat Max had wanted to take home but didn't mention it, hoping he wouldn't see it again.

"Doesn't look like anyone has been here since us," Zoe commented. "There's still an inch of dust on everything."

There was a loud 'creaking' noise above, and dust fell from the ceiling near them. They all pointed their flashlights toward the sound but could see nothing. They kept walking.

They heard Sparkles mewing in the silence. They looked at each other, and Henry took the lead. "It sounds like it's coming from this way," he said, moving through a door.

"Wait for me!" hollered Bridgett as she pushed through the others to catch up to Henry.

As soon as he opened the door, they were almost blinded by the daylight that hit them in the faces, just like before.

"Wow," Max said, "I remember that from the last time."

They strode into the middle of the large, empty room—the same room where they had found the disk. Sparkles was sitting on top of the desk where the disk had been, looking at them as if waiting. They moved slowly toward the desk, with Henry and Bridgett still at the front of the pack.

"Sparkles! I am so happy to see you! Are you all right? Have you found something for us?" Henry spoke to the cat as he approached him. He stroked his head when he reached the table. Bridgett also petted the cat as she looked around the room. The others approached.

"Okay, cat, what miracle do you have for us today?" Zoe asked sarcastically.

"Hello," they heard a voice from behind them! They all jumped and turned quickly. In the back of the room, where the daylight didn't reach, to the side of the door they had just entered, was a man in shadow sitting on a bench. The bench had probably been part of a production line of some kind. The five instinctively huddled closer together. Henry gathered the cat into his arms.

Finally, Alex asked, "Who are you?"

Just then, Sparkles jumped out of Henry's arms and ran over to the man.

"Sparkles! Wait!" Henry called.

They still could not see the man's face as it was in shadows. The cat jumped up beside him and purred loudly as the man stroked his back.

"It doesn't matter who I am," the man answered softly as he jumped down and came into the light toward them. "What matters is the message I've been given for you." He started walking toward them.

"Oh great!" Zoe muttered under her breath, "another message... "

He was of moderate height and slim, wearing a bright white t-shirt, light-colored blue jeans, and bright white sneakers, which was odd in this dirty, dusty place. He had long, thick, blonde hair and a calm look on his face.

They started to steel themselves as if for a fight if necessary.

"You need not fear me," the man said gently. He stopped to pick up Sparkles, who had followed him and rubbed against his legs.

"I have been sent to tell you that as soon as you are complete, there is something that you will be assigned to do."

"What do you mean 'complete'?" Zoe asked.

"And what do you mean we will be assigned something to do?" asked Bridgett.

"That is all I can tell you right now, but you must be strong, courageous, and faithful. You will be given all that you need when you need it."

"But…." Max started to say to the man, but just then, the man began to glow as if a sunbeam was showing behind him. Suddenly, he rose into the air, and with a soft '**pouf,'** he was gone!

They all just stood there looking at the spot where he had been.

Then, behind them, the large, heavy door banged open at the back of the big room! It was right in front of where their van was parked! They all jumped at the sound.

"Llllet's get out of here!" Bridgett said as she started walking quickly to the door.

"Not a bad idea," Max said as he followed her.

Alex and Zoe looked around the room, then at each other, then moved toward the door as well.

Henry started to walk toward the door but stopped. "But, where is Sparkles? He had Sparkles in his arms! Where did he take our Sparkles!" You could hear the panic in his voice. Just then, Sparkles appeared at the newly opened door and mewed as if on cue. "Sparkles! You are okay!" Henry rushed quickly past the others, scooped up the cat, and rushed outside.

When they were all outside, they looked back at the building.

"I need a minute," said Bridgett as she sat on the picnic table.

The others joined her.

"So, here we go again…riddles, unanswered questions," Zoe said disgustedly as she plopped down on the top of the table with her feet on the bench. "It's starting to tick me off!" She said as she rubbed her forehead.

"Yeah," Alex said. "What did that mean – when we are complete? Complete at something? Complete doing something? Complete what?" He looked perplexed as well. He looked at Max and Henry, wondering what this Messenger had meant.

"And, did that guy just disappear? We all can't be hallucinating seeing the same thing, can we?" Max questioned.

The others just shook their heads 'no' and looked confused as well.

"But at least Sparkles is okay," Henry said as he lovingly stroked the cat in his arms. "He didn't seem to be afraid of the stranger at all. Perhaps we shouldn't be either. Or at his message."

Zoe rolled her eyes at Henry's comment again, but he did not see her. "I've been feeding that cat for a while now, and I haven't seen him have any superpowers, Henry," Zoe said. "Let's get started; it's a long drive home."

They piled back into the van, Henry still holding Sparkles.

"Do we have everything this time? Bridgett, do you have your scarf?" Zoe asked.

Bridgett said, "Yes," as she felt for the scarf holding her pony-tail back.

They pulled away from the building, all looking at it, wondering what this all could mean.

CHAPTER 12

THE STOP

They rode along, mostly in silence, deep in thought.

They were startled out of their reverie as Alex swerved sharply, narrowly missing a large, rusty metal trash can blowing across the road as they got to the outskirts of the old town. Unfortunately, he didn't see the broken cement blocks strewn all over the side of the road, mixed with broken glass and other trash. He steered quickly the other way, but you could hear a tire blow. He fought to bring the van back in control as it sharply veered back and forth. He brought the van to an abrupt stop, sending everyone quickly forward in their seats. They all had held on as they were bounced around. The dust from the road encompassed the van.

Alex turned quickly. "Is everyone okay?" he choked out. He quickly unbuckled his seat belt to check on everyone. They were all coughing from the thick dust. He looked first at Zoe in the seat next to him. She nodded in the affirmative, saying she was okay, coughing. He turned in his seat and saw the others unbuckling and coughing at the dust still entering the open windows.

"I'm okay," Max half coughed and half yelled.

"I think we are okay back here, too," said Henry, covering his mouth with his arm as he looked at Bridgett as she coughed and straightened herself in the seat. Sparkles was now on the floor in front of Henry's feet, but he just looked up and jumped back on the seat between Henry and Bridgett.

"I'm pretty sure we have a flat," said Alex as he opened the door and got out.

"Sounded like it," coughed Zoe, who also got out.

Zoe opened the side door so the others could get out but shouted to Alex on the other side of the van. "It's here! The back tire is kinda shredded."

Alex and Max came and looked at it.

"Yep. Hope you have a spare, Alex," Max said as he pushed his hair out of his eyes.

"I hope so, too," Alex said. "The only one home right now is my mother, but I don't think she would know anything about fixing a flat on this thing; plus, I would have a LOT of questions to answer as to why we were in this area, to begin with."

Zoe nodded in agreement, hoping not to have to call anyone. She glanced over at the building across the street and thought she saw a figure behind one of the broken windows, but it was gone almost immediately. "Hey, did anyone see someone over there....?" She asked, pointing. "Oh, never mind," she thought better of asking since she couldn't see it anymore. The rest were busy looking at the tire and checking the van for dents.

Alex found the spare tire and jack in the back of the van under a floorboard. He, Max, and Zoe started to change the tire.

"Hey, thanks, Zoe, but Max and I have this."

Henry moved closer. "I would like to watch you do this," he said. "Someday, I would like to own a vehicle, and it is good to know how to handle emergency situations, is it not?"

"Ya, sure. You can watch," Alex said.

Bridgett and Zoe moved to the shade of a tree nearby in a grassy area on the side of the road about 20 feet away.

"Hey! Look at this!" Bridgett said as she peered behind the tree. "There is a stream down there! Here." She motioned for Zoe to come look. "You can see it between these bushes. It's down quite a way. Good thing we didn't go over the side. Come see!" Bridgett motioned again for Zoe to come closer.

"That's okay," Zoe said. "I'm kind of afraid of heights." And she moved toward some rocks farther away from the edge.

"YOU are afraid of something!" Bridgett turned back to her and made a smirky expression.

"I thought you were the tough one who wasn't afraid of anything! Miss tough girl!" Bridgett found it very amusing.

"Okay, okay. Enough, Bridgett," Zoe said, still deep in thought, trying to figure out all the messages and what all these things could mean.

Bridgett got annoyed by Zoe's dismissal of her as she turned her back to her and leaned against a large rock. Bridgett bristled. Zoe had always made her feel like she was inferior to her, that she wasn't smart or independent. She made her feel like a little kid. Zoe didn't understand why she didn't just tell her parents what she wanted to do and be done with it. Bridgett's frustration over her life, her anxiety, all that had happened to them all, all the unanswered questions – it all boiled up.

"You just think you are better than me, don't you? You think you are braver and smarter, that everyone likes you, and that you can take care of yourself, and I can't. Don't you think I would like to be like that!" She badgered Zoe as she followed her toward the boulder, talking to Zoe's back.

"I never said I thought I was better than you, Bridgett," Zoe said, sounding rather condescending. She didn't turn to look at her.

"See, you are doing it right now! You are dismissing me and not even acknowledging me." Bridgett got angrier now that she was finally saying what she felt inside instead of holding it in.

"Can't you even look at me when I talk to you!" Bridgett ran around in front of Zoe and got right in front of her with her hands on her hips.

"Drop it, Bridgett," Zoe said as she turned to look toward the van and the guys. "I'm tired and hungry and not in the mood."

"Well, isn't that too bad for you! I'm hungry most of the time!" She circled and turned back toward the bushes, talking furiously and looking very angry.

"It's not my fault your parents make you starve yourself," Zoe responded.

"Well, at least my parents care about me!" Bridgett turned and spit the words out at Zoe. She walked angrily back toward her. "I have people who want the best for me! Not like your mother, who doesn't even care where you are living or what you are doing!"

"Let it alone, Bridgett." Zoe now turned toward her, and you could see the anger rise in her eyes.

"I won't leave it alone! I'm tired of being the quiet one, not saying what I feel, and having people walk all over me! I'm tired of making people think I'm the pretty one with no brains or feelings! People like you who completely ignore me and think I'm not worth getting to know, or...."

"Bridgett.... stop...." Zoe began to move the five feet toward Bridgett, who was angrily walking back and forth. Her fists were now clenched.

"Maybe I'm better off being the pretty one people ignore than the angry one who says she doesn't need anyone – like you. Who doesn't even know where her father is..."

At that, Zoe rushed forward and shoved Bridgett – hard.

Bridgett turned her ankle at the blow and fell backward, clutching at the bushes, but she fell through them, to Zoe's horror. She screamed as she fell down the 50-foot embankment toward the moving water and rocks below.

Zoe froze where she was. She hadn't meant to shove her over the side! She brought her closed hand up to her mouth. Just then, something black, very large and very fast, ran past her through the bushes where Bridgett had fallen.

Zoe backed up and began yelling, "Guys! Guys! I need your help! Guys!"

Within a few seconds, a huge, black panther dragged a limp Bridgett in tow up through the opening in the bushes. The panther had Bridgett's jean jacket in his mouth and dragged her up to the top of the embankment, slid her over the top edge, pulling hard as Bridgett's clothing caught on branches, and dropped her at the front of the bushes. The panther looked at Zoe - gave a low growl, and ran off.

Zoe looked for a moment after the beast, then ran and knelt next to Bridgett, who was beginning to come around. She turned her over onto her side. She had a very large, bleeding gash on her right arm. Through her jacket, she could see the blood soaking into a 10-inch tear. You could also see a large knot, the size of an orange, forming on her forehead.

Just then, Alex, Max, and Henry ran up. They had heard Bridgett scream and had seen a big, black panther rush away from the clearing into the bushes in front of the van.

"What happened!" Alex shouted as he ran to Bridgett and knelt on her other side.

Henry knelt next to Bridgett, taking her limp hand in his. He nudged Zoe out of the way and called her name, "Bridgett, Bridgett! Are you okay? Please wake up! Oh my, look at her arm! There is blood everywhere!"

Max said, "Wow! Yes, that is a nasty cut even through the jacket!"

Zoe backed away, unable to speak, still with her hands across her mouth.

Alex shouted to Max, standing at Bridgett's feet watching, "There's a first aid kit in the van! Hurry, go get it!"

Bridgett started to open her eyes. She looked dazed. There was a cut on her forehead next to the raised, now grapefruit-sized bump. She looked at everyone, then at Zoe, then at her arm, and tried to sit up quickly, but she put her hand up quickly to her forehead, swooning backward again.

"No, wait!" said Alex, "Stay there for a minute. He removed his jacket, rolled it up, and placed it under her head. We have to stop this bleeding first. I don't want you passing out again."

Max ran back with the first aid kit. Alex opened it.

"Hey, I need some water! Did anyone have a water bottle in the van?"

"Yes, yes," Henry said. "I brought water. I will run and get it! Oh, please, please, Bridgett, be okay! I will be right back. Friends – pray, and I will too."

Alex pulled out gauze pads, antiseptic, and several other things. Henry came back with the water bottle. They cut the arm of the jacket off. Alex cleaned the eight-inch wound and dumped the antiseptic on it, at which Bridgett screamed, but Henry held her hand as she cried out.

Alex put pressure on the area and bandaged it as well as he could. Then they helped her up and let her sit on one of the smaller, round stones.

"Don't try to get up too quickly; you've lost a lot of blood," Alex said as he repacked the first aid kit after dabbing some peroxide on her forehead cut.

"You were amazing, Alex!" said Henry. "How did you know how to do all that?"

"Well, when you are into sports as much as I have been, my dad thought it a good idea to enroll me in a first aid/CPR class. I guess it stuck with me." Alex answered.

He smiled at Bridgett, who smiled weakly back.

Just then, Sparkles meowed in Zoe's ear from the top of the boulder she had backed into.

Zoe jumped.

"So, what happened?" Henry asked, looking back and forth between Bridgett and Zoe.

"It was all my fault," Zoe said softly from where she was. "It was all my fault."

She couldn't take her eyes off Bridgett sitting there with her bandaged arm. "I pushed her…"

"You WHAT!" Shouted Max. "You pushed her over the edge of a cliff?"

Henry sat back and looked at Zoe with disbelief and anger, then back to Bridgett and took her hand.

"What do you mean, you 'pushed' her?" asked Alex, looking sternly at Zoe.

Bridgett spoke up …" It wasn't all her fault." She said quietly.

They all looked at Bridgett, who went on.

"I got angry. All the feelings I've been pushing down all my life seemed to surface all at once, and I took it all out on Zoe. I said hurtful things." She looked at Zoe and pursed her lips. "I'm sorry for all the things I said…".

Zoe rushed forward and knelt in front of her. "Oh, my friend! I need to apologize to you! I'm so sorry I pushed you! I don't know why… I guess I've had some things built up inside, too. Can you ever forgive me?" asked Zoe as tears rolled down her cheeks.

Bridgett smiled at her through the tears on her face, too. "Of course I forgive you."

"But you know, the strangest thing happened," Bridgett said as if to herself, "as I started to fall,

I could see I was heading for a large, pointed rock about halfway to the river at the bottom. I knew it would not go well if I hit that. I called out to God in that moment, 'God! Help me!' and it was like this huge hand moved me as I fell, and I wound up about three feet to the right toward a clump of bushes sticking out of the side of the hill. I reached out my hand to grab it, then hit my head on something. The next thing I remember, I was up here..."

Zoe sat back and just looked at her for a moment.

"And as I stood there, frozen and too afraid to go close to the edge," Zoe recounted, "I saw a very large...." She looked at Henry before she continued, "No, a huge, black panther rush to the side and jump down into the hole between the bushes."

She looked around at the others to see if anyone believed her. "The panther was the one who dragged you back up here to the top."

"Yes, look at the teeth marks in the back of your jacket!" Henry shouted.

"And the scrape marks on your jeans and boots," Max pointed out.

"He must be some big cat!" Max said as they all turned to look at Sparkles, walking happily toward them. Sparkles then jumped into Bridgett's lap and curled up, looking at everyone as he did, almost smiling as if a cat could smile. Bridgett tried to pet him but winced in pain.

Henry looked at Sparkles, Zoe, Bridgett, and the others. "God has sent this cat to us to help us again. Thank you, the God of Heaven and Earth," he prayed out loud. Then he bowed his head and closed his eyes in silent prayer.

Alex and Max nodded their silent prayer of thanks as well.

Zoe looked at the cat in wonder. She didn't roll her eyes when Henry prayed this time.

Bridgett reached her good hand toward the cat and stroked him. He began purring loudly.

"We've got to get you home so they can get you to the hospital quickly," Alex said. They helped Bridgett up and into the van so she could lie down in the back.

The rest of the ride home was filled with questions that no one asked out loud. Henry sat on the floor in front of the bench seat where he insisted Bridgett lie down. He rolled his jacket up and placed it under her damaged arm, with Alex's jacket still supporting her head.

Max sat sideways on his two seats and stared out the window, looking back at the two periodically.

Alex fixed his eyes on the road and drove as fast as possible. Zoe sat in silent remorse.

CHAPTER 13

MRS. GRIFFIN

"I am so happy to finally meet you, Bridgett," Mrs. Griffin said, welcoming her into Alex's huge 'Better Homes and Gardens' kitchen. "I have heard so much about you. Can I get you all some beverages? We have iced tea, lemonade, and bottled water...".

Mrs. Griffin was a robust-looking, middle-aged woman. She wore a crisply ironed light blue shirt and chino slacks. Her bright pink painted toenails showed poking out of the sandals she wore. Her hair was thick and brown and pulled back into a high ponytail. She didn't look like a housekeeper, whatever a housekeeper is supposed to look like. Her broad smile and kind eyes immediately put you at ease.

As soon as she had given everyone something to drink and brought out the tray of freshly baked cookies, she sat down with them at the round table in the kitchen.

It was Henry, Max, Alex and Bridgett.

"I understand you have some questions, Bridgett," Mrs. Griffin said.

"Yes, but can I start at the beginning?" Bridgett asked as she sat forward and closed her hands together, wincing a little as she pushed her stitched arm forward.

"Of course, of course, dear, go on…" Mrs. Griffin also sat forward, ready to listen as she sipped her tea.

"You see, I was born with…. well, I have been gifted with looking…." She stumbled.

"You are very beautiful," Mrs. Griffin kindly finished her sentence for her and smiled.

"Well, yes, that's what I've been told," Bridgett smiled humbly. "And from when I was maybe two, my parents have gotten me into commercials, toddler beauty pageants, and modeling children's clothing for the store circulars. They have paid lots of money to have people show me how to walk, carry myself, dress, apply makeup, and do my hair…" she stopped. "Mrs. Griffin - I hate it," she said, looking searchingly into Mrs. Griffin's eyes.

"Have you ever told your parents this?" Mrs. Griffin asked.

"Well, no. I didn't want to hurt their feelings. It was something I just grew up with. It was our 'normal'. I didn't want to disappoint them." Bridgett looked down at the table. "

"Until recently, that is. Finally, I couldn't hold it back any longer." She looked up, searching Mrs. Griffin's face, "You see, my friends here, plus Zoe, our other friend, and I, we had a 'trip' and I …um, fell," she looked around the table at the others knowingly, "and cut my arm really badly." She showed the arm with the 30 stitches to Mrs. Griffin, who nodded at it. "I had to explain to my parents what had happened when my friends brought me home. I said I had been on a short trip with my good friends, and yes, I had close friends now, which they were pleased about, and that I had fallen and cut my arm. I told them that these friends had helped me.

On the way to the hospital, they freaked out that I was going to have a bad scar that would hurt my 'modeling career,' I finally blurted out that I didn't care if I would have a scar because I didn't want to be a model anyway. Whew! They were both stunned, to say the least. I thought the doctors would have to give them something so they wouldn't pass out!" She smiled at the group.

"But they seemed a little less shocked and sad when I quickly told them that one of my friends, Henry, was going to be a videographer and make movies and documentaries, and he had asked me to be in them." Bridgett paused for a moment, then went on. "My whole life has changed in the few weeks since finally being honest with them. I don't feel as stressed out all the time now. And I haven't had an anxiety attack in weeks!" She looked tenderly at Henry. "Well, my friend Henry has helped with that, too. Unfortunately, my parents don't know what to do with themselves since we had always spent most weekends going to casting appointments or getting modeling training, and things like that. They feel lost, but they are spending more time with each other, so it's probably a good thing for them, too?" Bridgett looked earnestly at Mrs. Griffin, "But you see, since I've met these friends –the first friends I have ever had – 'The Crew' as we call ourselves," and she smiled around the table, lingering a little longer as she looked at Henry who beamed, "I've learned to understand that perhaps I can be myself and people will like me for who I am not the way I look."

Mrs. Griffin smiled and nodded gently.

"The main reason I'm here to talk with you is that we have had a few 'unexplainable' experiences since the moment we met. These experiences have been quite intriguing, sometimes frightening, and have brought us closer together," Bridgett explained.

"Yes, I've heard about them." Mrs. Griffin nodded at the others around the table.

"Max has undergone a profound transformation since he had a conversation with a man at the Shelter and started reading the Bible. It's like night and day. His newfound spirituality has brought about a significant change in his outlook and demeanor," Bridgett shared, smiling at Max, who had a silly grin on his face.

"And, my friend here, Henry – I have seen many changes in him since he, as he explains it, has met Max's God of Heaven and Earth." Again, she smiled at Henry, who couldn't look more pleased.

"I haven't seen a lot of change in Alex. He was always a nice, giving, supportive kinda guy. But I know he has started talking Bible with Max, Henry, and other kids, too," she smiled at Alex, who smiled back sincerely.

"Then, just recently we…I had an experience with this 'fall' where I think I felt, maybe, the Hand of God. I mean, I called out to God as I was falling down this cliff by a ravine, and well, I felt like a big hand, or something lifted me and placed me near a bush about three feet from where I was falling to break my fall…. it's hard to explain, but I felt … *something,* and I knew it had to do with me calling out to God."

She looked at Mrs. Griffin and then around at the others… "I mean, then there's the cat, who turns into a panther…I've seen it. He even saved me from the fall." She glanced at Mrs. Griffin, who made no look of judgment at this comment, "He brought me back up from the cliff!" She looked at Henry, "And then I've listened to what Henry says about how he now feels peace inside where he used to feel fear and anxiety all the time." Then she looked at Max, "And I've listened to Max say how he doesn't feel like a loser anymore and that he knows God loves him like no one has loved him all his life, despite everything he has done…" Looking back at Mrs. Griffin, she said, "Well, I want what they have." She paused. "I have never really gone to church. I mean, I believe in God, I guess. I mean, I have heard about Him. But…. anyway, when I said this to these guys, they suggested I come and talk with you."

Bridgett continued to lean into the table expectantly, her hands folded in front of her, as she looked intently at Mrs. Griffin. The big, red scar showed under her pink T-shirt sleeve, and the bump on her forehead peeked out from under her bangs.

The others turned to look at Mrs. Griffin as well, waiting.

Mrs. Griffin, a wise and serene figure, sat back in her chair, her eyes fixed on Bridgett. After a moment of contemplation, she rose and walked to the counter, pouring herself a cup of tea. As she stirred in some sugar, her gaze shifted back to Bridgett and the boys, her expression a mix of understanding and joy.

She walked over to the sideboard by her room and opened the drawer. She pulled out a pretty, purple-colored bible and sat back down.

"Bridgett," Mrs. Griffin said gently, "there are forces at work in the world that most people are totally unaware of. There are forces at work in our hearts, both good and bad, that we struggle with – each and every one of us. At some point in each one of our lives, God's Holy Spirit, yes, God is three in one – God, Holy Spirit, and Jesus – don't ask me to explain it. It is just true. I had heard it explained like water can be ice, or steam and water too. But, in any case, His Holy Spirit will call to us. It will be our decision what we do with that call. The decision is ours and ours alone. Max heard the call and turned to his Savior, Jesus Christ. Henry has experienced God in a special way, and I've heard it said that once you've experienced God, no one can ever change your mind."

"That is very true, Mrs. Griffin. No one." Henry interjected, nodding his head solemnly.

"Alex," Mrs. Griffin went on, "has heard the Good News ever since he was a very little boy, although he probably didn't know it. But he had to come to a point of not just hearing the Word but admitting he needed to receive forgiveness even though he was already a 'nice' guy. He had to get it from his head to his heart. I thank God for Alex now being able to see how the whole world needs to hear this message, and." She looked over at Alex, who was sitting next to her, "that it's our privilege to tell others how God sent His only Son to die for everyone and explain to others how to receive that gift of salvation." And she put her hand on top of Alex's hand on the table. "You have been like a son to me all these years. I am so happy for you, Alex".

Alex put his other hand on top of hers and patted it warmly.

"Now, let's focus on you, young lady. You are aware 'of' God, but do you truly know His Son Jesus? I mean, have you experienced a personal relationship with Him? He endured a horrific death that He could have avoided at any moment, but He chose to go through it – for you, for us, and for all people worldwide. He is the key. He is the door. Jesus proclaimed this," And she opened the bible, pointing to a page, turning so Bridgett could see…. "I am the way, the truth, and the life. No one comes to the Father, except through me."

Bridgett nodded, "Yes, of course; I've heard of Jesus and seen pictures of him hanging on the cross."

"Well, Bridgett, the Good News is that He isn't hanging on a cross any longer. The Easter holiday that everyone celebrates isn't about bunnies and eggs; it's about the day Jesus was resurrected. And you know what? He's still alive today." She observed Bridgett pondering over this and smiling hesitantly. "No, dear, I mean He is alive – just like you and just like me. I mean, in a real, tangible sense." She noticed the understanding dawning on Bridgett's face.

"There's no magic here. There are no countless tasks you have to complete or special prayers you have to recite while performing some physical act. You can receive what people from the beginning of time to the end of time have and will receive – the gift of salvation and forgiveness."

"But what do I have to do? I must have to do something." Bridgett said. "Do I have to go to your church or read the whole bible first, or try to be a better person, or what?" She looked around questioningly at the others, too.

Mrs. Griffin smiled. "As I said, *you* don't have to 'do' anything, my dear; it's already been done – by Jesus. You have to believe, repent – which is an old-fashioned word for changing one's mind about sin, and trust in what Jesus has done for you – not what you, or anyone else, can do for yourself."

"But, I'm no big sinner," Bridgett said. "I've never really done much wrong."

"Have you ever told a lie?" Mrs. Griffin asked, "Or hated in your heart, or lusted after something someone else had or did? Taken a pen from school?"

Bridgett thought for a moment, then sheepishly nodded yes.

"Well, then, you have broken God's law. We are all sinners. See here; the bible says, *'for all have sinned and fall short of the glory of God.'* And she showed her that scripture, too.

"Seems too simple," Bridgett said.

"Yes, it does," smiled Mrs. Griffin. The others smiled, too.

Mrs. Griffin watched as Bridgett sat back and thought for a moment.

The others sat as they knew this had to be Bridgett's decision, just as it had been theirs.

Henry closed his eyes as he sat back a little behind so Bridgett could not see him. Mrs. Griffin thought he might be praying for his friend.

Finally, slowly, Bridgett sat forward again, put her hands in her lap, and, with big, soulful eyes, asked if Mrs. Griffin would help her make sure of her decision to trust in God.

Mrs. Griffin smiled softly, "Of course, dear Bridgett, but you mustn't base your salvation on having said a prayer. Reciting a prayer cannot save you. If you want to receive the salvation that is available through Jesus, place your faith in Him. Fully trust His death as the sufficient sacrifice for your sins. In the old days, it had to be an individual sacrifice of a lamb or other animal. Jesus became the spotless lamb of God for all. Completely rely on Him alone as your Savior. That is the biblical method of salvation. Do you understand?"

"I understand," Bridgett said.

Mrs. Griffin stretched her hands across the table and put Bridgett's in hers. The boys put their hands on Bridgett or Mrs. Griffin as she and Bridgett prayed. It was difficult to understand what Bridgett was saying because of her crying, but God understood. Afterward, Mrs. Griffin walked around the table and hugged Bridgett, being careful to stay away from her arm with the stitches. The others gave her pats, and Henry gave her a quick, 'friend' hug that perhaps lasted a bit too long.

CHAPTER 14

THE FINAL

The knock she had been expecting came at the door. "It's open," called Zoe.

In came the others: Max, Alex, Henry, and Bridgett. Zoe was sitting at the kitchen table and motioned them solemnly to sit as well. They all took chairs without speaking.

"Well?" Zoe said resignedly and waited, sitting back in her chair with crossed arms. She had a strange, tired look on her face.

The others looked quickly at each other, and finally, Bridgett began, "Zoe, we've come to tell you that I have received Jesus into my heart, as the others have."

"Ya, I figured something like that," Zoe said as she shoved the disk into the middle of the table. It now had all the lights lit up except hers.

"Wow," said Max as he looked at Alex and Bridgett.

They all saw that Zoe had a strange, stoic look on her face.

"Let me explain," Bridgett leaned forward toward Zoe beseechingly.

"Don't bother," Zoe cut her off and stood. "I've heard all this junk when the neighbors used to take me to church," she said glumly as she walked around the apartment. "Jesus died for me; He is alive and 'interceding' for me in Heaven; He loves me, blah, blah, blah." She stopped to look out of the window over the sink. The others just looked at each other uncomfortably.

"But, Zoe, it's true…." Alex offered.

"Just don't!" Zoe snapped back as she quickly turned, glaring at him with her hands on the sink behind her. "I prayed and prayed and prayed when I was a kid. I asked God to make my father come back. I prayed that my mother would love me and treat me nicely. I prayed for many things for many years," Zoe walked some more. "Well, this God that you have all turned to must not have heard me because none of those things I prayed for ever happened. My father never came around; my mother was mean to me and made me work like a child shouldn't have to work. I never got that hug I prayed for, never heard that 'I love you' I yearned for." Zoe came and sat back down at the table. She looked at them all for a minute. "So, you can keep this God that you have 'turned to.' I don't need Him or want Him. And if this," she reached over and held up the disk, "means I am no longer part of 'The Crew' – so be it." And she threw it back down on the table. "As a matter of fact, why don't one of you take this stupid thing with you? I don't ever want to see it again!" And she shoved it toward Alex's end of the table.

"But, my friend Zoe, please listen…" Henry said as he leaned forward toward her at the table, "your name is on the disk too. That must mean…"

Zoe cut him off. "It must mean nothing! I'm quite sick of this whole thing, anyway. I need to study things for my Police Academy Training courses that will start in high school in a couple of weeks. I don't need to waste my time with all this…" she looked both sadly and angrily around at them, "or with all of you. How about you guys just leave now."

"But, Zoe…." Bridgett started.

"Nope. Sorry about the scar and all, but nope." Zoe stopped her." I just don't want to hear it, okay? Please, just leave—all of you." Zoe said as she got up, went into the bedroom, and closed the door.

The four looked at each other, their eyes filled with unspoken words. They got up, and with a shared understanding, slowly walked to the door. Bridgett had brought a bible Mrs. Griffin had given her to give to Zoe. A beautiful, little teal-colored bible that would go with Zoe's colorfully decorated apartment. She placed it gently on the table as they left. Alex took the disk and put it in his backpack. Sparkles looked at them from his perch on the back of the couch as they solemnly walked out, their footsteps echoing the weight of their departure. Henry gave him a quick pet. Sparkles purred and settled back on the couch as the door closed behind them.

CHAPTER 15

THE BATTLE

Zoe watched them walk down the alley to the street from her bedroom window. She sat on the edge of the bed and cried, something she didn't allow herself to do very often. She felt very alone and sad. She grabbed a tissue from the box on the little table at the side of the bed and blew her nose. Even the brightly colored furniture she had painted didn't cheer her right now. She opened the bedroom door and got a bottle of water from the refrigerator. When she turned after standing at the window drinking her water, she saw the bible on the table. She picked it up and threw it. It landed with pages open on the couch, not far from where Sparkles lay, and he jumped quickly down. She sat down at the kitchen table and cried some more. Sparkles jumped up onto her lap and purred. Stroking the cat seemed to calm her and remove some anger and sadness.

"Cat, I don't know what you are, and I don't even like cats, but thanks for you at least hanging around. I can use the company right now." Zoe said to Sparkles as he closed his eyes and purred louder.

That night, Zoe couldn't sleep. When she finally dozed off, she had troubling dreams of running and being chased. She woke up sweating from a bad dream. Shaking off the night's dreams, she went in to take her shower. The steam from the hot water filled the small bathroom. The hot water felt good in the morning chill. Her muscles seemed to relax. She lingered under the hot water, letting it wash away her tension. Wrapping herself in a towel, she heard a slight sound coming from the kitchen through the closed bathroom door. She assumed Sparkles had knocked something over. The steam had fogged up the small mirror over the sink. She moved forward to use the towel to wipe it off so she could blow-dry her hair, but as she moved forward, she jumped back! She could see figures in the mist of the steam in the mirror! She turned quickly to see if these dark figures were behind her. They were not. In the middle of the fog, she could see these figures more clearly now, and they were …. demons! Black figures with fangs and claws stretching toward her! In the mist, she could see hundreds of them, all coming at her! She knew they wanted to kill her! She wasn't afraid of much, but she felt terror from deep within right now. In her fear, she froze and began calling out quickly, remembering they said God hears our prayers. "Oh God! Jesus, help me!" The fear she felt encompassed her. The demons were fierce-looking, with flashing eyes, sharp teeth, and skin-like scorched serpents. Then, through the mist in the mirror, she could see a being rise up behind her; it rose to about nine feet tall – so tall she could not see the face in the mirror! Now she thought she was going to die for sure! Then, as she cried out again, "Oh my God! My God! Please! Jesus, help me!" the being behind her began wielding a mighty sword and swung it around the side of her. It cut through the demons like butter every time she said the name of Jesus! Then she realized the being was on her side! Every time she said the name of Jesus, he swung his sword and killed more demons! Then, the steam began subsiding in the room. The mist on the mirror started dripping down, and she could see nothing more, and the being behind her was gone. She realized this whole thing had taken only perhaps 10 seconds. She realized she still had the blow dryer in her hand, so she placed it with a shaking hand on the small table next to the sink.

She put her hands on the sink to steady herself. What had just happened? I'm losing my mind! I couldn't have just seen that! She quickly opened the bathroom door, and the remaining steam dissipated. She quickly backed out of the bathroom, wanting to escape that mirror. Her breathing was labored, and her heart was racing. She turned and saw nothing out of the ordinary. A streak of sunlight shone through the window, and it shone on the couch next to the open bible. Sparkles sat upright next to the book, looking expectantly at her. For some reason, she didn't understand; Zoe ran to the bible. Picking it from the couch and sitting next to Sparkles, she saw the writing on the open page: *"Woman, go in peace, your faith has saved you."* Zoe looked at those words, and something made her realize they were for her. She got up with the open bible still in her hand and sat at the kitchen table. She pressed the bible to her still-damp chest, holding her finger in the place she had just read. She looked into the bathroom where she had seen the battle. She knew she had seen it! She remembered the power of the being behind her! She knew at that moment that he had been an angel of God sent to rescue her. She looked down at the bible in her hands and opened it to the page she had just read. She thanked God, her wet hair and tears dripping onto the page.

CHAPTER 16

DISK! ZOE! NOW!

They all received the text, dropping everything in a panic, and sprinted to Zoe's apartment! Arriving almost simultaneously, they dashed up the stairs and burst into the apartment, their hearts pounding with worry.

"What's wrong?" Henry asked as he rushed to sit next to Zoe at the table. He and Alex had been running laps in the park when they got the text, so they were both out of breath.

Alex stood looking at Zoe questioningly.

"Yes, what happened?" Bridgett asked, rushing in, trying to catch her breath after running from her job at the store down the street.

Max stumbled over the threshold, his entrance mirroring the chaos in his mind. His eyes darted around the room, his body tense with anticipation. "This must be something significant for you to summon us so urgently, especially after... well, especially now."

Zoe's countenance was a revelation, a gentle and peaceful aura they had never witnessed before. She guided them to the table, her smile a beacon of serenity. They exchanged puzzled glances, intrigued by this uncharacteristic shift in her demeanor.

Zoe got up and spoke without looking at them. She told them about the dreams and about the demons in the mirror, then the being who had stood behind her and cut through the demons like butter when she said the name 'Jesus.' Then, finally stopping and looking at them, they noticed the teal bible in her hands and her finger holding a spot open within the pages. She came and stood by the table and explained how, in anger the day before, she had thrown the bible, and it had landed on the couch open to this page. Looking into each of their eyes, she explained how she had, in panic, felt led to go to the Bible after seeing the demons and all. She saw these words and immediately knew they were for her. She read the words to them, closed the book, and waited.

She had a totally different look on her face. That anger that was always lurking behind her eyes was gone. She finally sat down at the table and looked at each of them. "I know it's hard to believe, but it happened! I mean, *really*. After I had read that, something inside me had changed! The fight went out of me. I got on my knees right here and told God how sorry I was that I had blamed Him for everything bad that had happened in my life. I told him I was tired of being angry. I told him about every evil thought I had in my heart towards my mother. At that moment, I knew He knew everything about me and forgave me still. And He still loves me!"

She looked excitedly at the others. "I know what you mean now, Max! And you guys, too!" She had tears in her eyes. "When I was praying, it felt like the weight of the world had been lifted from my shoulders!"

Then, she wept. Heavy sobbing cries that shook her shoulders. Bridgett got up and stood behind her, putting her hands on her shoulders as they shook from weeping. Henry put his hand on her arm. Max got up, brought the box of tissues to the table, and placed them in front of her.

Alex reached down and pulled the disk out of his knapsack. All the lights on the disk were now lit up. He slowly put it on the table in front of Zoe. He smiled broadly at her. The others saw, too, and smiled.

Zoe looked at the disk through her tears, having forgotten about it. A wide-eyed look of amazement appeared on her face.

"So, it was true," she said softly as she blew her nose.

Then, suddenly, with a soft *'pouf,'* Mrs. Griffin – who was now dressed in what looked like armor, the messenger guy from the vacant building, and a 9-foot tall, very formidable looking fellow with arm muscles the size of Alex's head, also in armor, appeared in the room.

Zoe thought the 9-foot guy with the sword was probably the guy who 'fought for' her in the bathroom mirror experience.

And another *'pouf'* and Sparkles turned into the huge Panther Henry had seen before. The panther strode over, stood beside Mrs. Griffin, and sat with a heavy plop. The room barely had enough space for them all, and except for the high ceilings, the protector would have had to stoop down!

They all jumped up and huddled together behind the table for fear of the power they felt from the visitors.

"Mrs. Griffin?" Alex said in awe. "Is that you?"

Mrs. Griffin smiled, nodded, and moved a few feet toward them. "Zoe, you have been a tough cookie, but you are right. God has changed you, and we thank Him you finally saw your need."

"Me too," whispered Zoe, with Henry, Bridgett, and Max all so close they touched shoulders.

"Now that you are complete," Mrs. Griffin said as she sat down on one of the chairs (which barely fit her and creaked under the weight of her with her armor), we need to talk."

"Ah, so that's what that means! We are all believers now – complete…" Alex said.

"Yes, dear Alex, that's what that means," she said. "Show me the disk you have, please."

Alex reached his hand over and took it from the table, hesitatingly reaching out to give it to Mrs. Griffin.

"You see the larger circle in the middle?" she asked as she held it toward the five.

They all looked, and there was now a word in the big circle – 'Learn.'

"There will be several things that you have been entrusted to do. You will not be given future instructions on what they are, but the word will change to give you simple directions for what you are to do now."

"But how will we know what to do?" Max asked. "What does 'learn' mean?"

The large fellow in the back, with a booming voice that sounded like thunder (and scared the five who jumped almost simultaneously) whom they will now call 'the Protector,' said, "If you are told to 'go,' you will not know where –go. Your steps will be numbered and directed. If you are told to 'stay and fight,' you must follow the commands as they are given to you – just like men of old in the bible. You would faint from fear if you were told now what lies ahead of you. This assignment affects the entire world, and you have been entrusted with it."

The messenger, who looked almost tiny next to The Protector, stepped forward. "You each have been given a 'gift' from God. Something that will help in your journey.

Alex, you are the one who will develop the actions of this group, 'The Crew', as you call yourselves, just like your 'game plans' in sports. You have been called to be The Leader.

Henry, you already have the gift of creativity, but you will also have the ability to understand the vision of what needs to be created for your various tasks to achieve the end result. Your gift is that of The Architect.

Max - you will be able to figure out how to make those things happen through technology. Your gift name will be The Adapter.

Bridgett - your ability to draw will be surprisingly handy during your journeys. You, too, have the gift of creativity - but to make those things real. We will call you The Maker.

And Zoe - dear Zoe, you will be able to see into the motives and intentions of others by discernment. You will see the big picture. We will call you The One of Perception."

"I'm kinda scared," Bridgett said weakly. Henry and the others nodded their heads in affirmation.

"As I told you in the warehouse," the messenger said gently, "you must be strong, courageous, and faithful. Just trust in the power of God, and you will be successful. He will go before you; if you listen to His voice, you will know what to do."

"We, as well as others, will be with you even though you may not know we are there to protect you as the enemy will seek to destroy this mission," Mrs. Griffin continued.

"Why us?" Max asked. "We're just kids."

Mrs. Griffin smiled at his question, "Because you have been 'named' as our friend here," she nodded toward the colossal soldier, "told you in the park at the beginning. God has looked at your hearts, not your appearances. You were chosen from before you were born for this task, and everything you have experienced in your lives has led you to this moment, both good and bad." She got up and walked back to the others. Sparkles, who had been sitting, stood up. He was almost as tall standing as Mrs. Griffin. "We must go now. She pulled a small scroll out from her belt. This will explain what you need to know for now. And she handed it to Alex. Don't worry about telling anyone you will be gone on a mission; we will take care of that. They won't even realize you are gone."

"But..." Zoe started to say, but **'pouf'** they were gone, except Sparkles, who was now 'just a cat' again. He walked over to Henry and rubbed against his legs.

CHAPTER 17

THE SCROLL

They all visibly relaxed when they were alone again. Max flopped back onto the couch as he sprawled out in emotional exhaustion. "That was intense!" he said, closing his eyes as if squinting what had just happened into the back of his brain.

Henry repeated Max's statement. "It was definitely 'intense,' as you say, Max. Who would even believe us if we tried to tell them of all these things? No one would believe. I've tried telling my mother just a few things, and she changed the subject quickly and began making dinner or something." Henry sat down in the chair by the couch. Sparkles jumped to the chair where Henry was and into his lap.

"How can you be so sweet and cuddly but then a fierce panther, too?" He asked the cat. "I do not understand, but it is true. There are a lot of things I do not understand lately, but I know them to be true." Henry reflected as he stroked Sparkles. "At least the others have seen your change now too."

"So, what's in the scroll, Alex?" Bridgett asked as she sat down beside Zoe, whose olive skin looked pale.

Alex remembered the scroll and sat down to open it. He unrolled it onto the table and began reading out loud.

"There have been evil men in the world from the beginning of time," he paused and looked at the others. "You five have been named to carry out a mission. The assignment is to stop a new one who seeks to destroy innocent souls and lives and has already done evil in my eyes. He wants to be a god; he wants to be like me. He is under the control of the ultimate deceiver, the once mighty archangel Satan, who was cast from Heaven because of his pride with the 3,000 he deceived there. Like those Zoe saw in the mirror this morning."

When Alex read that, he looked at Zoe in amazement. Zoe looked astonished that it had been written since it had just happened to her earlier.

Alex went on, "I, the Great I Am, has allowed this evil one a time on earth to try to confound the sons of man. This new pawn of the devils has taken the name of Zagan - once called the king of hell. He has cloned human beings… mere Shells of flesh and bone who have no souls since no one can create a soul but Me." Alex looked at the others, who sat in silence and listened. "These beings have been created using foul means and today's advanced technologies. The creators have developed what looks like a piece of jewelry: a tiny computer that connects wirelessly to their brains and DNA once inserted. They wear them willingly. These computers are all controlled from one of seven locations around the world. They have already been releasing these beings, the Shells, slowly into the world to deceive and convince humankind that there is no need for any god and that intelligence and wisdom are enough. All will seem good to everyone in the beginning. They have been sent into churches, schools, and businesses. They appear 'nice' but are devoid of conscience, feelings, or free will. Zagan, working for Satan himself, at a designated time will instruct these Shells of humans to eliminate all those who love God or who won't turn to

Zagan. I have allowed these things for a time. But you are being sent to confound the enemy's plan until the time and result I have determined, which no one knows but Me alone." The scroll then fizzed in Alex's fingers, and he had to drop it as it burnt itself up on the table in front of him and was gone.

They all just sat and looked at each other, Alex gingerly wiping his fingers and the top of the table where the ashes were.

CHAPTER 18

DISK – 'GO'

"**M**y God in heaven," Henry said. "Have we come so far in technology that this is possible?"

Max stood and said, "Unfortunately, yes. I had a class about cloning, and the reality is pretty scary. They have developed ways to clone already; think of Dolly, the sheep. It is very real. There are a couple of ways to clone, both being rather complicated from what I remember and not without many failure attempts before a viable living thing is created. A high number of them are born but have very short lives or multiple physical deficiencies, so they have to be 'terminated.' I think the most successful have been using embryonic or stem cells, like those from aborted babies."

"But," Zoe said, "there must be laws?"

"Again, unfortunately, not many," Max responded. "One of the sticking points has been with many major religions who are totally against this. But scientists and technologists don't put much weight on their 'religious or moral' arguments. Others worry about the potential diseases and conditions this process might inflict on a cloned baby or society. If I remember, there are only 30 countries that have banned human cloning experiments, and in the US, there are no Federal Laws against cloning humans. Multiple states have laws prohibiting cloning for any purpose. Still, some states allow the creation of human-cloned embryos but prevent the embryos from being implanted, which doesn't sound very wise to me. I remember this because I was surprised in class discussion that there were so many proponents of it. They argued it could help parents who could not have children naturally, replace lost limbs, and even raise people from the dead! In their opinion, it was the next step – the new frontier!"

Bridgett piped up, "I even heard of one of the big movie stars who had their dog cloned when it was dying."

"Yeah, I remember hearing about that, too," Zoe agreed.

"This almost sounds like a book I have read," Henry said. "It was one of your Star Wars books - you know, with the insidious dark side force and the Sith lord trying to cheat death. He cloned storm-troopers. It was an exciting book, but who would think it could be remotely possible." He shook his head.

"I guess truth can be scarier than fiction," Zoe said. She got up to get a bottle of tea out of the refrigerator, pouring it into plastic cups and offering some to all. The last couple of days had been emotionally charged for her—a lot to take in, for sure.

"With all this stress and weirdness, I wish this was something a little stronger than water," Max said half-heartedly, almost to himself, as he took the cup of tea.

"Max!" Henry shouted. "God has changed you. You said it! You told me He took those desires for strong drink out of you."

He startled Max. "He did, Henry. I was just…. It was just a comment," Max backstepped, looking embarrassed.

"He just had a weak moment and was trying to be funny, that's all," Alex said as he walked over and patted Max on the shoulder. Alex took a cup of tea off the counter for himself and handed one to Max as well. "Remember, Mrs. Griffin always quoted this scripture – *'Be alert and of sober mind. Your enemy the devil prowls around like a roaring lion looking for someone to devour'.*... This applies to all of us, especially now, I am sure." He stopped and grinned. "Hey, I'm surprised I remembered that scripture! All my reading must be sinking in!"

Sparkles sat up and quietly growled as if in agreement with his comment about resisting the devil. Alex looked at him and smiled.

"Ok, so what do we do now?" Zoe said as she stood with her back against the kitchen counter, her cup of tea in her hand.

As if on cue to her question – the disk **'binged.'** Alex walked to it and picked it up, and they saw the middle light had come on. **'Go,'** it said. Alex relayed the message to all.

They looked at each other.

"Go, where?" Henry asked.

No one offered an answer because no one knew.

"Hey, you are supposed to be the guy with the game plans who leads us into action," Zoe said as she looked at Alex.

"Yeah," Bridgett agreed. "I guess it's game time, friend."

They all looked at Alex.

Alex had an odd look on his face, not knowing what to do, which quickly turned more resolute. He looked at the disk, then back at the others. Then you could see him steel himself, stand more upright, and put on his game face. "Ok! It's time to go, as the disk has told us. I'm unsure where, but we need to step out in faith – like Abraham did in the bible. He wasn't told where to go, just go!

142

Let's hit it!" he said as he put the disk back in his backpack and stood taller.

"But what about our parents? Shouldn't we go home and tell them we are going somewhere? Shouldn't we pack some clothes or something?" asked Bridgett as she stood up, looking anxious.

"Yes, that would seem logical," Henry agreed as he stood as well.

"No, guys, we just need to go - *now*. Remember, Mrs. Griffin said they would take care of all that," Alex stated forcefully as he started toward the door.

"But…." Zoe started.

Alex was out the door before she could finish her sentence. She looked at the others, shrugged, and followed Alex down the stairs. The rest gave each other raised eyebrow looks and followed.

When Alex got to the bottom of the stairs, he stopped for a moment. You could see he was trying to figure out which way to go. Sparkles rushed down in front of him and ran off toward the park. He smiled a half-smile when he saw Sparkles and then determinedly strode off that way too.

The rest looked at each other and then followed, trying to catch up with him.

Zoe almost ran because she, being of short stature, had short legs.

The rest of them were tall, except Max, who was just 'normal' height for a young guy but still much taller than Zoe.

There was traffic and shoppers, but no one seemed to pay any attention to the group; Alex strode in front of everyone. When they got to the park, there were some picnickers, a couple of families with kids on the swings, and one group on a bench by the trees that seemed to watch them out of the corners of their eyes, but Sparkles kept running toward the back of the park, back by the boulders where Alex had found the tunnels.

No one usually went back there as it wasn't kept up like the rest of the park. With the large boulders strewn around, it would be difficult to mow with the tractor they used elsewhere. They got around the boulders to where the tunnel door and the shed were. Sparkles had been first to arrive. He was sitting at the top of one of the large boulders, head high, waiting for them, wagging his tail as if ready for play.

Alex got there and stopped, hands on hips. He looked around, trying to figure out his next move.

"Well, we know to avoid the tunnels," he said as if almost to himself as the others arrived.

Everyone nodded and stood watching him.

"There's nothing back there," he said as he looked up the hill separating the park from the expensive houses behind. He made a running attempt to get up the hill, but it was too steep, and there was too much brush. "I don't think that's where we are supposed to go," he said as he stumbled back down, holding on to the bushes so he wouldn't slide. He stood with his hands on his hips again, looking around. He opened the shed door and peered inside. "Nothing in there but wheel barrels and pitchforks and stuff." He shut the door with a sigh and stood with a frown on his brow.

Sparkles had jumped up onto the next boulder that was about 12 feet tall. He sat there looking at everyone, wagging his tail.

"OK, Sparkles, where to now?" Alex said to the cat halfheartedly, as if he was going to answer.

Everyone stood around uncomfortably.

Sparkles jumped down in front of Bridgett and began rubbing against her. After she stooped to pet him for a moment, she laughingly said, trying to lighten the situation, "Maybe I'll just draw a door into this boulder, and we can get where we need to go!" She took her finger with a flourish and began outlining a door on the side of the boulder.

Suddenly, there appeared what looked like a laser beam coming from the end of her finger. It startled her and everyone else.

She pulled her finger back and looked at it, trying to see where the beam had come from, but saw nothing unusual. Tentatively, she kept going with her drawing. Wherever she drew, a deep line appeared in the rock. She stopped momentarily as she registered the shock of what was happening but continued. She looked back at everyone, who also showed amazement at what they saw. As she drew, an old door appeared, then a door knob. Then **BAM!** it became real! It freaked her out, and she jumped backward at a few paces. Henry stopped her by grabbing her shoulders from behind. She turned and gave a questioning, wide-eyed look into his eyes.

"Yes, I know," Henry said.

They all stood looking at the 'real' door on the side of the boulder.

"Well, that was rather freaky," Max said as he inched forward to touch the door.

"Hold on, Max, we need to be smarter about how we handle things now that the game has changed. Let me try first in case there's something or someone in there," Alex said as he pulled out his hunting knife and moved slowly past Max and touched the door knob. The knob turned to his amazement. He slowly pulled the knob toward him, and the door opened. It wasn't a small, dark tunnel like they had entered before. It was a large entrance to … somewhere. As he moved inward, the lights on the smoothed rocks on the sides turned on. He turned to look at the others, not understanding what had just happened, but shrugging and deciding to go with it, he went in.

"Oh my gosh!" Bridgett whispered, still in shock, "How…."

"Well," Zoe offered, "they said your drawing ability would be of great help to us. And, like many things lately – we can't explain it, but there you go!" She lifted her hands and shrugged, pointing to the door.

As Sparkles jumped down from the top of the boulder, he became the panther, scaring them as he did it so quickly in mid-air. His big body paused momentarily as he looked at them and then went through the open door. You could see the strength in his shoulders as he walked. He got a few feet behind Alex inside the opening, then turned and looked back at them as if waiting for them to follow.

"I guess our tour guide is waiting for us," Zoe said, half-smiling at the others.

"I guess so." They returned the smile and walked forward into the opening. Max was next to go, then Bridgett and Henry, with Zoe the last to enter.

They walked for about 20 minutes; then, as they rounded a corner, the passageway opened up into what looked like an old-fashioned military war room that seemed to be on the side of a mountain. They, indeed, weren't anywhere near the park anymore.

It was a large room filled with big windows looking out into the valley before them. There were many desks with computers, TV screens on the walls, maps, and other equipment. Through the windows, they could see a vast green valley below them, with trees, a stream, gardens, and people in the valley going in and out of a castle-like structure on the next hill. The castle was near a high, lush, craggy mountain.

Sparkles, the panther, sat in front of the window looking out with a twitching tail.

Max was very interested in the technology; he rushed around, touching the keyboards and looking at all the equipment.

"This is high-tech stuff!" he exclaimed. I've heard and read about some of this technology but have never seen anything like it in person. Look," he touched a few keys on a board, and a 3-D image of an apple appeared in the middle of the room over a big, round table.

"How did you know how to do that?!" Zoe asked.

"I ... I don't know," Max responded, "But this is some cool stuff."

Just then, Sparkles gave a low growl, stood, and looked out of the large window more intently.

"What is it?" Henry asked the panther as he walked closer to the window next to him.

Suddenly, with a **whoosh**, a very large, winged animal with a head that looked like a bear, the body of an eagle, and arms and legs like those of a man flew up and banged into the window. It looked in at them, growling loudly with fangs bared. The hands held a large sword, and the animal held it out menacingly.

Henry jumped back at the sight of the strange beast! The rest heard the bang on the window and saw the winged beast as it flew at Henry and Sparkles. They gasped at the sight.

"What the heck!?" shouted Max as he pushed himself back in the desk chair he had sat in by the consoles.

"Looks like they've been cloning other things besides people," Zoe said, clutching her chest.

Alex stood next to her as they all gathered at the window. Watching, they saw other winged beasts, all different-looking, flying around. Some looked like eagles with different animal parts attached. Some were as big as ostriches, with gangly legs and horns on their heads. They could also make out other giant beasts on the ground in the valley. Some things had the bodies of elephants with heads of serpents or ones that looked like horses but had clawed feet and long tails like alligators. They seemed to be all outside the perimeter of where the people were. Others looked like men, perhaps nine feet tall like The Protector, but had heads like lions and tails with things that looked like stingers. Those beasts were stationed at the doorways of the castle and around the perimeter where the people were. They looked like they may be guards.

"Hmmm. That's not a great-looking route if we have to go down there." Alex said.

"Not great at all," Zoe agreed.

"Let's sit at that big, round table in the middle of the room. It looks like it was where they made decisions," Henry said. Perhaps we will get some ideas there."

"Good idea," Bridgett said as she moved to the table.

The rest joined, and Alex pulled the disk out of his backpack as he sat. "Let's see if the disk has anything to tell us."

As he put the disk on the conference table, it *'binged'* softly, and the word changed to "watch."

They looked at each other, then toward the big window, where Sparkles was still sitting, looking out, wagging his big tail.

They talked for a while and came to no conclusions other than to do as the disk said—watch the activity below and anything they could see on the screens Max could bring up on the many computers in the room.

Max seemed to be having a great time with all the technology. They were amazed that he could somehow figure out how to use it all so quickly.

Later that day, Alex sighed as he got up from the table to stretch after their many discussions about their situation.

"I have a feeling this will be the easy part," he said and went to stand next to Sparkles. He looked briefly over at the panther as they stood. "We really need to change your name," he said as he put his hand on the shoulder of the cat, who was as big as he was as he sat there.

CHAPTER 19

WATCHING

Henry, Zoe, and Bridgett found food and water supplies in one of the side rooms. Whoever was here before must have left abruptly. The food wasn't very tasty as it was military issue in pouches – Alex had seen it before at the sports outfitting store. He said they were called MREs that could last for a hundred years, but it was food. The water was all self-contained in small pouches and had long expiration dates on them as well. There were enough sleeping bunks, towels, and blankets for many people, even a small kitchen and laundry room. There was even a hot water tank that Max had figured out how to turn on. The facility was built for long-term military use. None of them could figure out for what specifically, but it had what they needed for now.

Max and Alex spent a lot of time trying to figure out what all the technology was and how to use it. Well, it was mainly Max, but Alex helped where he could and did a lot of head-nodding.

Henry was able to listen and offer suggestions about how they could use the technology to help them in their tasks.

Bridgett practiced drawing things that became real. She made a little flower pot, a bar of bath soap, and a non-military-looking coffee cup. It surprised and delighted her every time it happened.

She knew it was a gift God had given her and thanked Him for it often.

Zoe kept watching the activity around the castle and marveled at the strange-looking beasts she saw daily. In a pink notebook that Bridgett had drawn for her, she took notes on when the Shells, as God had called them, went out into the gardens to plant or pick food, where the lion-headed guards were stationed each day and their movements.

She watched as the group gained knowledge and grew closer together as a team, especially Bridgett and Henry. She sensed that their feelings for each other were more than friendship, which made her smile.

She watched as Max grew in confidence and skill. She watched Alex become more and more ready and able to become a leader and call the shots as they went along. He was, perhaps always had been, a good, kind leader and friend, always considering others. She watched as all of them, including herself, read the little bibles Mrs. Griffin had given them. She felt more and more comforted and at peace because of its words.

She marveled at how God had brought them all together, given them time in their own walks to come to him in their hearts, and how He had trusted them, just kids, really, with this huge assignment.

She watched Sparkles go off and disappear for a day or two, assuming he was transversing the tunnels, then come back and sit and stare at them before taking long naps. He never turned back into a cat.

After some time of **'watching,'** Alex called the group together to the big, round table.

"Let's regroup and try to figure out what we are supposed to do now," Alex said, standing up from one of the chairs at a control station and walking to the big, round table. "Hey, Max! Bring up the aerial view we found and the schematics, would ya?" He hollered toward Max, sitting at the biggest control station.

"You got it!" Max turned and punched things into a few keyboards, and a 3-D image appeared in the middle of the big, round table in front of them.

"It is amazing what all this technology can do," Henry said, looking wide-eyed at the images hovering above the table. It surprised him each time he saw it.

"It is," Zoe agreed, "but what do we do with this information?" She asked as she moved from the table and stool she had set up by the window. She sat down at the round table, staring up at the images as they moved before them. "You can almost see each detail on their faces. They look like those tourists I used to see periodically around town." She paused, and you could see a light bulb go off in her head. "Hey! I bet those were clones!" she said to everyone as she had the epiphany. "No wonder they never talked or smiled or anything. They've been all around us for a long time now, and we didn't even know it!"

The others nodded their heads.

Alex agreed. "We've all seen these kinds of people, too, thinking they were just strange tourists."

"Yup," Max muttered that he had seen them too, then turned back to the control board and equipment. He said almost to himself, "I've seen this kind of technology in movies but never thought it was real or that I would be the one pushing the buttons," Max swung his chair around and, not being far from the round table, climbed the couple stairs down to the table and joined them. He stared at the images, sitting in a chair with a thump. "It's almost too much information. Too much data," he said, looking overwhelmed.

"It is a lot to take in," Alex agreed.

"But just think, perhaps it can be used to help us," Henry continued.

There was silence for a moment as they all stared at the images above the table of the Shells and the beasts moving about as if in a movie.

"So, what do we know so far?" Zoe asked as she pulled her notebook out.

Max sighed and sat forward to address them all. "Well, a lot…. That's where it gets confusing. What will we do with all this information? Okay, here I go…"

They all sat forward and listened intently, Zoe taking notes. Alex stood and moved behind his chair, resting his hands on the back, looking at the images as Max talked.

"Where do I start…. OK, we know there are seven of these, oh what do I call them – camps, for lack of a better word? They are on seven continents but seem to be linked to what seems to be the main hub here. We can 'see' into most of the buildings of the Hubs, like the castle over there, but I cannot get into some areas. They must be blocked somehow. The activities are all rather boring. If they are supposed to be 'taking over the world,' nothing indicates that. There is no military training, tanks, guns, nothing— just similar guards, like the lion-headed ones here and the Shells. Most of the hubs are in remote locations like this one, wherever we are. We seem to be remote in Michigan's upper peninsula – somewhere. But the GPS has no signal here. I have no idea how we got all the way here from Central Park in a 20-minute walk, but that goes along with all the other strange things we've experienced. Perhaps the Hub locations are blocked by something I haven't found yet. I don't know. There are a few small planes and unmarked buses going in and out, but nothing exciting. The buses take Shells, as we know the clones are called – they take them out - but don't bring any back. I haven't spent much time tracking where those buses go yet. There's too much other stuff to try to figure out. This building and that Hub across the valley seem to have been former military outposts, so a lot of security is in place. We have been able to see and 'listen' somewhat to the other Hubs through some of this technology and with translation devices. But any conversation they have been having seems pretty benign. They are training the Shells at each location on things like religion - of all things, politics, languages, math... 'school' type of stuff. Things pertinent to the areas of the world where they are located. There are things they call 'Hospitals' where they create the Shells, but they aren't created as babies. They look like they are maybe 8 or 9 when they come out of the hospital and then go directly to the school, well some of them, others are 'terminated.'" He looked around solemnly at the others when he said that. "The animal clones are created at places outside the camps and are designed to protect. They are experimenting with using various body parts of different animals, as we have seen. Some are pretty scary beasts. Neither the Shells nor the beasts think for themselves but are programmed to do whatever they want them to do."

Max sat back as if exhausted from all the information he had just given. "There's more, but you get the main ideas."

There was momentary silence.

Alex spoke as he walked toward the windows. "Some other interesting information we have found is that the Shells and other Hubs consider one a 'king' who calls the shots. That king is Zagan, who God told us about." He turned to the group and kept talking as he approached the table again and sat down. "We discovered his real name is Carl, but he changed it to Zagan. He worked at a big bio-med company. He and three very wealthy guys, whose real names we can't find because they kept changing them as Carl did to Zagan. These four wanted to use cloning many years ago, but the governments they were from shut them down. No one has seen the other three in many years, and we don't know what happened to them. In the beginning, the four had many meetings with the best of the best in science, but no one knew why those meetings were stopped or what happened to those other scientists and medical people. There have been many mysterious disappearances of people who had attended those meetings."

"When we looked up this name - Zagan," Max continued, "He was from mythology and was supposed to be a fallen angel, like Lucifer." He looked at all of them before he continued. "As far as fallen angels go, he was a particularly nasty one. The things I read called him 'the president of hell' and said that he was the protector of people who perpetrated fraud by fake means of exchange. He was also able to give 'wisdom' to foolish people."

"Why would anyone want to be like him?" Bridgett said.

"Well, when you think of what's going on here, it kinda fits," commented Zoe.

"And," added Alex, "it says this demon hates all humans."

The five looked at each other.

Henry, feeling a growing unease from the demon talk, rose from his seat and walked to the window. His voice, almost a whisper, broke the silence, "And he *did evil in the eyes of the Lord.*' I was reading that scripture last night - in the book of Kings."

Bridgett stood up and walked gingerly back and forth around the table as she talked, "So, let me get this straight - some rich guys and this Carl - alias Zagan - a demon who hates humans, among other things, got together and wanted to do cloning for some evil reason. Whatever they wanted to do was shut down by the governments they were from, and these guys, except for our fallen angel wanna-be here, Zagan, are nowhere to be found. And we have seven places throughout the world where 'clones, 'er Shells' are being created that are seemingly mostly peaceable but are going to annihilate any human that doesn't want to follow Zagan, and we are supposed to 'confound their plans' – whatever those plans are and defeat Zagan." She paused and added, "And that's with flying beasts, and millions of Shells, and who knows what else out there…." She turned to look at the rest, who just sat there with resigned looks on their faces.

"Yep, that's pretty much it…" Max said as he slumped farther back into his chair.

CHAPTER 20

DISK – INFILTRATE

A s they sat, the weight of the situation heavy on their shoulders, the disk on the table emitted a sharp sound. The word on the large, circular light shifted from 'watch' to 'infiltrate. 'Everyone's eyes were drawn to it. Zoe, the closest to the disk, picked it up, her gaze fixed on its message.

She looked around the table at everyone, placed the disk back on the table, and let out a big, resigned sigh through pursed lips as she sat back in her chair.

No one said anything for a few minutes, understanding the enormity of what was being asked.

Alex walked over and looked through the window. Sparkles came and stood beside him and nudged him with his big head. Alex looked over and petted the big cat, who began purring, which was pretty loud coming from a panther.

"I think Sparkles is telling everyone not to worry," Henry offered.

Alex stood for a moment silently, then closed his eyes. Then turned to the group. "OK, guys, we are being told to go down to the valley and get into the mix. I've just prayed that God would direct our paths because I've got nothing right now. I have no plans for when we get down there. Maybe it is another 'don't ask, just go' type of thing."

Henry stood and said, "That's a great idea, Alex - prayer! We are all believers now; we have been given an assignment from God through His Angels. To us, this assignment seems to be insurmountable. But, let us, as a group - The Crew - also pray for guidance and wisdom in what to do. We need help to be strong, courageous, and faithful, as the Messenger had told us to be. We must ask our God to give us, you, Alex, that game plan we need and wisdom about how to accomplish what God has asked of us. Before I trusted in Jesus, this would have caused a massive panic attack, but now I know in my heart that I do not need to fear."

"That's right," Bridgett said, moving to stand next to Henry. "I just read this the other night - so glad Mrs. Griffin had given us all these small bibles to keep with us. I read in Deuteronomy," she started flipping through pages, "Ah, here it is, Deuteronomy 31:6 'Be strong and courageous,' yes, just like the Angel Messenger had told us, Henry, here, I'll read it: *'Be strong and of good courage, do not fear nor be afraid of them; for the Lord your God, He is the One who goes with you. He will not leave you nor forsake you.'* And she closed her little bible and put it back in her shirt pocket.

Zoe said, "You know, in the past, I would have rolled my eyes at that and relied on myself to 'fix' things, but in this short time, I have come to understand that there is one higher than me who knows much better than I, how my life needs to go and how to fix things. It is kinda a relief to know I'm not responsible for everyone and everything anymore - like I ever really was." She chuckled. "Yes, let's ask for guidance on our next move. Alex, you've been at this a lot longer than any of us. How about you pray out loud?"

Alex smiled calmly and approached the table. He sat down, put his head down, and prayed out loud as the others joined hands, closed their eyes, and nodded in agreement.

CHAPTER 21

THE HUB

"Are you sure this is what we are supposed to do?" asked Max as he walked back and forth, pushing buttons and using different keyboards as he looked at the screens. "There seems to be a lot more activity at all the Hubs right now, and many buses have arrived at all of them, too."

"I'm as sure as I can be, Max," Alex answered as he prepared himself. "The only thing we have to figure out is how Zoe and I are going to get down there without getting plucked up by one of those monster-flying beasts."

"And you are sure we need to stay here and that just you two go down there?" Bridgett asked, looking a bit worried.

Zoe answered as she stood by the window, "Yes. We need Max here to monitor the equipment, and you and Henry are here in case Max needs help getting us back out. And you, Bridgett need to be here in case you need to whip something up with your fancy drawing fingers." She smiled at Bridgett and gently pushed her arm as she walked by. They had become fast friends since the accident.

Max brought up the close-up visual of the Hub and hovered it above the big table. He also brought up five or six moving images of the seven other remote locations.

They all looked at each other with grave looks on their faces.

"They seem to be making ready for something big," Henry said solemnly. "Speaking of drawing things, wouldn't it be good if Bridgett could draw you the same kind of clothing that all the Shells seem to wear so you don't look out of place?"

"See, that's why we need you here!" Zoe said. "Great idea!"

Bridgett nodded. "Max, get me a close-up of a couple of Shells so I can see what they are wearing, would ya?"

Max went to work and brought up a male and female Shell that appeared 3-D in the middle of the round table. "How's that?" he asked.

"Perfect," she said and began drawing their clothing. As she did, the clothing became real-looking instead of a flat picture. When she was finished, she touched the edges of the drawing hanging in mid-air and gently pulled, and the fabric lifted and became real. She grabbed it as it fell. She handed the outfits to Alex and Zoe.

"Amazing, amazing - always amazing," Henry said as he watched the process.

Bridgett smiled at his comment.

Just then, Sparkles strolled into the room. He came and sat down next to them. He held something large and round in his huge mouth like a toy ball.

"What the heck?" Max said.

When Sparkles saw he had all their attention, he dropped it with a thud, and it rolled across the floor and stopped at Henry's feet.

Max rushed to pick it up. "It's a... cantaloupe? Where in the world did he get a cantaloupe? It's real and smells wonderful!"

Then he had a lightbulb look on his face. He rushed to one of the monitors and brought up a close-up picture over the table of some of the Shells working in the garden area outside the castle. They were harvesting ... cantaloupes, which looked just like this one! Sparkles brought this from down there!" he said, amazed. "But, how....?"

Henry went to the big cat and petted him lavishly. "Once again, my wonderful cat, you have been sent to help us. You are so wonderful!" Sparkles purred very loudly and rubbed against Henry's hand. Henry rested his forehead on the big cat's head and closed his eyes. Sparkles rubbed Henry's forehead with his face lavishly.

Alex stood, his eyes wide with wonder, as he saw the cat and the cantaloupe. "All this time, I thought he had just been roaming the tunnels and caves, but he's found one that must go underground to the garden area down there. I guess we have our answer – follow that cat!" he chuckled, a sense of adventure sparking in his eyes.

Zoe smiled at the panther. " Good kitty," she said as she walked over and petted the big cat on the head. Sparkles loved it.

"Well, bud," she said as she looked at Alex. I guess this is as good a time as any. Let's get changed and go?"

Alex nodded and went to the men's quarters to change. Zoe did the same to the women's side.

"I don't like this," Max said as he sat glumly in front of one of the computers. "There are so many of them, and we don't even know what we are supposed to do once we get down there. I mean, once 'they' get down there. And I don't like sending them off by themselves."

Bridgett put her hand on Max's shoulder, a reassuring gesture. "Don't worry, Max. Remember Mrs. Griffin said she and the others, the Messenger and the Protector - our nine-foot-tall buddy, are with us ...somewhere. We're in this together, Max, and we'll find a way through."

Alex came out in his 'Shell uniform.' "Good fit, Bridgett!" He looked like a superhero or something in the uniform; it fit so well. His, like the Shells in the valley, fit closely. It was a bright blue color with a symbol on the left chest area. "And don't worry, Max. You haven't had time to read all the scriptures yet, but there are many where God sent his people into battle where there were only a few of them, and it appeared they were outnumbered, but then He went before them, and they won all the battles against all odds. When you get to them, there are some pretty exciting stories in the Old Testament."

"Yes," Zoe said as she came out into the room, "And after I saw that the Protector cut through that army of demons like butter that I saw in my bathroom mirror, I am not afraid either,"

She was wearing her Shell uniform. She looked strong and fierce— even for a 5'2" short girl.

"Here are a couple of small flashlights and knives," Max said as he tossed the items he had found in the storage cabinets. The uniforms were close-fitting, so they didn't have much room to hide things, but they put them in the side pockets of their pants.

The rest stood and looked at their friends, being both impressed and apprehensive.

Zoe and Alex smiled at them, no fear on their faces.

"Okay, Mr. Sparkles," Alex said to the panther, then stopped mid-sentence and looked around at the others, "can we please change his name when this is over? Anyway, Mr. Sparkles, lead the way."

As if Sparkles knew what he meant, he licked his paw, ran it across his muzzle, and sleepily jumped down from the bunk he had been lounging on, giving a big stretch.

"Well, he is not anxious at all," Henry said as he smiled at the panther. "Let's give it one more prayer before you are off," he said as they huddled and prayed for their friend's safety and protection.

When they broke, they saw Sparkles had moved to the entrance of one of the cave tunnels and was sitting there waiting. As soon as they were finished, he turned and bounded off.

"Hey! Wait for us!" Zoe laughed. She gave them all a quick hug and a smile and followed the panther.

Alex moved that way, too, but stood at the tunnel entrance for a second, pausing and turning back to the others. "Don't forget my friends– 'strong, courageous and faithful.'" He gave a short wave, turned, and ran to catch up.

Henry, Bridgett, and Max moved to the window.

"I hate that we never get instruction #2 from the disk so we could figure out a plan or even understand what we would have to do next. It would be so much easier if God would tell us His whole plan," Max growled as he looked out the window.

"I guess then there would be the danger of us becoming proud and thinking, 'Look what WE did,' don't you think, my friend? Where would the faith be in that? We should do nothing without the guidance and power of the Holy Spirit of God anyway - especially on this assignment." Henry wisely said.

"Plus, remember The Messenger said we would freak out if we knew all we would have to do," Bridgett reminded them softly. "I've done enough freaking out in my lifetime. I'd rather follow God's instructions at this point."

They stood at the window for a long time.

CHAPTER 22

THE TUNNEL

S parkles was much faster and more agile than Zoe and Alex, but he seemed to know when to stop and wait for them. The tunnel took many turns. They sometimes had to climb over fallen rocks and crawl through smaller openings, and without Sparkles leading the way, the two would have gotten lost quickly. When it looked like there was no way out of an area, Sparkles would slip behind a large outcropping of rock and be gone, returning to ensure they were following. They made their way for what seemed like hours, but it was only minutes.

"Sparkles, wait up a minute, would ya? I've got to catch my breath," Zoe said as she sat down on a smooth rock near her.

Alex stopped and looked back at her.

"My legs are shorter, so it takes me twice as many steps as you tall folks…. and you, Mr. Panther."

Sparkles lay down on the top of a large rock near the ceiling in the hollowed-out area in front of them as if understanding.

Alex came and sat next to Zoe on the rock, taking a deep breath. They sat for a moment. Zoe stretched her legs and took her shoes off to remove some stones. Alex wiped the sweat from his brow, frowning a bit.

Zoe looked sideways at Alex. "You are concerned?" Zoe asked.

"No, no, I'm fine. Just a little out-of-breath, that's all," Alex responded.

"Don't forget, my gift is discernment, Alex, so don't try that on me," she raised her eyebrows slightly as she smiled at him.

"Oh yeah, I forgot," he laughed. "I'm confident we are supposed to go there among them and that God goes before us, but not so confident that I am going to know what to do or say when we get there."

"I hear ya," Zoe said solemnly as she looked toward the panther.

She looked at Alex again, "Hey, I never told you …. Well, I never thanked you for not giving up on me before, and for…well, trying to tell me the truth about Jesus and salvation. I guess God had to use that bathroom mirror thing to get through my thick head. It's such a relief not to feel like I have to claw my way through life anymore and that God is in control and has my best interests at heart."

She paused, looking straight ahead, then said, "And it's nice to know that even though I might not be 'good enough' in my mother's eyes, I am in God's eyes, but only because He sees me through Jesus, who is perfect."

She paused again. "Forgiven, acceptable, good enough – that's hard to comprehend. I've always had to work hard just to be okay, even in my own eyes."

She spoke without the hard edge to her voice she used to have. "I still don't understand all of it, really, like how God would allow **me** to come to Him - **me.** And how Jesus paid for **all my** sins through His death because He was the perfect sacrifice - the lamb of God. I never related the two when they talked about them at church when I was a kid - the lamb people had to sacrifice every year and Jesus being the perfect Lamb that sacrificed Himself for everyone, for all time. The part I like the best is that He didn't stay dead, but is alive now watching over us and ...," she turned to him, "what's that word you guys used, oh yea, 'interceding' for us who trust Him in faith. It's almost too simple. Just turn from the sin in our hearts and believe. Wow. And I almost missed it because of my anger."

Alex looked at her face, which seemed different now, at peace, without a perpetual frown. He smiled. "I know. That's why so many don't believe it - it's too simple. They feel they have to 'do' something hard, to be perfect on their own, to say certain prayers, or go to certain churches to get to heaven when all they have to do is realize they can't 'do' anything to get there themselves and surrender in faith to God's perfect plan of salvation. The 'doing' has already been done." He stopped, then looked at her again with a smile on his face. "And you are welcome, Zoe. Now you can use your story to tell others about what you have experienced and learned and tell them the good news too."

"And what a story it will be," Zoe said as she turned to him again and smiled, quickly wiping a tear from her eye. "But, come on! We have work to do - whatever that might be," she said as she jumped down and moved toward Sparkles.

Sparkles, in turn, got up and, after stretching his long body, turned to move through the tunnel.

Alex smiled as he got up to follow.

CHAPTER 23

THE VALLEY

Sparkles began moving slowly in front of them, almost as if he were stalking something. The light in the tunnel became brighter, and they could faintly see sunlight now. As they slowly moved forward, taking the cue from Sparkles, the mouth of the cave became visible and narrowed considerably. Crouching and staying to the side, they saw they were at the tunnel's entrance leading to the outside. Peering around a rock in front of the entrance, they could see the valley spread out before them. They were about a football field away from the garden area near the castle. There was a lot of brush around the boulder, so the tunnel wasn't readily visible unless you knew it was there. The entrance looked like it had been closed by the debris around it but was now open enough for a person, or a panther, to get through.

Here they were.

There was enough room that as they crouched and peered around the stone, they could see through the tall weeds that many Shells were near the entrance and that a couple of buses had just pulled up next to the garden area between them and the castle. They watched as Shells came out of the castle and began getting onto the buses, all looking somewhat happy in an unemotional way, kind of like Spock on Star Trek. The garden workers stopped what they were doing, yelled congratulations, and waved at them - again in a strangely unemotional way.

Zoe wondered how people could be so happy and excited and not show it on their faces.

"With all this commotion, it's probably a good time to get out there without getting noticed," Alex whispered to Zoe. "Let's go, now!"

He squeezed around the boulder and into the weeds, stood up, brushed himself off, and quickly reached behind to help Zoe out of the small opening.

She stood, and they moved quickly to the garden area to get close to the Shells, who were all facing the other way and looking at the buses. Sparkles did not follow. It appeared they were on their own now.

Zoe and Alex separated and tried to look like part of the crowd. Like the others in the garden, they joined in the clapping for the Shells going onto the buses. When the vehicles were full and they had pulled away, the Shells in the garden returned to work pulling weeds and harvesting fruit and vegetables.

The two tried to look like they knew what they were doing, although Alex, a rich kid, had never had his hands in the soil before, and Zoe had an aversion to gardening ever since her mother made her do the weeding when she was like four years old.

The fruits and vegetables looked so good to them. They had been on 'not real' food for so long that Zoe wanted so badly to pop some of the beautiful strawberries, blueberries, grapes, and other things into her mouth as she stood beside the vines and bushes; she could hardly stand it. Alex looked at her sideways, and she could tell he was having the same problem reaching for peaches hanging from the trees near him.

"Hey!" yelled one of the Shells toward them. Zoe and Alex froze.

"You! Tall guy! I need you over here!" the Shell hollered at Alex. The Shell yelling at Alex was stocky with dark hair and big muscles. Alex looked briefly sideways at Zoe and walked toward the Shell, who was calling him. Zoe tried not to look concerned but followed him with her eyes as she moved to where they were pulling carrots from the ground to see better where he was going. She began pulling carrots out of the ground and putting them in a basket, glancing at Alex, trying not to look conspicuous. She couldn't hear what was being said, but the Shell, who had called to Alex, pointed to an apple tree on the other side of the driveway and a ladder, indicating that he wanted Alex to pull some of the ripe apples off the taller tree limbs. He handed him a basket. Alex nodded, took the basket to the tree, and climbed a few steps up the ladder. He positioned himself so he could see Zoe, trying to look nonchalant.

Zoe kept working. There were so many big, beautiful carrots to pull. Everyone just kept working. None of the Shells around her said anything to one another. They didn't look happy, mean, angry, or .... well, anything. They didn't interact with one another at all.

She wondered what Alex would say would be their next move. She prayed in her head, "OK, Lord, we need a little help here, please."

One of the younger Shells slipped over toward Zoe as she worked. "Hi," she said very quietly.

Her whisper startled Zoe.

"Oh, hi," she whispered, trying to look calm.

"I don't remember seeing you in the garden before," the young girl said again very quietly. No other Shells were within earshot, but the girl spoke cautiously, looking around at them.

She was a beautiful little thing, perhaps eight years old. She had big, soulful hazel-colored eyes and red hair that shone in the sunlight. It was pulled back into a ponytail that swung as she moved.

"You don't?" Zoe responded, not making eye contact.

She moved a little to the next patch and pulled strawberries from their post on the ground. Zoe's mouth watered as she looked at the beautiful, big, red strawberries.

"Oh," the young girl said pensively, following her to the strawberry patch. "I'll bet you must have just gotten out of school and are going on one of the next buses. Right?"

"Ah, yes, that's right…. school. Next bus…" replied Zoe, still not looking at the girl.

The girl came closer and knelt beside the strawberry bush near Zoe. She looked around to see if anyone was looking, pulled a big, beautiful strawberry off, and popped one into her mouth.

She giggled. "Don't tell, okay?" she said as she grinned from ear to ear ducking down behind the bush as she chewed. "I know how we are supposed to collect everything for the community and nothing for ourselves, but sometimes I just want one for me! She looked at Zoe. "I could tell, somehow, you wouldn't tell on me." She smiled sweetly at Zoe again.

 Zoe could tell that she was different from the rest.

Zoe smiled back at her and, after looking around to make sure no one was watching as well, reached over and popped a strawberry into her own mouth. It was wonderful! She smiled at the child, who snickered and held her hand up to her mouth to muffle the childlike giggle.

"I like you," whispered the girl as she studied Zoe. "You are different. Your eyes are different, and you have feelings on your face, like I get sometimes."

"I like you too," Zoe responded, getting a little scared. The girl could see she was different. She hoped no one else could.

"Wow," the little girl sat back on her heels, "No one has ever said that to me before. Hardly anyone here seems to have any feelings at all. I know that's how it's supposed to be, but it can be lonely sometimes. Why are you different? Did you ask for feelings in school?"

Zoe just smiled at her and kept pulling strawberries and watching Alex. The empty basket she had found was getting full by now.

"What's your name, little one?" Zoe asked.

"My name?" said the little girl, stopping to look at Zoe with a weird look on her face. "You know I won't have a name until I graduate from school, like you, and then I will get to pick one when they give me my life jewelry."

The girl looked at Zoe. "Hey, where is your jewelry? I don't see it behind your ear."

"Oh, I forgot it," Zoe said nervously.

"Forgot it? But how did you get it out after they implanted it for you?" The girl asked innocently.

"Oh....it was faulty and fell out. I have to get a new one." Zoe said, knowing she was getting into trouble with this conversation.

"Hey, let's go pick some of those blueberries over there," Zoe told the girl as she stood up.

Just then, a chime sounded, and everyone stopped what they were doing. Like robots, they started moving toward the castle, no one talking or smiling.

"See you!" the girl called out and skipped toward the castle, catching up with other young Shells who were not looking as lively as her.

Zoe glanced at Alex, who saw what was happening, got off the ladder, and started moving along with the rest of the Shells.

The huge lion-headed guards on each side of the door looked at them with their fierce golden, yellow eyes as they entered with the crowd but made no move toward them. The vast door banged shut after the last of them entered the castle. Zoe's heart skipped a beat at the sound.

CHAPTER 24

THE CASTLE

Zoe and Alex did their best to get closer to each other as they walked amongst the crowd. It was odd to be amid this many 'people' and not have any conversation or anything going on. It was pretty creepy, actually. Alex and Zoe dared not speak to each other.

The foyer was a large stone area with grand, curving staircases on either side and tall, impressive stained-glass windows adorned the tops of the walls. The light caught them and sent beams of different colors of light into the room. It looked like the Queen of England would come down the stairs at any minute, or maybe Cinderella. There were many more guards inside the castle than outside, who were also not saying anything, just watching – almost like statues. But then, do lions speak, Zoe wondered, trying to amuse herself from the tension she could feel in her shoulders. Bigger, thick, carved doors were opened into a domed hall. This hall had brightly colored motifs of kings, chariots, and animals, and many scenes of battles were painted on the high walls. It looked like a warrior's version of King Tut's tomb. There were enormous 50-foot curved tables in a semi-circle on each side of a 20-foot tall, raised, curved platform at the front. Underneath the platform was another set of doors. No one stopped in that room but walked silently toward the doors under the platform. The crowd caught Alex and Zoe and, moving along with them, entered another seating area.

This area looked more like a mess hall. It didn't have any of the colorful paintings or stained glass, but the tall ceiling was still domed, and many small windows were at the top. There was a tall, raised area in the front of the massive room with a throne on it that was cast in gold. Jewels of many colors were embedded in the gold covering it. There were guards all around it. Zoe tried not to stare at everything, even though it was beautiful.

Some Shells, dressed differently near the throne, seemed to have a different role. Some wore brightly colored robes, and some held trumpets. Everyone sat at a table. These were not curved but long from the front of the room to the back and had chairs on each side. There was a wide aisle in the middle. The tablecloths were black, and the candlesticks and serving dishes were a combination of marble, silver, and gold. Each place setting was made of a different, brightly colored porcelain. The silverware was of intricately carved silver, each a little different.

Zoe and Alex gently pushed and nudged to be able to sit across from each other. The Shells didn't seem to notice. The two glanced at each other periodically without being obvious, trying to fit in and do what the others were doing: sitting and unfolding napkins and pouring water from the ice-filled canisters. Very little conversation was heard except, 'Please pass the water,' or 'May I have some of that salad, please.'

Very delicious food was served, much to Alex and Zoe's enjoyment after eating only military-issued food for some time.

Zoe tried not to gulp her food down.

Strangely, everyone ate mainly in silence. Zoe thought the Shells seemed pleasant enough; there was just no conversation, only the occasional, "Please pass the rolls." There was little to no eye contact. Some kind of meat, cooked to perfection, was the main course. The many vegetables and fruits grown around the castle were on the table in wonderful sauces and creams. Zoe stole glances at the others around her. The fellow next to Alex looked quite Mediterranean, with dark, thick hair and a dark complexion, and was very handsome. The fellow on his other side looked more Scottish, with red hair and a ruddy complexion, and his green eyes had a bit of a glint as he looked toward the bowls near her. Still, no emotion showed on anyone's face. Zoe looked at the girl to her right. She was very fair-skinned with long, almost white-blonde hair and the brightest blue eyes Zoe had ever seen. Gorgeous. Even prettier than Bridgett, she thought. To Zoe's left was a dark-skinned woman with coal-black eyes and curly, thick, dark hair that fell in ringlets below her shoulders. They were all quite beautiful people.

During dinner, after Zoe heard the occasional, 'Please pass the cantaloupe' or 'May I have the tea jug, please?' she thought she would venture into a conversation. She looked at the ruddy fellow next to Alex and said, "Your hair is a delightful shade of red, almost like the strawberries," she said and smiled at him.

The red-haired fellow stopped chewing and stared at her wide-eyed. Everyone around her stopped what they were doing with forks or cups in hand and turned to stare at her.

"Oops," she thought. Alex gave her a wide-eyed look like –"Don't do that!"

The girl to her right said to her, "Is that 'conversation'?" she asked incredulously. "We don't learn that until we go to the School of Excellence." The girl looked around at the other Shells. "So, you have you been to the School of Excellence? Then, you should have been on the bus today," she continued, almost uncomfortable in her speech.

Alex stuttered, "...Yyyes, we have both been to the School of Excellence but were detained and will be on the next bus tomorrow." He said as he looked around to see if they bought his story.

The Shells beside them looked at each other and slowly returned to eating. Zoe did not attempt to speak again, especially after Alex gave her an almost indistinguishable, stern look across the table, narrowing his eyes at her.

Zoe thought the Shells would have been uneasy after that conversation, but that would have meant they would have had to have feelings, so she guessed they were out of the woods. The Shells glanced at each other occasionally and then at Alex and Zoe but said nothing more.

When everyone was finished, the dishes were collected, and some after-dinner drinks were brought and placed in very beautifully decorated, small glasses in front of them all. The liquid was bright blue. Alex and Zoe looked at each other.

Alex almost imperceptibly shook his head 'no' to the drink. Zoe understood and snuck hers into the girl's cup next to her when she turned to look at something on her other side. Alex pretended to drink his but put his large, dark-colored napkin in the cup, which soaked up the liquid nicely when he put it down. Then, he deftly pushed the napkin to the floor. Zoe couldn't say anything, but you could see the look on her face was 'very ingenious of you!'

Suddenly, the Shells at the front of the room sounded the trumpets! The noise startled Zoe and Alex, but none of the others seemed to notice at all. With the trumpets, everyone silently stood, turned to the middle aisle, and looked toward the back of the large room. Alex and Zoe awkwardly stood, trying to mimic the Shells, wondering what this meant.

A procession had begun at the back of the large room, with 20 finely dressed Shells in the front throwing blood-red rose petals onto the floor. More trumpeters followed them. Then, some grotesque creatures with heads of varying animals and bodies of men walked in front and the back carrying a finely decorated litter upon which was a very ornate chair covered in blood-red velvet. A man sat in the chair. He wore a red robe with long black feathers all around the collar and cuffs, and he was wearing a mask that looked like a bird of prey with a long beak. More trumpeters were behind them, and then more creatures on leashes made of heavy chains, snarling and spitting at the crowd. The lion-headed guards were straining to hold them. As the creatures passed, Zoe could smell their putrid breath and feel the heat of their bodies as if they were on fire. She could sense the intense inner pain they were in. She almost felt sorry for them.

When the procession reached the front of the immense hall, the trumpeters went around the side. Then, the platform, which was 20 feet in the air, was lowered, and the man on the throne was ushered off and up to the throne on top of the platform. Standing there, he raised his staff with an eagle's head on it, and everyone chanted, 'Zagan, our king, Zagan, our king – long live Zagan.' The trumpets sounded again, and everyone applauded. The rest of the procession left the hall through the side doors.

The man lifted off the mask and handed it to one of the Shells with the brightly colored clothing next to him, who then backed away from him as if in reverence.

There stood a man, his sandy-colored hair and slight build reminiscent of Max, yet there was something more. An aura of darkness clung to him, an unmistakable air of evil. Zoe could feel it immediately. This must be Zagan, she thought to herself, her curiosity piqued.

"You may sit, children," Zagan thundered as if on a stadium microphone and lowered his arms and staff. Everyone sat in unison. Alex and Zoe took the cue and awkwardly sat as well.

Zagan strode out to the front of the platform. Everyone looked up at him. He said in a loud, booming voice that Zoe thought surely was being projected through some hidden microphone in his robes. "Today, we have made history, children! Our final segment for our initial takeover has gone out into the world from each of our capitals worldwide. Tomorrow, our deputation will begin!" Zagan's words hung in the air, heavy with anticipation, as the audience held their breath, waiting for what was to come. As he raised his hands, the crowd cheered - in a most unnatural and unemotional way.

"It will only be a matter of weeks before all of you will be able to go to the School of Excellence and join your brothers and sisters in our venture to save the world from everyone and everything that is currently destroying it!"

There were more cheers if that's what you could call them. Zoe thought it almost sounded like a soundtrack.

"I will review our plan for you again," Zagan continued as he walked from one side of his platform to the other, speaking to the crowd of perhaps 500. "As you know, my dear children, when you receive your 'graduation jewelry,' you are instructed by it on how to feel about anything happening. I know you don't know yet what feelings are, but you will. These feelings control most of the world right now, but they are wrong feelings. They are feelings of greed, hate, and pride. You will receive new feelings directed by me. They won't hurt you, my precious children, and the wonderful thing is you won't have to decide which ones to act upon. I have taken that burden from you. The outsiders believe their feelings, that they control themselves, are of the utmost importance. But because of that 'freedom of choice,' as they call it, there have been wars and murders throughout history. Their selfish ambitions and greed have destroyed the environment. Your brothers and sisters have been sent among them to their churches, companies, schools, hospitals, and neighborhoods, and tomorrow, when the alert is launched, we will introduce 'The Decision' to the outsiders. **The Decision** will be explained to them through the internet, their televisions, their cell phones, and through your brothers and sisters so that all will know. We will explain why *Our Way* is better for the entire world and how their transition to becoming like one of you will be for the good of all. Their assimilation will be painless, and they will become brothers and sisters by the insertion of their graduation jewelry similar to what you have received. They will never have to worry about making wrong decisions again and will be taken care of their entire life. Any children or babies will automatically receive jewelry from one of us since we understand they cannot decide on their own. Then we will live together as one, all over the world. There will finally be world peace, and every nation and people will share all their resources with each other. There will be no more fighting or wars. Everyone will think the same." He strode to the side of the platform closest to Zoe and Alex. "Unfortunately, if they reject *Our Way*, we will be kind enough to destroy them quickly and mercifully, adding them to the resources used for others."

Cheers and applause followed. Zoe turned quickly and looked at Alex gravely.

"The world will then become clean from pollution by self-centered companies, the environment will heal itself, and there will no longer be hunger or poverty because I will control everything with my wisdom. I will decide everything that will make life on earth as it should be, and we will all be as one living in harmony – one being just like the other – no one individual any different than the rest! I will be your King forever and will tell you what to do, to think, and to feel so you won't have to concern yourselves with anything!"

"Hooray for King Zagan! Long live King Zagan!" The chant began.

When the applause died down, Zagan backed up and sat on his throne. "You may sit, children; it is soon time to rest your bodies. But, before you do, I want to introduce you to two visitors - outsiders."

Zoe's skin crawled. She hadn't noticed the guards approach their table.

"Guards, please bring them forward."

Two guards, one on each side of them, roughly grabbed their arms and dragged them to their feet and toward the platform. Even Alex, who was a pretty big guy, looked like a shrimp next to the lion-headed guards. Everyone just blankly stared at them as they were brought forward.

"These, my children," Zagan said as they were dragged toward the throne, "are the kinds you will be encountering in the world: small-minded, emotional, self-seeking, people who want to live their own lives, not considering how their actions affect the lives of the rest of the world. Each thinking they are right and good."

Zagan stood as he walked to the front of the platform. He looked down at Alex and Zoe as they stood, squirming. "Turn them around," he said gruffly to the guards. They swung them around to face the Shells. "See them and remember," Zagan shouted.

Zoe and Alex stood in front of the assembly. They looked out at the blank faces before them. Except for a few, like the young girl she had talked to in the garden, Zoe could neither see nor feel any heart in any of them. She immediately felt sorry for them all. Then she felt very afraid for her and Alex. She looked over at Alex, and he just smiled and winked at her, like, 'It will be okay.' For some reason, she felt calmer then.

Zagan stood and motioned the assembly to rise.

They chanted again, "Zagan, our king. Long live Zagan!"

"Children, go to your beds and rest your bodies. Tomorrow, we have a world to save! Guards, take these two to my study."

As they were dragged between the huge guards, the assembly filed out silently. Zagans attendants gathered his belongings and ushered him into his study through a door behind the platform, bowing low before him as they left.

Alex and Zoe were dragged to a side door on the platform and up some dark stairs to Zagans study.

His study was totally different than the rest of the castle. It was modern and sleek.

"Guards, place them in these chairs and stand away," Zagan said to the guards, who shoved Alex and Zoe into two chairs that looked like they had been carved from ice; the intricate carvings caught the light from the windows and sent prisms of many colors dancing around the room. The desk was even more intricately carved from this thick, glass-looking material.

Zoe had never seen anything as beautiful as this before. The desk had jewels of many colors embedded in it as well. The study had been created to look like it belonged to someone with much prestige and money. There were expensive-looking fineries everywhere, from the black velvet curtains to delicate porcelain figurines and an immense portrait of Zagan himself looking like King Louis XIV. The top of the desk was made of fine marble, and the window casings looked chiseled out of marble, with beautiful designs in many panes of glass. Zagan slowly walked around their chairs, not saying anything to either of them. Zoe's skin crawled. He handed one of his attendants his cloak as he slid it off. He had on dark, red velvet pants and a black satin-looking shirt with a high collar. Many rings adorned his fingers, as well as many chains and jewels around his neck. Strangely, once his mask was off, he looked like any other guy on the street. A middle-aged guy with a greying beard. He picked up very elaborately decorated eyeglasses and looked through them at a stack of papers on his desk. He put them down and sat back, looking at the two for a moment with a smirk.

"So," he said, "my fortune tellers told me there would be visitors, and here you are. Unfortunately for you, we let you in. You won't be getting back out, though," and he smiled an evil smile.

CHAPTER 25

DISK – THINK/PRAY

Henry, Bridgett, and Max had been watching the 3-D images that Max brought up over the table.

"Oh no!" Bridgett cried as she watched Alex and Zoe get captured and taken behind the throne. They could not see any further into the Castle or where they were taken after that. "What are we going to do now?! How are we going to help them!?"

Max and Henry looked at each other with no answer on their lips.

Max got up and walked to the window. "With all this equipment and technology, I don't know how to use it to get in there and help them," he snarled. "I feel helpless. And where is all that help we were supposed to get? Where is Mrs. Griffin, the Messenger, and that big guy now when we need them? Even that stupid cat has left us," He turned to look at the other two. "I need to get out of here! I haven't had a decent meal, fresh air, or sunlight in weeks. Now it looks like we are going to have to watch the rest of our team be murdered at best. I can't take it right now," and he turned and stormed out of the room into the barrack area, kicking a chair over on his way out.

Bridgett watched him go and felt his anger.

She also walked to the window and looked out. "What are we going to do, Henry?" She asked frantically. He could hear the panic rise in her voice.

Henry sat for a minute, staring at the Castle Hall on the 3D overhead.

"Okay, my Lord and God, I was given the gift of Creativity and Organization. If you would, at this time, please, I think I need to get creative and organize some way to help our friends and accomplish this mission you have given us." He prayed out loud to the empty ceiling.

He sat waiting expectantly. Nothing happened. He waited some more. No idea came to him. He looked over at Bridgett, who was still standing and staring out the window. She was crying now.

He got up and walked to stand beside her. He was a little behind her so he could look at her without her realizing it. Her long, shiny blonde hair was pulled back in a thick ponytail. She had no makeup on that he could tell, but she was more lovely than he could imagine. She was dressed in clothing she had found in the women's barracks: baggy camouflage pants with a belt trying to tighten them around her tiny waist and a military green tank top, which would have caused her parents to cry. But to him, she was more beautiful than she had ever been with all her fancy clothes and perfectly applied makeup.

"Please don't cry," he said and touched her shoulder.

She turned to face him. "You are quite lovely," he said softly.

"Henry, you're a great guy," she said as she wiped a tear from her eye and put her head against his shoulder. "But what are we going to do now?"

Henry lifted her chin and briefly looked into her bright blue eyes, then could not stop himself. "Bridgett, I know I am beneath you in so many ways, and I don't even deserve to say this, and I know this is probably a bad time to talk about this, but…. well, I, uh …. I have very strong feelings for you."

She looked at him tenderly. "I have feelings for you too, Henry," she said quietly. "And you are not beneath me in any way."

"But I am without much money, and I am from another country which may not please your parents, and have dark skin, and…....." he started.

As he talked, she leaned forward, gently touched his arm, and kissed him on the cheek.

He thought his heart would explode. She put her head on his shoulder and began crying again. "We have to do something…." She sobbed into his shoulder.

"I know," he said as he held her, not believing she hadn't rejected him. He looked at the valley, trying to think of anything to help their friends.

Just then, they heard a **crash**!

As they quickly turned, they saw Max leaning against the wall near the men's barracks. He had knocked over a metal table near the doorway, and everything had fallen to the floor.

Bridgett ran toward him, "Max, are you okay? Are you sick?" she asked as she quickly tried to gather all the papers, tin cups, and books that had fallen off the table.

 Henry ran toward Max and tried to grab his arm, but Max slid down the wall and wound up splay-legged on the floor. Max started laughing.

"Max! What's wrong with you?" Henry knelt beside him. That's when he saw the bottle in Max's hand. "What is that, Max?! You reek of alcohol. Where did you find that?"

"Here, you want some, my naïve friend?" Max slurred. "I found it when we got here in one of the lockers. It's pretty bad, but… here, try some! I've been sipping at it all day and just chugged a lot. I think it just hit me." Max laughed as he extended his arm with the almost empty whisky bottle toward Henry.

Henry grabbed the bottle out of his hand and handed it to Bridgett. He nodded for her to take it away. She placed it behind the cabinet next to them.

"Max, my friend. Why?" Henry asked Max sadly as he continued to kneel beside his friend.

"Oh Geeze, Henry! I'm sorry, okay. I found it when we first got here. I knew then I should have dumped it out, but I didn't." Max said as he tried to get up but slumped back against the wall again when he couldn't get his footing. "Then every time something happened that frustrated me or scared me, all I could think of was that bottle….it just stuck in my head, Henry."

Henry helped Max get into a nearby chair. Bridgett steadied the chair for them.

Now Max was crying. "I'm not worthy to be on this assignment with you guys. I'm a jerk who can't even control my own thoughts. I'm not a good person like the rest of you. I'm a trash kid. A loser, like my mother always told me …... I'm sorry. I just couldn't take it anymore… I feel helpless."

Bridgett came over, pulled a chair beside them, and handed Max a paper towel to cry into. "You are not a trash kid, Max. Remember, you are a child of God now. None of us are 'worthy'. God makes us worthy. And, don't apologize to us - your 'sorry' needs to go to God." She patted his arm as he nodded and cried louder. "Remember Mrs. Griffin always told us we would not be perfect even after giving our lives to God, and that if we sinned to honestly confess our sins and, let me see if I can remember the scripture – 'If we confess our sins, he is faithful and just to forgive us our sins, and to cleanse us from all unrighteousness." Yes, that was it."

Max just stared at Bridgett between his sobs as she spoke, then put his head down. "But I've screwed up…big time."

"You are okay, Max. You did mess up, but God forgave you for that the day you trusted in Him. God has shown you and us how the power of our thoughts can control our actions if we allow them. They can make us do things that displease our Lord. But if we are truly sorry, He forgives us."

"Here," Henry said as he stood up and pulled Max up, "Let us get you back to the bunkroom and let you lie down for a while."

Bridgett held his other arm, and they were, not very easily, able to get him onto a bunk. Bridgett grabbed a blanket and threw it over him as they left.

"Thanks guys…I'm sorry…" Max said as he waved weakly at them. His arm fell down on the bunk next to him, and he began quietly snoring.

As they returned to the central control room, Henry walked toward the big, round table and saw the disk had changed. Now it said, 'Think and pray.' He put it back down and looked around the room at all the equipment he had no idea how to operate, and the beautiful girl who was looking at him for answers.

CHAPTER 26

QUESTIONS

Alex's mind raced as they sat in the big chairs in front of Carl, alias Zagan. He knew he had to think of some action plan to get them out of this, but how, with all these guards, and then what about the assignment?

Carl's voice broke his train of thought.

"So, what brings you two into my humble abode?" Carl asked as he sat back in his chair and folded his hands together in front of him. "I'm sure you weren't sightseeing up here in these mountains, especially since you went to all the trouble to dress like my children. What is it you want? Ask me anything. You won't be any trouble to me shortly, anyway. I might find your questions amusing."

Zoe looked at him defiantly and asked, "Why?"

Carl laughed. "Yes, I guess that would sum everything up, wouldn't it? Well, the short answer would be because 'they' said we couldn't."

"But what about all these soulless lives you've created? What about the people your 'children' are about to kill when they won't submit to you?" Alex asked fervently, sitting angrily forward in his chair.

"Phish!" Carl spat. "Humans! All self-centered, egotistical, know-it-alls who think whatever they think is the 'right' way and will argue their point even after they have been proven wrong! They are destroying the environment, polluting the air, using earth's resources, and each side will fight for their beliefs!" he got more incensed, sitting forward with clenched fists as he spoke. "They kill each other, abort babies to the god of self, have wars for power and political gain, steal, maim, and lie....do any of those humans care about each other?" he stopped his rant, visibly calming himself, and sat back in his chair, "I could go on, but no need."

He stood and walked around his desk, in between their chairs, just looking down at them, then back toward the wall where the fine porcelain and other beautiful things lay on a table. He lightly touched some of them as he spoke, not looking at them or the guards. "Our vision, the thing we have put all our money and efforts into for these years, has been to eradicate the hate, the greed, the need for self-justification. When we found a way to clone successfully, even after we were told it would never work and that the ethical ramifications were too high, we pooled our resources, got funding from other believers who wanted a different world, and developed what you see here." He turned to face them. "We can create any being we want! Animals, humans! Isn't that glorious? We can develop them into doctors, lawyers, scientists, anything - by using the right stem cells – anything!" He raised his hands into the air, "And, whallah, the best part is, none of them care about themselves. They simply all work together as a team to make things better!"

"You mean to do YOUR will," Alex said, glaring at Zagan.

Carl glanced at him angrily from his reverie, "Ah, yes, well, someone has to lead the show, don't they?"

"They are merely robots with human bodies," Zoe said. "And, what is that 'jewelry' thing you put in them anyway?" she asked.

"Ah, finally, a good question!" Carl smiled as he sat back down, leaning forward delightedly. "That was such an incredible discovery by one of my partners. That small dot contains a microcomputer combined with specific DNA we develop that, once inserted through a tiny pin-prick of a hole, shoots strands that attach to the DNA of that …uhm, recipient we shall call them, and they become one with the main computer here! Isn't that ingenious! And they said that couldn't be done either! Hah!" He sat back with a delighted look on his face.

"So, like I said, they are merely robots with human bodies," Zoe reiterated angrily.

Carl looked at Zoe with an evil glint in his eye. "Your questions are getting boring. No, young lady, they are more than robots! They have been taught what to think pertaining to their specific professions, how to react to certain outside stimuli…" he looked at Zoe laughingly, "such as irritating human arguments." He laughed to himself. "They are taught how to grow food, build things, use technology, perhaps go to space. They will not produce waste as humans do now. They will make our world healthy again. Then, when their bodies are no longer of use, they will be used for either food or fertilizer. The ultimate in recycling!"

"How lovely," Zoe said sarcastically, "But they don't even have emotions!"

"And more importantly, they were not created by God, so they don't have souls," Alex chimed in.

Carl jumped up angrily, slamming his hands on the desk. "Ah! There it is! The God argument! There is no 'God'!" Carl shouted. "I spent my entire young life trying to 'find' God! To find a logical reason for Him or proof of His existence. When I went to college, at age 12, by the way – since I was and am a genius," he smirked," I realized there are over 4,000 religions in the world, and they all say they are the only right ones! Blah! I have found no reliable evidence that there is any god that consists of anything more than traditions and the stupid desire in humans to be controlled by something higher than themselves." He calmed down a bit and sat back down. "I will fill that role for my 'children'. They know I created them, have given them intelligence, and will tell them how and what to think and what to feel. They know they will be going out to fulfill a great work for the good of all, and they worship me blindly – just like most religions!" He glared at them menacingly. "Now, enough! You tire me. Guards, take the male to the hospital and the other to the kitchen." He turned his back on them as the guards dragged them out of their chairs and pulled away.

Zoe and Alex looked at each other as they were roughly taken out of the chamber and in different directions.

"Don't lose faith! Be strong and courageous!" Alex shouted over his shoulder to Zoe as she was pulled away.

CHAPTER 27

DISK – DEVELOP/RESCUE

As Bridgett and Henry sat forward anxiously watching the images projected over the big round table, they saw Zoe and Alex being dragged away from the room they hadn't been able to see into but in different directions. Just then, the disk binged, and when Bridgett picked it up, she saw it said 'develop/rescue.'

"Oh my gosh, Henry! It's time! We have to do something! We have to help them!" Bridgett announced.

"But that is our problem, Bridgett. What do we do?" Henry replied. "There are 3 of us, well, two at the moment, and thousands of them, plus those guards and beasts. We would surely be going into our own deaths."

"But you and Alex always say to have faith and to trust God, and…. and now you…. well, now I'm scared again," Bridgett said as she looked into Henry's face with a frightened look on her face.

Henry looked into Bridgett's eyes and saw the look he recognized so well. The look of impending panic. He knew he needed to do something, think of something, use the gift he had been given, and trust God to get them through whatever it was they were going to have to do.

Then, it came to him! Like a small voice in the back of his mind. 'Use a weapon to distract'.

"I think I have an idea, Bridgett," Henry said excitedly. When I was a young boy in Sudan, there were many weapons of war around us. My Father and his friends had obtained many rifles and weapons to try to protect our homes. One of the weapons was something that looked like a tulip bulb on the end of a long tube. That was my recollection as a boy, anyway. But this thing, whatever it was, could shoot very long distances and made a deafening noise that frightened all of us - the mothers and children- when it exploded. If we had one of those, we could distract everyone long enough to get Alex and Zoe out of there somehow!"

"But where are we going to get one of those things?" Bridgett asked. "And we would have to know exactly where they had taken them to save them, wouldn't we?"

Henry contemplated her questions. "Yes, we would need a perfect plan; that is a sure thing. God will give it to us as we need it. But where we will get that weapon is - your gift, Bridgett. If Max were functional, he could probably make one using all this technology to modify some of the items around here, but I think he will be asleep for a long time, so it has to be you."

Bridgett's brows furrowed with concern, but then, a glimmer of determination replaced it. "Henry, you'll have to guide me. I'll sketch it, and it will materialize - just like the door. But, will it truly fire?"

They looked at each other solemnly.

"I think that is what we will have to find out, Bridgett, and trust His hand in this," replied Henry, looking more determined as he sat more upright. He unfolded his hands, which he had been wringing without realizing it, and placed them firmly on the table. "If David could go out and defeat Goliath with a slingshot because he had the Lord with him, and if his army of 600 could defeat the army of thousands through the power of God, we can do this with the help of our God too!"

Bridgett brightened. "Ok! Let's do this and hurry! They need our help right now!"

Henry and Bridgett huddled as Henry talked Bridgett through what the weapon looked like. Bridgett drew into the air as they stood next to the table. What looked like a long tube-shaped cannon with a large, round, pointed end came into being as she drew. It had the fixings of a rifle and a shoulder rest. When she was finished, Henry reached up and, looking sideways at Bridgett, touched the weapon's handle and brought it down to his shoulder. It was real now!

"That still kinda freaks me out," said Bridgett in a calm voice, "but thank you, Lord, for giving me this gift for such a time as this!"

"That is a pretty wonderful gift," Henry said as he looked at the weapon in his hands.

"Now, how do we get down there?" Bridgett wondered.

Henry looked at her blankly.

Just then, Sparkles bounded into the room and stood at the entrance to the same tunnel Alex and Zoe had taken. He looked at them, gave a slight growl, turned around, and faced the tunnel again.

"I think he wants us to follow him," Henry said.

"I think you're right. Let's go!" Bridgett said and rushed to follow Sparkles.

Henry quickly followed, lugging the long, heavy weapon.

They ran for what seemed like a long time when Henry shouted as he ran, "We forgot to get the exact locations of our friends on the castle schematics!"

Bridgett didn't stop to answer; she just said, "God will lead us!"

Henry smiled at her answer as he ran.

They got to the entrance behind the big boulder near the garden. There were now a lot of buses in the front of the castle, and lots of Shells were being ushered onto them. They seemed excited in a non-feeling kind of way – if that's possible.

"Let's just make a run for it!" Bridgett said breathlessly. "We didn't make ourselves uniforms, so they will immediately notice us. We've gotta get in there and help our friends!"

"Wait a minute, Bridgett," Henry said. "We must first use this to detract them from the entrance. Those guards look pretty fierce. And I think I remember them saying they would take Zoe to the kitchen. The kitchen is that building over there. I remember Max and Alex saying it when they looked at the map." He pointed to a low building next to the castle.

"I guess we'll have to split up then," Bridgett said as she looked him in the eyes. "I'm praying for God's help and protection right now! For all of us!" She looked at him for a moment more, then headed toward the hospital building. She stopped abruptly, turned back, and kissed Henry on the cheek. She took off quickly and ran behind some of the bigger rocks on the path to the kitchen. Sparkles followed her quickly, passing her by on the way to the kitchen building.

Henry looked after her and also prayed at that moment. Then he took a deep breath, raised the weapon, and pointed it toward the trees to the side of the castle on the other side of the buses. He pulled the trigger and immediately fell backward at the strength of the weapon as it propelled him backward.

A very, very loud explosion and fire occurred almost immediately where the shot had gone. When the Shells screamed (he guessed they had enough emotion to know when their lives were in danger) and started running wildly around, not understanding or knowing what to do, he ran toward the big doors of the castle. The guards had all run quickly toward the location of the explosion, leaving their posts. He ran quickly into the castle, ducking behind columns as more guards ran out to see what the explosion was. He looked around, trying to figure out where they might have taken Alex. He noticed the little girl hiding behind a chair not far from him. She was the one they had seen Zoe talk to in the garden. He ran behind chairs and columns to where she was. "Little girl!" He leaned over her way to speak to her, "I know you are frightened, which is a good thing actually, but could you please tell me where they might have taken my friend – the boy you saw them take to the front of the assembly at dinnertime."

She looked at him wide-eyed. "I don't know who you are. And I am having things going on inside of me that I don't understand."

"Those are called 'feelings,' little one," he said as he moved closer to her, "and the one you are feeling right now is called fear. I have experienced that myself and my friends are probably feeling that right now, too. But I need you to help me quickly. I don't have much time."

She looked at him, and you could see she felt better because he told her what was happening to her inside and that he had the same 'feelings.'

"No one has ever been able to explain these things to me. I always thought I was flawed, as they said some of us were and would be terminated before long."

"Please, I need to find my friend quickly. I can explain more to you later," Henry pleaded.

The little girl looked at him for a minute, at all the guards racing past them, and then grabbed his hand. With Henry closely behind, she ran to a doorway between columns and high furniture. She looked both ways, then opened the door and went through. Henry followed.

As he stepped into the room and closed the door behind him, he could see this was different than what was represented in the hall and foyer. This room was also totally modern in appearance. There was a lot of metal furniture and technological equipment, whatever it was. He silently wished Max were here. They had not seen this before when Max brought up the screens, so some security must have blocked it. The little girl quickly brought him down a hallway to another door that opened to a stairway and an elevator.

"They probably would have taken him to the place where they get stem cells from subjects. I learned that in my brief classes before they decided I was flawed. It's up on the fifth floor above the schools and such. I had to deliver something there once, so I saw all this. I am breaking the rules, but it seems, inside, like it's ok. Come this way," she said and pushed the elevator button. The elevator was a marvel, its walls made of a clear, heavy glass that allowed a breathtaking view of the floors they passed. As they ascended, the little girl pointed out the activities on each floor. "This is the first level of school," she said, "where we are taught how to grow food and keep the planet clean." She pointed to the next floor, a bustling hub of desks and technology. "This is where we would learn what our king wants us to know, like other languages, politics, economics - things like that." She beamed, being able to show her knowledge. "Then, on this floor, they are taught things they wouldn't tell me about, saying if I got to school, I would find out. Then, the last floor before 'the hospital' is where they are tested, and if they graduate, they are allowed to pick a name and get their jewelry." She looked at him, smiling. "Isn't that cool?" She asked.

"No, little one, it isn't cool. The things being taught are not good, but I will have to explain all that to you later." Henry said to her. She looked crestfallen. "You are very intelligent, though, and I am going to give you a name right now! I am going to call you …. Ivana! It was my friend's name in my country, and it means 'gift from God'!"

The little girl was first in shock, then beamed. "Wow, I have a name…. But who is this God you speak of, and what is a god anyway…and what is a country?"

"That, my young friend…. oh, wait – that **Ivana** is a conversation for another time." He smiled down at her.

"I like this… I have something going on inside right now… you called it a feeling? I like it!" She almost squealed in delight.

He took pleasure in her newfound joy.

"This is it," Ivana said as the doors opened. I've never been up this far, but I will accompany you. There will be brothers and sisters here."

As they got off the elevator, they saw what looked like many incubators in the room. They saw other older children, like Ivana, who didn't move or look back at them as they moved through the room.

"Perhaps they haven't been activated yet." She whispered.

They walked further and saw many drawers labeled with statistics such as tall, blonde, athlete, or brown hair, intelligent, stocky. They looked like the old card files that used to be in libraries but bigger. Then they saw the clear beds containing humans, looking unconscious with many tubes and wires coming out of them.

"That's probably where they harvest the stem cells; they make us out of," Ivana said quietly. "It's a most reverent procedure."

Henry just looked at her and whispered, "I have much to teach you, Ivana."

She whipped around and stared at him, "You are going to teach me things?!" she whispered a little too loudly.

"Yes, many things," Henry answered. But we need to get my friend out of here first."

Then he saw them. Two Shells were placing Alex in one of the coffin-like, clear beds. He looked drugged and wasn't putting up much of a fight. Three Shells were maneuvering Alex around at the back of the room.

"There he is!" he whispered. But wondered how he was going to get Alex out of there without winding up in one of those things himself. Get creative, get creative! He thought to himself. He looked over at the wall next to the column they were hiding behind and saw some of the lab coats the Shells were wearing. He reached over and pulled one off the hooks and saw a wheeled cart with medical-looking items on it. He put on the lab coat and stood, motioning to Ivana to stay there and stay quiet. He stood up straight, lifted his head, and started pushing the cart as he walked toward the group handling Alex.

"Ah, good," said one of the Shells as he approached. This one is heavy, and the sedative doesn't seem to be working as well on him as it does on the others. Here, you take this side…."

As he said that, Henry grabbed Alex's arm, looked him in the eye, got a look of recognition, and swung around and hit the Shell with the tray on his cart. He had never been forceful before! It felt good!

The Shell fell to the ground and didn't quite know what to do since he had never experienced violence before. The other Shell was quite shocked as well and backed away. Alex shook his head, trying to clear it, and stepped down from the bed, almost falling as his legs were weak. When the other Shell he had knocked down stood and came toward them, he roughly kicked him, and he fell backward again, hitting his head on another bed and knocking himself out. The other female Shell stepped back momentarily, unsure what to do. They had not had any of the physical training to handle fighting since they were programmed to be scientists.

"Get back!" Henry shouted as he picked up one of the syringes that they had ready to administer to Alex and pointed it at her. Come on, Alex. I need to get you out of here quickly. Lean on me!" They backed away from the Shell. The woman looked utterly bewildered about what to do. She hadn't been programmed for anything like this.

"Get to the buzzer to call the guards!" shouted the Shell on the floor who had come to. The woman started to run to a console in the middle of the room. Alex picked up what looked like a metal cube of some kind used for testing and, using his weak but still strong pitching arm, threw it at the woman. His aim was perfect, and it hit her on the side of the head. She tried to grab something to keep from falling but went down like a sack of potatoes. The Shell, who had been on the floor, rushed to the console before they knew it and pushed some buttons. An alarm went off as the Shell turned to them again but slowly backed up. Henry didn't know if the Shells felt fear, but this one was definitely afraid of something. He backed away from Henry and Alex and ran out of the back door. Henry turned to look, and behind them was the 9-foot Protector. He was just as frightening here as he had been before. Seeing him, Henry was glad he was on his side!

"You must come now," The Protector said in his loud booming voice.

Henry motioned to Ivana to come quickly from behind the column on the side of the room. Ivana hesitated seeing the Protector, but Henry urged her to come. She did and hid behind Henry, holding onto his shirt tail, as they followed The Protector toward the stairs.

CHAPTER 28

THE KITCHEN

Zoe tried her karate moves, kicking, struggling, biting, anything she could do to escape the guards, but she was like an annoying flea to them. Nothing she did phased them at all. They took her to a building on the side of the castle. When they opened the door, Zoe saw that everything was clean and shiny, with lots of chrome and porcelain. There were some Shells in the large room they entered first, who seemed to be preparing food. One of them turned to the guards and said, 'Take her to the prep area.' They took her to a smaller room that led to several different enclosures. The enclosures were made out of some thick, clear material. Some had farm animals in them, some had wild animals, and some had animals that had obviously been cloned using different species. It was pretty noisy with the sounds the animals were making. Then she saw the enclosure with the humans in it. One of the Shells who was working there punched in a code, and the large gate to the human enclosure opened. The guards shoved Zoe in. She fell forward as they did.

The other 'humans' in the enclosure just looked at her blankly as they stood or sat, none of them moving.

She stood, brushed herself off, and looked around the room, trying to take it all in. The reality of what the meat might have been that they had served for dinner now made her retch. When she composed herself, she went to one of the younger females in the enclosure, who was sitting on the bench that went all around it.

"What are they going to do to us?" Zoe asked with fear in her voice. "Are we going to be dinner tomorrow?"

"Perhaps," said the girl stonily.

This took Zoe aback. How could this girl and the rest of them be so calm?

"There's got to be some way out of here," Zoe's voice raised as she walked around the large, square area. She examined every inch of it. It seemed to be a solid, thick plexiglass-type material, welded somehow at all the seams. The only opening was the gate and some air holes at the top. The door had thick, square bars of the same shiny material, but they were black and contained a large, electronic-type lock.

"There is no way out," one of the other Shells said as he stood up. "Don't worry, it's painless and quick. You won't suffer."

"How can you all be so....so nonchalant about this!?" Zoe screamed at them. "This isn't right!"

The Shells just looked at her and each other, not saying anything, as she banged on the gate in frustration.

One of the other Shells, a woman, said quietly, "It *is* right. Our King has explained it to us. If we are inferior in some way, mentally or physically, or if we have served the purpose for which we were created, we are to give our bodies back to our family, just like the animals and plants. It is all part of the universal moral code. King Zagan has told us it is our way to promote peace in our collective hearts and life everlasting and ......".

Zoe cut her off. "Your 'king Zagan' is a liar! He is just using you all for his own purposes! He wants power and to be adored, just like the ones he says are bad out there in the world!" She paced and shouted, "There are many good people in the world. And there is a King who is higher than Zagan or any other king - that is King Jesus, the Christ! He's the only One who can truly give peace and life everlasting...." She caught a glimpse of them and stopped as she saw their blank stares.

"It's no use talking to you. You have no hearts, no souls.... I can see that. You might have physical hearts, but the heart that can understand God is not there...." She plopped down on the bench dejectedly.

A Shell came from across the room and up to the console that operated each gate. She opened one that contained sheep, and someone else led one out. As she stood there, she glanced at Zoe. Their eyes met for an instant before the Shell looked away. Zoe could see in her eyes that she was 'different.'

Zoe ran up to the bars, clutching them. "Miss! Miss!" she yelled to the Shell.

The Shell was not as tall as most of the others and was a bit plump, but she had beautiful, long brown hair and a flawless complexion. When Zoe called to her, the Shell looked back at her.

"What is it?" the Shell asked as she walked closer and studied Zoe. You must be from 'outside'. Most of us they bring in here don't attempt conversation." She walked over to Zoe, who was holding onto the square bars.

"I can see you are of short stature, like me," Zoe said gently, trying to find common ground.

"Well, not as short as you, but yes, I am inferior in that way," the Shell answered as she stood and studied Zoe.

"That doesn't mean you are inferior, just different," Zoe responded. Looking into her eyes, she could see a glimmer of heart in them. "Why were you not terminated if you are considered inferior?"

The Shell came closer to study Zoe. "I was the product of an outsider and a Shell, so they are watching me and the others like me to see what happens with this type of mix," she answered. She slowly walked back and forth, looking at Zoe, then asked. "You have a lot of feelings, don't you?"

"Well, yes. Yes, I do. Right now, I am angry, frustrated, and afraid if I must admit it." Zoe responded softly.

The Shell approached the bars and momentarily looked into Zoe's eyes. "I can see that. I often have many feelings inside of me that I cannot explain. Perhaps they are some of the ones you mentioned."

Zoe saw an opportunity! "If you let me out, I can explain what you feel inside, these feelings, these emotions."

The Shell frowned. "I can tell you are smart as well. A different kind of smart. You make your own decisions." She paused as she stood looking at Zoe. "We are told what to do, what to think, when and how to act – and that's okay with us. But…." She tilted her head as she came nearer to the bars, looking more intently at Zoe, "but …sometimes I don't think it's okay … but I don't know why."

She walked slowly back and forth in front of the bars, looking at Zoe and turning her head as if trying to comprehend something.

 "You see, if I let you out as you ask, it would be going against protocol and considered treason to the king. Then I would be terminated immediately by the device behind my ear."

"But, how would they know?" Zoe responded quickly, "You are here by yourself now since the others have left. And have you ever thought of taking the device out? Has anyone ever taken it out?" Zoe asked. When she asked that, she saw an astonished, questioning look on the gatekeeper's face, and all of the Shells in the enclosure looked at each other almost in horror—if they could feel that.

"Take it out?" the gatekeeper asked incredulously. "I don't think any of us would have ever thought to do that. It was a cherished gift to us when we graduated from school. A symbol of family and belonging. It contains the name that we chose and gives us identity. We were awarded it when we were educated enough to serve the king and the family. It was a great honor to receive it. Plus, it made all your nerve fibers feel so alive when it was attached." The Shell pulled over a chair and sat in front of Zoe and the square bars, almost like she was weak in her knees.

"But," Zoe said. "That's merely propaganda from the man who wants to control all of you. He wants to make all the rules that come out of his perverted version of what life should be like. He makes all this sound so…, so benevolent and noble, and like he cares about the environment and his 'family'! But he is an evil overlord working for the devil himself! The only thing he cares about is having power over you and the rest of the world!"

The Shell looked shocked at Zoe's words and looked at her with wide eyes. "Something stirs in me with your words."

"That's your real human part," Zoe said softly. "It's probably confusion and doubt at what you have been taught all your life. It is probably the part of you who wants to make your own decisions. It's probably the part of you who understands truth when you hear it," Zoe said gently as she sat on the floor in front of where the Shell sat on the chair on the other side of the bars. "Can you imagine being able to make your own decisions, to have your own feelings about things, to feel happiness and joy, to be able to sense the truth?"

The Shell silently looked around as if trying to make a decision. She put her hands on each side of her head. She kept blinking her eyes. Finally, she looked back at Zoe.

"Something inside me tells me to do what you say." The Shell said softly.

"Do you have a name?" Zoe asked gently.

"Yes, I chose Mary when I graduated." The Shell said quietly.

Zoe smiled at her. "I like that name," she said. "Mary, there is so much more than this. There is truth, there is peace, there is happiness, and there is the free will that God has given to us who are created by Him because He truly loves us. I found that out just recently. We can choose good or evil." She paused, "He *really* loves us; we are His children, but He doesn't just want robots who are programmed to worship Him as Zagan wants; he wants it to be our decision."

"But we are taught that there is no real god; all we need is a king to care for us. We were taught that there are thousands of gods in the world and that you outsiders use them to find ways to try to make yourselves feel better about yourselves and all the bad things you do to each other and the planet. We were taught that Zagan, in his benevolence, takes away the trouble of us making our own decisions, which won't be right most of the time, and programs us to know what to think. We were taught we are going to heal the planet, stop killing and being mean to each other once those like you, and I guess like me, are eradicated, and that it will be one big family across the whole earth where we will live in peace forever."

Zoe stood and came within inches of the bars and looked more closely into Mary's eyes. "Those are lies, Mary. There is some truth that we make wrong decisions sometimes and that there is inhumanity in the world. Still, God, the only real god, gave us our own free will so that once we realize our bad ways and how we can't make ourselves better, we can *choose* to give our hearts to Him, and He will guide us and help us and love us – for our good not just His. Yes, we may still make bad decisions, but He forgives us if we truly ask with sorrow, and then we can do better. We are not manipulated or made to worship Him. It is our decision, and the feelings inside you get when you turn to Him are, well, indescribable – kind of like falling in love. How do you describe that? But you don't know what that feels like either, do you?"

Zoe watched Mary, who was turning her head to try to understand, as a puppy would. "But you *could* know what that feels like, Mary. It's wonderful."

"But why would this God want to let the earth be ruined or let you outsiders kill and maim and hurt others – even be cruel to animals?"

"I can't really answer that, Mary, other than there is evil at work; there is an enemy of God called Satan. He will use humans to do bad things. The humans who are not in love with God, that is." Zoe responded gently. "I'm kind of new to this myself, but I know, that I know, that I know, that I have been changed – inside - by simply having faith in God's sacrifice for my sins. The One who paid the penalty for my sins is His only Son, Jesus. A filling of God's Holy Spirit is something amazing. And, once you truly receive salvation, no one can ever change your mind about the reality of God."

"His Son, Jesus?" Mary asked.

"Mary, this is a whole conversation we would need to have, but in the meantime, just believe this: Jesus is God, then became a man, then died, but came back to life and is living today and intercedes for those of us who turn to Him," Zoe said. "But right now, I have to get out of here, help my friends, and complete an assignment God has given us. Will you help me? Are you willing to experience real feelings of your own and truly live a life of your own?"

Mary looked deeply into Zoe's eyes for a few minutes. She rose slowly.

Zoe held her breath, not knowing what Mary would decide.

Then Mary walked away.

Zoe's heart sank.

But Mary silently walked to the console, looked at Zoe one more time, stopped briefly with her fingers above the keyboard, punched some things in, and opened the door to the enclosure.

Zoe jumped back so as not to get stuck as the bars moved.

"Come on, guys! You're free!" she shouted to the others. None of them moved but just stoically sat where they were.

"No, thank you. We are here for the family," one of the women said to her.

Zoe looked at them incredulously and felt sad, but ran out and ran to Mary. Mary, you need to remove the jewelry now!"

Mary looked at her, slowly reached behind her right ear, and haltingly and painfully tugged at the small, brightly decorated metal thing embedded in her skin. When it finally came out, she held it in her hand and looked at Zoe, and then it looked like she was going to pass out. Her eyes rolled back in her head. She became very pale and began to faint. Zoe grabbed onto her and pulled the chair over. Mary weakly sat for a minute, her head down and her arms dangling, a trickle of blood running down her neck.

Oh no! Zoe thought - I killed her! "Mary…. Mary…" she said frantically as she squatted next to the chair. "Can you hear me? Are you okay? Mary, Mary…...?" Zoe quickly prayed for her in her head.

Within a few minutes, Mary began to sit more upright. Zoe dabbed at the trickle of blood from behind her ear with some towel she found by the console. The bleeding stopped.

Mary's eyes fluttered, and she raised her head slowly to look at Zoe. "I…., I…feel very weak, like I have broken something inside." She said faintly.

"You have, my new friend, but it's a good thing." Zoe smiled at her. "Can you stand?"

"I don't know." And she tried standing only to wobble. Zoe caught her. Mary tried standing again and held on to the side of the console. Zoe held her up the best she could. Eventually, Mary stood a little straighter.

"I feel little pops inside, like random electric shocks here and there," Mary said.

"That's a good thing, I think," Zoe said as she held onto her new friend. "Zagan's power is being short-circuited throughout your body and brain. I don't know how long it will take to get it completely out of you, and I know you are weak, but we need to find the central computer hub and find my friend, who they took away somewhere else. Do you know where the Hub is or where they might have taken my friend?"

"Was your friend healthy-looking and smart?" Mary asked.

"Yes, I guess so. Why?"

"Well, they probably took him to the Hospital where they extract stem cells to make more clones – like me," Mary said.

That frightened Zoe – a lot.

212

"We need to find both the Hub and my friend. Quickly! Can you make it?" Zoe looked at Mary, who looked weak and confused.

Yes, I think so." Mary said. "I will take you."

She started to walk but had to hang on to Zoe and other things as she moved. She seemed to get stronger with each step, though still weak. "It's back in the main castle."

"We will need to look like we are taking food to the castle," Mary said as she picked up a tray and handed Zoe a dome-covered platter. They moved slowly through the kitchen past other Shells, trying not to look at them. Except Zoe stole a glance out of the corner of her eyes to make sure they weren't noticed.

Since Zoe was still in their 'uniform,' they didn't attract much attention. But Zoe kept her head down since Zagan had 'introduced' them to everyone at the dinner. She didn't want to be recognized.

Mary guided them to the castle's side door, where there were no guards.

CHAPTER 28

DISK - STOP ZAGAN

They walked quickly across the castle kitchen with no one paying much attention to them, entered the main foyer behind the castle's platform, and made their way to the elevator area. Too many Shells were trying to get on and off the elevator, so Mary motioned for Zoe to follow her.

"Come this way," Mary whispered. We can take the stairs to one of the other floors. She led the way to the stairway behind the elevators.

They quickly started climbing stairs, 1st floor, 2nd floor, 3rd floor - Mary was getting out of breath; she was still very weak and experiencing internal electric-like shocks.

"Can we sit for just a minute?" Mary asked as she struggled to hold on to the railing.

"Yes, but just for a minute," Zoe said as she helped her sit on the stairway.

Mary looked up at her. "Do you have a name?" she asked.

"Yes, my name is Zoe," Zoe she answered.

Just then, they heard first, then saw, a guard coming down the stairway! Mary stood quickly and backed up against the rail.

Zoe grabbed her arm, "Hurry! We need to go back down!" Zoe tried to pull Mary back down the stairs, but Mary stumbled. They were near a doorway. Zoe opened the door only to see a bunch of Shells and guards milling around. They saw her. She quickly slammed the door shut. There was a broom leaning against the landing wall. Zoe quickly grabbed it, stuck it into the long door handle from inside, and lodged it into the door frame to prevent them from quickly opening it. Zoe knew they had no way to overcome the nine-foot guard with the head of a lion who was closing in on them. She prayed – out loud this time, "Lord God! We need your help here!" and she pushed Mary behind her against the wall and stood with closed eyes, ready to accept the assault she would soon feel. She could feel Mary shaking.

She could feel a swish of air out of nowhere as something rushed past her from the stairs below, heading toward the guard above them. She quickly opened her eyes – it was Sparkles! The big cat sprang at the guard who had reached the landing just steps above them. There was a fierce fight with bared fangs, loud growls, and claws flashing everywhere. It was like watching a lion and a panther fight to the death, which it was.

Just then, someone touched Zoe's arm from behind and made her jump. It was Bridgett!

"Oh, my goodness, Bridgett! I've never been so happy to see you!" Zoe said as she saw who it was.

"I got here as quickly as I could! I saw you two walking back into the castle and followed you!" said Bridgett loudly, trying to be heard amid the growls and fighting above them. She held a weapon of some sort. "I found this lying on a table near the entrance as I snuck in." Bridgett pointed the weapon, with shaking hands, at the two fighting above them. "I'm... I'm afraid I am going to hit Sparkles," she said with a quiver in her voice.

Zoe straightened, pushing Mary against the wall to steady her. She took the weapon from Bridgett's shaking hands, walked forward a couple of steps, and pointed the weapon. "I've been to the firing range many times with Charlie in preparation for my police academy training. I don't know what this weapon is, but ... stand back!"

Bridgett and Mary backed up a few paces and held onto each other. Zoe moved forward a few more steps, steadied herself, and pulled the trigger. The weapon threw her back, almost falling backward down the stairway behind her, but she grabbed the railing, the two reaching forward to steady her. The smoke from the weapon didn't allow them to see what had happened right away, then it cleared.

Both Sparkles and the guard had stopped fighting. The big cat lay on top of the lion guard. Neither of them moved. They both looked like they were dead.

"Oh no!" Zoe shouted as she dropped the weapon and ran up the steps toward the two. "As she got to them," she saw Sparkle's paw, which was the size of her head, move slightly. "Oh, Sparkles! Are you all right?!" Zoe said with tears in her eyes. "Please don't die!" she said as she tried pulling him off the bloody guard. He was much too heavy for her to move. She put her head down on his bloody shoulder and cried into his matted fur.

Bridgett and Mary came to them as they could hear the guards banging on the door they had blocked off. They knew it would only be moments before they would be on the staircase.

Bridgett cried too. Mary just looked at the scene, at the two girls, and you could see a tear in her eyes as well. She wiped it away, looking at the tear in confusion. She had probably never cried before.

216

Bridgett shook her head like she was remembering and said, "Hey! I can draw some bandages and medicine." And she began to draw things that Zoe used to dab at the bloody gashes on Sparkle's shoulder and face.

"And I can pray," Zoe said. She prayed silently for the big cat who had saved their lives many times now as she dabbed at his wounds.

Bridgett drew quickly, and Zoe bandaged as best she could, as fast as she could, stopping the bleeding.

Zoe saw the large, bleeding hole in the chest of the fallen guard underneath Sparkles. She guessed her aim had been pretty good.

Then slowly, Sparkle's eyes opened a slit, then bigger, then he made a great effort to get up! All three girls did their best to help the big cat stand up on the stairway. The bleeding had stopped, and he stood over the lion-headed guard and growled loudly into the air above him!

"Oh, Sparkles! Thank you!" Zoe said.

"We're so glad you're okay!" Bridgett couldn't find a spot to pet him that didn't have deep knife gashes on it.

The door was now being banged on with something heavy and metal.

"We have to get out of here!" Bridgett said.

"We still have to get to the main control room and stop Zagan! And we have to find Alex!" Zoe said. "Can you still show us the way, Mary?"

"Yes, of course," Mary said as they stepped over the dead guard. Sparkles turned slowly, and you could see his pain as he followed them up the stairs. He gave a loud growl that reverberated loudly in the stairwell!

They were now up to the fifth floor. As they approached the landing, the door banged open in front of them! The girls gasped and hugged the wall as they stopped mid-stride on the stairs just below it. Two people rushed into the stairway! It was Henry, Alex and the little girl!! The Protector was behind them but could only bend his head into the stairway to look in as his shoulders were too big for the doorway!

The Protector said in his booming voice, "I will meet you in the Command Center." And he was gone.

"Henry!" Bridgett shouted and rushed into his arms! They held onto each other for a minute, then realized the others were watching and broke apart quickly. "You're all right!" she said to him. "And you found Alex!"

"It was with the help of my new little friend here. Her name is Ivana." Henry said as he smiled at the child.

Ivana beamed.

Mary, Zoe, Bridgett, and Sparkles climbed the few stairs to the doorway and followed Henry, Alex, and Ivana out into the hallway.

"Shut the door! Shut the door!" Zoe said as she rushed to shut the door behind them.

"Alex! It's so good to see you! Are you okay?" Zoe asked, seeing he, too, looked weak.

"Mostly," Alex grinned. Then he looked at Mary questioningly.

"Oh, this is Mary. She is helping us." Zoe said. "And hello, little one," she said, smiling at the little girl.

"Her name is Ivana!" Henry said to Zoe with a smile.

The little girl beamed again, smiling from ear to ear. "You are the one who ate the strawberry in the garden with me!" Ivana shouted in delight.

"Yes, little one – oh, I mean Ivana," Zoe said as she patted her on the head.

Alex looked at Mary, nodding to Zoe, like, 'Are you sure about her?'

"She's okay. I'll explain later." Zoe nodded her head. "She's taking us to the command center. We have to hurry!" Zoe saw a lock on the stairway door and locked it. Then she and Henry slid a heavy cabinet in front of the door.

Then Henry saw Sparkles, who had slid out of the stairway just before they locked it. He was licking his many wounds. Sparkles tried walking toward Henry but was limping on his front paw, and he could see his shoulder hurting him. The big cat had clawlike marks all over his body and a large gash on his shoulder that had started bleeding again.

"Sparkles! Oh my, what happened to you!" he rushed over to the panther and touched his injured shoulder as he knelt beside him.

"He saved our lives," offered Mary, speaking for the first time to the boys.

"Again," Zoe added.

"He will be okay, I think, but we need to go before they get through that door down there," Zoe said as she turned, urging Mary to lead them.

They went to the elevators down the hall and looked around. No one was around, but the elevator was already going up–possibly to their floor.

"We have to go to the 10th floor," Mary said. "That elevator looks like it's coming up already and may be coming to get us. Quickly. There is a utility elevator in the back. Come this way."

She led them down another hallway. The rooms looked like classrooms. There didn't seem to be anyone on this floor. They got to the utility elevator, and all got on except Sparkles, who bolted down a hallway.

Henry tried to call after him quietly, but Alex whispered, "Shush! Don't worry. Sparkles is more than capable of taking care of himself. He wouldn't have fit in here anyway." Henry reluctantly stepped back into the elevator as he saw Sparkles round a corner and disappear.

They tried to steady themselves as they rode the elevator silently, not knowing what awaited them on the 10th floor.

Alex broke the silence. "Lord God," he prayed aloud, "we need your help. Please go before us; give us the wisdom, strength, courage, and faith to do your will. I pray this in the name of Jesus."

Everyone but Mary and Ivana, who looked quizzically at him turning their heads, quietly said, "Amen."

The floors ticked off: 6, 7, 8, 9, 10. They held their breaths as the door opened to a long hallway leading to a bright, polished room with more electronic equipment than any of them had ever seen, even more than the room back at their dugout, and they could only see part of it. There were many Shells doing things at the various pieces of equipment.

Alex motioned them to be quiet by holding his finger to his lips and motioned them to back up and hug the wall. He inched his way to where he could better see the large room. There were perhaps 100 Shells doing things at consoles that all faced the throne in the front of the room. The throne was raised, and the back of it was very high and ornately decorated, but with modern scrollwork and precious gems – diamonds, rubies, emeralds. It was facing outward, looking out through the large, wrap-around windows out over the valley. Perhaps 10 Shells, five on each side, stood near the throne facing into the room. They had on the more brightly colored uniforms he had seen in the dining room. Their jobs must be to serve Zagon personally. From his standpoint, Alex could see that, in the distance below, many buses were driving out of the valley. At the back of the room, he could see 3D images being shown over some of the console tables, like the images Max had been able to bring up back at the compound. It seemed all the Shells in the castle were ready to board other buses coming into the valley.

He inched his way back to the others and stooped to whisper to them. "Okay, there are a lot of them," he said to them, then looked around and looked perplexed. 'Come on, Lord, I need a plan here," he said almost as if to himself as he thought for a moment.

Then he turned to Mary.

"Mary – hello, my name is Alex," he whispered. "Can you tell me anything about what they are doing?"

"No," she whispered back. "I've only been up here once when they questioned those of us who are mixed with outsiders' blood. I think each one of the big consoles in the back connects to the other locations in the world because they would shout questions at us as well, and sometimes we wouldn't understand their languages." Mary rubbed her forehead. "You will have to excuse me. I am not used to having conversations."

"It's okay. Take it slow. So, there are others like you?" Alex asked.

"Yes, she is mixed with one like us," Zoe whispered to him.

"Ah," he nodded.

"Yes, there are perhaps 200 of us in various stages of life," Mary answered.

"Is there any way you could find them and talk to them? Tell them what I told you. Get them to take the jewelry out?" Zoe asked. "We need their help."

Mary looked at Zoe for a moment. "I don't know if I can explain it very well. I don't fully understand it myself, but I can try."

Zoe put her hand on Mary's shoulder, closed her eyes, and whispered, asking God to go before Mary, give her the words, and help the others understand.

"Please take Ivana with you," Henry said, smiling at the little girl and nodding.

Mary nodded, actually smiled at them, stood from their crouching position, motioned Ivana to follow, and went back down the elevator.

Ivana looked at Henry, not wanting to leave him, but followed Mary at his insistence. "It's okay," he mouthed at her.

The others crouched with their backs against the wall.

"Got a plan, Alex?" Zoe whispered. "Time is running out here."

"I know, I know," he answered. He thought for a minute." Okay, Zoe, you and I are the only ones with the uniforms on, so we have to get in there and figure out which one of these pieces of equipment is the central unit that controls the Shells. If we can short-circuit it or break it or something, maybe all the Shells will not know what to do?"

"And, then what?" Zoe asked.

"I don't know, but it will come to me," Alex answered. He looked at Zoe, who had raised her eyebrows at him. "Yeah, yeah, but that's the best I got right now."

Henry asked, "What are we to do?"

Alex thought for a moment. "It looks like this corridor goes to the room's other side. Those big pillars are spaced every ten feet, so you should be ok if you can hide behind them and move when no one is looking. See if you can spot the central console; if you do, point us towards it.

 Zoe turned to Bridgett, "You didn't happen to bring that weapon you had, did you?

"No," Bridgett answered. I dropped it when we ran up to Sparkles. Want me to draw another one?"

Zoe nodded, "That's okay. We have a better weapon—God." Henry and Bridgett nodded.

They all moved quietly forward. Alex and Zoe nodded toward each other, took a deep breath, stood up, and moved into the large, open room.

They separated, Alex, nodding to Zoe to look around the other side. Zoe picked up a notebook from a table as she passed, making it look like she was checking screens for something. Alex kept his head down, trying to look inconspicuous, moving toward the center of the room. He could see nothing that looked more important than any of the other consoles or screens. He glanced at Zoe, who gave a slight shrug. She kept moving slowly amongst the different stations, pausing to pretend to write in the notebook. He looked to the back of the room and could see Henry in the shadows, slightly shaking his head and raising his arms.

Just then, the throne swiveled around to face the inside of the room. Zagan sat on it and glared directly at Alex as he turned.

"So, we meet again." Zagan rose and climbed down the throne steps to where Alex was standing. "You and your friend over there," he motioned to Zoe, who froze, "have caused me to lose a guard. I just got notified of the problem on the stairway." He paused. "And you," he strode to Zoe, "have caused some confusion in some of my children. This will cause me to lose some time, and some workers who could have proven good research will now have to be terminated."

He walked menacingly around Alex as he stood still. "And you have disrupted the Hospital Zone immensely. Unfortunate. You could have produced some interesting clones." Then he told some of the Shells to bring Zoe nearer since she was still at the back of the room. They roughly pushed her forward to stand next to Alex.

"Do you not understand the best security known to man is in place here? But I should have remembered how cunning and deceitful you humans can be and put more guards on you two." He laughed. "And do you think the two in the hallway are hidden from me?"

He motioned to have them brought to where Alex and Zoe were standing as well.

The four stood there. You could almost hear their hearts pounding. Zagan walked menacingly and slowly in front of the four, inches away from their faces.

Alex said so the others could hear, "Have faith." He could see Bridgett shaking a bit and Zoe's fists clenched. Henry stopped slumping then and stood more upright with a determined look.

Zagan continued, "Ah, yes. Faith. And see where that faith has gotten you?" He laughed again. "Well, you picked the perfect day for your irritating games. You will get to see the worldwide annihilation begin of those who refuse to be mine. People like you. It won't take long. I've been sending my children out into the world for over a year now. They have been placed in schools, churches, office buildings, grocery stores, the government.... everywhere in the world." He got an evil look in his eyes as he walked in front of them. "By the press of this button," he moved to his throne and opened a hidden panel on the arm to display a ruby button, "My children will ask the question of any humans they have encountered – 'will you bow to King Zagon and receive his mark?' If they say 'no,' which most humans will, because they don't want to be part of anything they didn't create or that they don't understand, they will be terminated on the spot!" He raised his hands to the sky. "Then I will be King and ruler of the entire world!" he said excitedly.

"What about your 'partners'?" Zoe asked.

Zagan's mood broke as he heard Zoe's question. "They were a convenience I needed in the beginning. We didn't see eye-to-eye on many points. I didn't want to subject the world to disagreements or power struggles again, so they were.... well, let's say, they are no more of a problem to me."

"So, you killed them, just like you are going to kill the human race to replace it with your clones who will worship you blindly! You are an evil man....' Carl'!" Zoe said through clenched teeth.

Zagan whipped around and slapped Zoe on the face. "Don't call me that! I am Zagan now!"

Alex and Henry made a move to go after Zagan but were restrained by the Shells around them.

"Bind them!" Zagan yelled at the Shells.

The Shells in brightly colored clothing motioned into the air, and a rope that looked like it was made from electricity came from nowhere. It wrapped itself around the four of them and pulled them together.

"Now, if you will excuse me," Zagan said as he started walking toward a special-looking elevator with jewels on the walls all around it. "I will be getting onto my jet now to go to my new home in … Paris; yes, I think I will start there. I will be able to watch it all happen from the technology set up there and at other chosen points worldwide. Then I can take journeys anywhere I choose to see my new earth and welcome my children," he said as he strode to the elevator, then turned back to them. "Oh, by the way, this building will be destroyed by these children when I leave. They know it is the best for the family and don't mind that they will be destroyed with it - along with you, of course." He laughed an evil laugh.

He got on the elevator with his entourage, and the elevator door closed. You could hear his evil laugh as it went down.

The Shells went about their duties, ignoring the four tied together in the middle of the room. They could not shake the glowing rope. It seemed to float and move as they struggled against it.

Bridgett tried talking to one of the Shells. "Can't you see this is a lie?! You don't want to die, do you?" The Shell didn't even acknowledge her.

"It's no use talking to any of them," Zoe said. "None of them have heart, I can tell."

Bridgett motioned to Alex and Zoe. Bridgett had quickly drawn a pistol while she and Henry were in the back hallway, one for her and one for Henry. Henry could, only slightly, move it from his pocket to his hand and point it. Bridgett's was kept pointing down by the rope. One of the Shells started walking toward the throne, looked out to see if Zagan had left the building yet, and then began to move to where the button was. They assumed he was about to push it to start the takeover of humanity, and Henry yelled, "Stop. I have a gun, and I will shoot you!" The Shell didn't stop or even slow down, so Henry shot him. There wasn't much blood, so they supposed him to be unconscious. One of the Shells near Henry took the gun out of Henry's tied-up hand. Another Shell pulled the unconscious one they had shot out of the way, and then he moved toward the button.

Suddenly, all the Shells froze in whatever they were doing, mid-air as if in a movie.

"What in the world…?" Zoe said.

Zagan's elevator door opened, and a drone flew into the room.

Then, like out of nowhere, the Protector stood before them. Holding a glowing sword. He raised his massive hands and cut the electrified, glowing rope around the four.

"Oh, thank you!" Henry said. Then, as an aside, "Hey, what took you so long?"

The Protector didn't reply; he just took a few steps back from them and seemed to be waiting.

"Hey guys! Guys! It's me!" a voice from the drone said as it wobbled in front of them.

"Max?" Alex asked questioningly.

"Yes, Max!" the voice called out from the drone. "You don't have much time. I've intercepted the program that controls the Shells, but they will only be frozen for a few minutes. You have to disconnect the 'start' button, as we will call it. The one on the throne."

"How.... You were not functional the last time we saw you, Max," Henry said.

"I know, I know, but when you wake up alone and then pull up the screens and see what's happening to your friends, it sobers you up really quick!" Max said through the drone microphone.

"And where did you get this flying thing?" Henry asked.

"I found it in one of the cabinets here before but didn't think we would need it for anything. And, by the way, getting a drone up ten flights of stairs wasn't easy! Luckily, I saw Zagan exit, and I flew this into his private elevator before the doors closed. The drone was able to push the only button to this floor," Max replied through the drone.

"Okay, okay - so what do we do?" Alex said as he moved toward the throne and button.

The drone flew and hovered over the throne.

"There is a panel on the side of the throne you will need to open, but do it gently because from what I can see from these drawings I found, it can trigger an explosion to set off the others that were intended to destroy the building."

"Okay, Max, walk me through this," Alex said.

"No, it has to be me," said Bridgett. "My fingers are longer and more agile. You hold footballs; I hold pencils."

"Ok," Alex said hesitatingly as he backed away from the chair.

One of the Shells near them groaned a bit as he stood a few feet away, frozen in a walking position. They all looked at each other.

Bridgett hunkered down next to the step up to the throne.

"The big blue stone on the side is the key to the secret door," Max said. "Hey, you have to move a bit so I can see on this camera. Okay. Press the blue stone, no! Not that one, the bigger one on the side. Yes, yes."

Bridgett pressed the stone, and the panel door opened to reveal just a few wires and gadgets.

"This doesn't look too complicated," Bridgett said. Is it this one or the other one I have to take out?"

"Don't touch those!" Max shouted. "They are a decoy! The real panel is behind this one. See that small screw; you will have to remove it."

"We didn't exactly come with tools, Max!" Alex said.

"Silly boy!" Bridgett said and drew a small screwdriver that became real in her hands. She smiled at Alex.

"That will never stop amazing me," Alex said.

"Take it easy when you pull the panel away. According to this schematic, there are a lot of wires behind it," Max said through the drone. Then, as if to himself, he said, "I wonder how this schematic got up here anyway. Well, in any case, do it–slowly."

Bridgett slowly removed the screw and gently pulled the panel away. They noticed another Shell near the throne start to move his finger. They all looked at each other.

"Now, remove the pink wire from the terminal it is plugged into," Max instructed.

"Max, none of these are colored…" Bridgett said as she stared into the panel.

"Oh…. well, ok. Uh. Ok, ok. This picture looks like it is the …. Let me count…. fifth wire to the right of some round kind of dial. Yes, the fifth to the right and then…. hang on a minute – this has to be right…. then the 12th one down from the top. As long as it is not the one touching the dial."

"Huh?" she said. She looked at the others and looked scared. They could see her hand start to shake.

The others looked at each other.

Henry said quietly, "I have the architect gift – you know, in case something happens while doing this, so why don't you let me take over from here? I can figure it out by what he says." He turned to The Protector, who was standing on the other side of the platform, "Unless you want to do this?"

The Protector didn't answer or move.

"I didn't think so," Henry said.

Bridgett slowly backed away, and Henry moved forward, looking nervously at her and then at the others. He took the small screwdriver out of her shaking hand. You could see sweat appear on his forehead.

"You can do this, Henry," Zoe said confidently. He nodded back at her.

"Draw me some tweezers, too, please," Henry asked of Bridgett. She did and handed them to him.

"Ok, Max, give me the count again," Henry said.

Max repeated them, "Fifth to the right from the dial, yes, that dial, no, don't count that one, it's not attached to the dial, yes, yes, that one… Okay, save your place. Now count down from there to the 12th one, which is in the same row. Move your hand a little so I can see what you are doing better. Yes, now you are 12 down. "

"Count this little wire too, Max?" Henry asked as he got to a smaller wire than the others.

"Um, let me see closer in there…" Max's voice said, and the drone moved closer. As he did, the propeller hit the side of the chair, and the drone flew off sideways into a table and then fell loudly to the floor. Max's voice was garbled, and you couldn't understand anything he was saying.

"Oh no!" Bridgett squealed.

She made Henry jump a bit.

"Don't do that!" Zoe said to Bridgett. "Okay, Henry, if you were the person who made this, would you put in a smaller wire just to confuse anyone trying to disconnect the device, or does it look like it fits the plan? Think," she said to him calmly.

Henry stopped where he was with the tweezers inside the panel. "I am going to use my head to figure this out. Creativity is the gift that has been given to me by God; I will use it to understand this puzzle as if I were building it myself."

Henry stopped and recounted out loud… "Fifth to right, 12 down. This is seven down, that little wire - wait, it looks like it might be connected to something behind this round dial …. It wouldn't make sense to me to use different size wires…. I will skip it and count the rest of the way down. 7, 8, 9, 10, 11 ……12. Max had said to pull the connector out." He placed the tweezers at the base of the 12th wire, closed his eyes for a moment, looked at the others, then…. pulled.

The wire came off the dial easily. Nothing happened. He, still hunched over the panel with the tweezers and wire in his hand, looked to his side at the others. No one moved. Nothing happened still.

Alex looked at the red jewel button on the chair's arm, and the light behind it had died.

"I think it's disconnected," he said.

"You mean we, did it?" Henry asked questioningly.

"No, Henry, you did it. With the help of the Lord," Zoe replied.

They heard movement behind them. The Shells were coming to and starting to move.

"Let's go!" Alex shouted. But as soon as they turned around, they saw the Shells standing, fully awake now but staring at them.

Alex quickly stood and moved to the front of the group, looking like he could take on the world. Zoe was to his right, and Henry and Bridgett were to his left. They looked around them, and The Protector was gone.

"Did you draw any more pistols, Bridgett?" Zoe asked.

"No, unfortunately not, and there are way too many of them anyway. I don't know how to draw weapons that fast that could take out all of these. I don't really want to kill anyone anyway, even if they aren't really human," Bridgett answered.

"Ok, friends, again - if David could kill Goliath with a stone, we will ask God to go before us and just watch what happens!" Alex said.

"Amen," said Zoe.

'Yes, amen," said Bridgett.

"And yes, we need also to get Zagan before he gets away. Lord! Help us, please! Amen," Henry said.

The Shells started to come toward them. As they did, the elevator and stairway doors opened, and Mary and the rest of them, who were half-human like her, came into the room behind them.

"Good job, Mary!" Zoe called out with relief in her voice.

Mary smiled at her. The smile looked good on her face.

Zagans Shells began moving forward toward them. As they came, those with Mary came at them from behind. They started picking up chairs and any objects they could find to help in the fight. Bridgett quickly drew some swords and handed them to Zoe and Henry.

The elevator doors opened again, and many more of Zagans Shells streamed into the room. They were severely outnumbered. Obviously, some of Zagans Shells had been taught how to kill as part of the takeover. Mary's Shells had not. They were severely outclassed in the ways of war.

Then, suddenly, when it seemed all was lost, all the Shells, even Mary's, stopped fighting. They stood and stared at the area behind where The Crew were clustered in front of the throne. Zagans Shells began backing up, staring at the windows. Mary's Shells just stood looking with open mouths. Zagans Guards rushed into the room and stopped short as they, too, looked out the window. They all backed out and left the floor through the stairways or the elevators. Soon, The Crew and Mary and her injured group were the only ones left in the room. Alex and the rest just looked at each other, wondering why the fighting had stopped.

Mary pointed to the window behind them. As The Crew turned, they saw Mrs. Griffin standing on the throne chair, with the Messenger and Protector beside her. Then, behind them, outside the window, they saw legions of angels hovering—some very fierce-looking—thousands of them!

"Wow," said Bridgett breathlessly as she stood in awe. "Is that what they call an Angel Army?"

Mary and her group approached the window to look at the Angels. "See what I mean? "She said to the others, "These outsiders understand things we have never heard of before… Angels."

She repeated the word. "What are they? They look wonderful," she said as she moved slowly closer to the window. Her people all stared and then began asking her questions. "Who are they? What is their purpose? Where did they come from? Are they clones, too? Are they for us or against us?"

Zoe could see that those who had come with Mary had removed their 'jewelry.' She smiled and tried to quickly answer their questions, "Yes, they are for us. No, they are not clones." But, saying there would be so much more to learn for them now.

CHAPTER 30

THE LAST CHALLENGE – DISK - FINISH IT!

"Mrs. Griffin!" Alex shouted as she came down the stairs from the throne. "Can I hug you!? I've never been so happy to see you in my life!" He stopped after he gave her a side hug. Somehow, she had gotten taller than him. He stepped back and looked up at her," You look so...so... 'fierce' now! And the armor is a good look!"

Mrs. Griffin chuckled. "You have always made me smile, Alex."

The Messenger came down to them as well. "You have stopped the immediate danger, but your task is not finished." He said to them. He, too, looked different, more like a wise sage or something. His long, blonde hair was now white, and it glistened in the sunlight from the windows. He had on white clothes and a long white tunic.

"What do you mean?" Zoe asked.

The Messenger sat down on a step of the throne. "Zagan is smart. He has a backup console on the plane. If he doesn't see this building blown up by the time he takes off, he will activate the plane's alternate takeover alert."

"Excuse me, sir," Henry sidled up toward the Messenger. And looking up at the Protector asked, "Sirs, do you have names?" The Protector was standing with arms folded at the top stair of the throne. "Our names are not important. Just remember God has sent us to guide and protect you.

"Okay, so, you are angels, I assume. And there are thousands of angels out there, so couldn't you all just take care of this? Do you really need us? We have nothing to give. We're just kids."

The Messenger answered, "Yes, of course we could." He continued to sit calmly on the step.

The five looked at each other quizzically.

"Ok, stupid question. Then - why don't you?" Alex asked.

Mrs. Griffin answered. "Because the task was given to you. God could always do things on His own or through some of us since He is the creator of everything and has all power and might. But He has always chosen to work through man, or in this case -you young people." She smiled at them. "The assignment is yours to complete."

Sparkles strolled in and sat next to The Protector, standing at the top of the throne. It looked like his injuries had been healed. Henry and the others smiled at the big cat.

"We told you we would be here to help you. You have asked God for guidance and help and to go before you all along. He has done that even though you could not see it at times," The Messenger said.

"Now, you must go." Mrs. Griffin said loudly. She turned to the large windows, waved her hand at the thick glass of one of them, and the glass disappeared. They could feel the breeze from the valley come in. A long, clear-looking stairway appeared down to the valley. "You don't have time to take the elevators and make your way through the castle." She turned to the big panther, "Asher, lead them down!" the cat sprang to the window and stood waiting at the top of the broad stairway.

"Asher! Well, that's a whole lot better name than 'Sparkles'!" Alex shouted with a grin on his face. "Come on! We need to hurry!"

Alex was the first to reach the stairs, which were actually very long and frightening. They led to the garden area next to the castle behind the trees. They wound back and forth, with slight landings at each turn. He turned to look at the others determinedly and followed Asher down the stairs.

Henry was the next to go. He grabbed Bridgett's hand, and they ran toward the stairs.

"Thank you...." Zoe said as she turned to The Messenger, The Protector, and Mrs. Griffin before she raced toward the stairs. When she got to the top, she stopped short. "Whoa!" she thought to herself. A clear stairway ten stories tall was a very frightening sight for someone afraid of heights, but she said a silent prayer for courage, took a deep breath, steeled herself, and followed the others down.

CHAPTER 31

RECLAIMED!

As they reached the bottom of the stairs, they could see a motorcycle and rider approaching very quickly from the other side of the valley. It kicked up a dust plume as it came. They steeled themselves for a fight from the rider, but when the dust cleared, they could see it was Max!

"Max!" They all shouted. Alex, Henry, and Zoe ran up to him to pat him on the back, and Zoe gave him a short hug.

"How…." Bridgett started, "I wasn't there to draw a motorcycle…"

Max took down the old t-shirt he had wrapped around his face, coughed from the dust, and answered breathlessly. "When the drone crashed, and I didn't see the building explode because you had chosen the wrong wire…." he rolled his eyes at them," I knew I had to get here as quickly as I could. Then I saw all the angels and knew this was it! I had found this bike in one of the back sections a while ago and tinkered with it when I needed a break from what was happening in the console room. Then, strangely enough," he winked at them, "today, I found a door in that same area I hadn't noticed before. It led to a path down the mountain to the valley!"

"Not strange at all. It was a 'God thing,'" Henry smiled.

"But we need to get to that plane before it takes off!" Alex said. "It looks like Zagan's jeep has stopped to talk to that group of Guards. The Guards are probably telling him we are not dead and about the Angels in the sky. They are facing the other way, so we can get to the hangar over there without being seen.

"I know you are the game plan guy," Henry said breathlessly, "but thinking creatively and looking at the valley, if we stage a distraction in front of the plane so that it cannot take off, it will give some of us the time to get to Zagan." Zagan's jeep was getting closer to the plane as they spoke. Other jeeps drove toward him, probably telling him about the angels, Mary's group, and how the start button was disconnected.

"What kind of distraction?" Alex said.

"Well, since Max has this motorcycle," Henry responded excitedly, "what if he just drives really fast, doing his best to avoid being killed, I might add, and drives in circles in front of the plane, kicking up lots of dust. That area is more desert-like, near the plane, and sandy, like my old country. That could give some of us time to get to Zagan somehow. Wouldn't that be better than all of us just rushing in and getting killed or captured? I've seen a maneuver like this in my old country when my father tried to delay a plane that could take some of us to freedom." Henry was excited by this plan.

"That actually sounds like a good plan, Henry," Alex patted him on the shoulder.

"OK, Bridgett, when you guys get to the hangar, draw some very loud weapons and quickly, please. Zoe, you are the sharpshooter. Do you think you can keep us from getting killed if we can get you to that hanger and behind some of that equipment?"

Zoe nodded yes.

"There is a large loader over there, Henry. Can you drive it and get me close to the plane so I can jump off and get onto it or at least prevent Zagan from getting on it?" Alex asked quickly.

"Uhm, I think so. I don't have much driving experience, but …. with the Lord's help…" Henry answered.

"This all has to be timed and coordinated for it to work, and of course, we need God to go before us…." He looked toward heaven and said, "Once again, Lord, your help, please?" Looking around at his friends and into each one of their eyes. "We have been brought together for such a time as this. Remember, we go forward with strength, courage, and faith!" They all knew this was their last chance. "Now, let's go!"

Max took off as fast as he could go. When he was seen, Shells near the plane sent gunfire at him. They would have no problem with killing him, he thought, if they could see him. He swerved back and forth and kicked up enough dust to create a cloud. Whatever weapons they were firing at him created enough smoke cover that the others could race toward the hanger, a football field away from where the buses were parked. There were no Shells or Guards anywhere to be seen now. They were probably all sent out or in the castle waiting to be blown up - as instructed.

Henry and Alex veered off toward the large loader. Bridgett and Zoe ran to the hangar and hid behind some of the equipment as Bridgett began drawing the same kinds of loud firearms that Henry had used to distract the Shells before. Zoe picked them up and began firing them at the Shells, who were shooting at the motorcycle. These that Bridgett drew were very loud and caused a lot of smoke as well. She had to make sure she didn't hit Max, which was getting more difficult because she couldn't see him that well through the heavy smoke and dust and because he kept swerving and going in circles. She thought of trying to blow up the plane but didn't know if Zagan had put in a safeguard that would activate the takeover if the aircraft was destroyed.

Henry climbed up on the large loader and turned the key. He had never really driven before. He let out a heavy breath between pursed lips and looked around at the controls on the dashboard. Alex climbed onto the back of the front bucket, which gave him some protection. The loader jerked and started. Some gears were heard grinding, but Henry was able to get the big, yellow piece of equipment moving. No one could see his hands shaking, but he continued - trusting.

Zoe could see the loader approaching the plane, and Zagan's jeep was now stopping at the end of the plane stairway. She asked Bridgett to draw a couple of rifles, which she used to send fire on the stairway to prevent anyone from going up. She didn't want to hit the gas tank on the plane, though, again fearing that might set off the termination signal. Her arm was getting tired from the heavy, tulip-shaped mortars she was firing, keeping the Guards at bay. Now, the rifles rebounding on her shoulder were making her sore, but she kept up.

They didn't see the Shells come up behind them in the hangar.

They were roughly grabbed from behind and, at gunpoint, restrained.

The Shells tied them up with the glowing ropes and then ran toward the loader.

"I hate these ropes!" Zoe yelled, struggling.

Alex yelled back to Henry, "We've lost fire cover, and I see Guards coming out of where the girls were. You need to drive faster!"

Henry yelled, "I will try!" and pushed the gas pedal to the floor. Alex started to bounce as the large equipment went over bumps, but he held on. Henry and Max were pelted with gunfire from behind as the Shells ran toward them.

Just as they neared the Jeep Zagan had gotten out of, Alex saw him starting to climb the stairs of the plane. Alex jumped off and ran to stop Zagan. He didn't get very far because Zagan's private Shells tackled him and held him. Henry tried to ram the stairway with the loader but got the bucket stuck under the side of a vehicle, and it wouldn't move.

The Shells ran from behind, grabbed him out of the loader seat, and pulled him down where they were restraining Alex.

They saw Zoe and Bridgett being dragged toward the plane by some Guards.

Then Max's motorcycle sputtered and stopped. He had run out of gas! The Shells ran to him, grabbed him, and dragged him to the same spot near the stairs where the others were.

Zagan stopped on the second step and turned and looked at them with fury in his eyes.

When the five were shoved together in one spot, with Shells all around, Zagan said, "Release them!" He seethed and walked down the steps toward them.

The ropes around the girls disappeared, and they were left rubbing their arms. Bridgett moved closer to Henry and put her hand in his. He looked at her, but neither had fear in their eyes.

"I am weary of the problems you have caused me!" Zagan yelled at them. "I have a world to take over! You cannot stop me! You are like flies buzzing around my head! Pesky, little irritants!" he pushed at Alex with his fist.

Then he got an evil look on his face. "I'll tell you what. I will allow you to live and become one of my family if you bow before me right now and accept me alone as your king." He stood looking at them with folded arms.

Alex looked at the others but boldly stood apart, "I bow before no one but my God."

"Nor will I," Max said, standing firmly beside Alex.

Henry and Bridgett looked at each other hand-in-hand and stepped forward, "Our King is Jesus Christ."

Zoe maintained her stance, "Neither will I bow to you, Zagan. Whatever may befall us, our God is Lord of all."

"Arghhhh!" Zagan lunged at Max's throat, but Max sidestepped in time. "You young fools! Kill them!" he shouted at the Shells. They raised their weapons towards The Crew.

Suddenly, the ground shook violently! The Shells and Guards wobbled and fell over. Zagan grabbed the railing of the stairs on the plane. The plane rattled and creaked. The Crew held onto each other, trying not to fall over.

The mountain on the other side of the runway shook violently, and peals of thunder and lightning strikes came from the top of it! A dense cloud came down and encompassed the mountain. All the Shells fell to the ground from the shaking. The five continued to clutch each other to keep from falling, but also staggered onto the ground next to each other.

Zagan tried to run up the plane's stairs, but the stairs creaked and broke loose, and the aircraft fell sideways. He ran backwards. Looking up, he tried backing away from the mountain.

Then, the loudest booming voice they had ever heard, which shook the ground even more, came from the cloud. "You have defiled my name and done evil in my eyes."

Zagan tried standing, but he kept looking up at the mountain and stumbling backward, now crawling as the earth trembled at the sound of the voice.

"I know who you are!?" Zagan shouted, his voice shaking with fear. "What do you want of me?!"

The voice said, "Demon, come out of him!"

Zagan screamed, shook violently, and fell face forward to the ground.

The voice said, "Rise and face me."

Now free from the demon within, Carl had a different look on his face as he rose to his knees.

"Carl," the voice boomed, still amid lightning, thunders, and smoke, "The demon you welcomed in is now gone. You know who I am, the God of the Universe. You need to repent of your evils. You need to understand who I am and who you are. There was another who wanted to be like me, and I cast him out of heaven. He has been the one leading you. I have given you the grace to believe even now. You will be forgiven if you chose Me over your own evil desires.".

On his knees behind the plane, Carl began weeping. Still looking up at the mountain. "You...you *are* real.... I sought you for years when I was young. Trying to find you in wisdom, learning, and all the world's religions, but you weren't there. I called on the underworld in my ignorance. Now I see my eyes were blinded by what I wanted - power and riches. I was doing what was right - in my own eyes." His face showed the sorrow he felt.

"But, Lord, I... I have done too many wrong things for your forgiveness." He wept more, his whole body shaking. "How could I ever be forgiven for what I've done...?"

"My Son, Jesus, has already paid the price for your sins. It is up to you now to believe, repent, and receive forgiveness or reject that gift. What will you choose, Carl?" The voice boomed.

Carl looked up at the quaking mountain and said in a quivering voice, "I ask your forgiveness, my Lord and my God," And he fell prostrate to the ground.

The voice said, "Get up, my son. You have been forgiven." Carl slowly rose to his knees, still sobbing, his whole body visibly shaking.

The ground stopped shaking.

They looked at each other and slowly walked toward Carl. Henry reached his hand out to help Carl get up. Carl looked at the five incredulously, wondering how they could be helping him after all he had said and done.

They looked around, and between them and the mountain stood Mrs. Griffin, The Protector, The Messenger, and Sparkles (alias Asher). They were all smiling, even the Protector, which was quite a sight.

The Shells, who had believed Mary, slowly gathered from the castle to behind the plane, looking up at the mountain.

Zagan's Shells didn't know what to do, especially after seeing their former king change and hearing the voice from the mountain.

"I allowed you enough worldly wisdom to create flesh and bone, but in my compassion, I will now give them what man could never create – a soul." Said the booming voice that shook the ground even more, and there was a barrage of lightning and thunder.

Then, suddenly, all of the Shells, even Zagan's – or Carl's, clutched at themselves and stood up with a look of shock and enlightenment on their faces. They looked really alive for the first time, looking around at each other in wonderment. The jewelry behind their ears fell off.

The voice went on, "They will now have the free will to choose their destiny."

The Messenger moved forward, "Alex, you will explain the good news to these now."

"Me?" Alex asked, looking rather shocked and kind of scared. "But, how? They are all over the world, and what can I say…. I'm just a kid…"

"With Me, all things are possible," the voice said from the mountain. Then the cloud lifted, and the lightning and rumblings stopped.

Mrs. Griffin moved closer. "Again, you make me smile," she said to Alex. "Max, you will go back and get into their system in the castle after you disengage the termination switch on the plane. You will then program the system to allow Alex to give the good news to all former Shells worldwide through it. God has already changed them. The metal objects will disengage and fall off, and they will be like all others, free to think for themselves and choose their own destiny. God has made it so the rest of the population will not remember or notice any of this happening around them, and the Shells will not remember any of this former way of life but, unlike the rest of the world's population, will be allowed to hear the Good News all at once."

"Wow, that's possible?" Bridgett asked but then smiled to herself. "Why would I even say that after everything? Of course, it is!" She laughed.

"I feel so unworthy to give such an important message to so many," Alex said as he looked at Mrs. Griffin. "Shouldn't one of you do it?" he asked. "Perhaps he could do it?" He said, looking toward The Messenger.

Mrs. Griffin smiled at him, "Remember the scripture, '...*do not worry beforehand about what to say. Just say whatever is given you at the time, for it is not you speaking, but the Holy Spirit.*"

Alex nodded solemnly.

Asher came up and rubbed his big head against Henry and purred. Henry didn't need to stoop to rub his head and began stroking the big cat. Bridgett joined him, giving Sparkles a big hug around his neck.

Mary came forward hesitatingly, "We want to learn more. We desire this relationship you have with the God we just witnessed. We need to know all about Him." The others behind her looked at Zoe beseechingly.

"I'm kind of new at this...and Alex will be explaining it..." Zoe responded.

The Messenger came to Zoe, "You have that little bible Mrs. Griffin gave you?"

Zoe searched in the uniform pocket and pulled it out.

"I do!" she exclaimed.

"I will help you in explaining the basics," The Messenger said, "and then they will be able to decide what to do with that information.

These are special ones. They will learn more as time goes by. It is sometimes a lifelong process to obtain fullness with Him,"

The Messenger walked over and sat on a rock in a grassy area near the runway under shady trees. He motioned them all to follow.

Mary's Shells eagerly followed and sat in the grass or knelt near him, eager to hear the words he and Zoe would say.

Zoe looked hesitant as she walked with them. Sitting near The Messenger on another rock, she looked at him and opened the little Bible to the only passage she knew by heart so far, *"For God so loved the world that He gave His only begotten Son, that whosoever believes in Him might have life everlasting...."* She looked up to see them all, listening raptly. She could feel the searching in their hearts.

Bridgett and Henry watched Max and Alex go back to the castle with Mrs. Griffin. They saw The Messenger sitting in the grass next to Zoe, speaking to Mary and her Shells, who were all listening intently. They looked over and saw The Protector kneeling on one knee next to Carl, with his hand on Carl's shoulder as he wept and wept.

It had been quite a journey.

CHAPTER 32

DISK – ASSIGNMENT
FINISHED – WELL DONE

The Crew were all sitting around Zoe's brightly painted kitchen table. It was a time of reflection, talk, and laughter at some of the things they had experienced. They also recounted some of the frightening and dangerous trials. They had become the closest of friends and had seen the Hand of God at work many times through their journey. They had changed as individuals and found God, becoming new, each in their own unique ways. They had found strengths within themselves they didn't know existed. They knew that none of it was of themselves and were grateful to the Lord…. for all of it.

The conversation died down, and they sat pensively, each within their own wondering.

"So, what do we do now?" Max asked quietly.

Zoe sighed. "Well, I guess we go on and live our lives as normally as possible after all we have seen and been through. Do the things we had chosen to do, but now with the knowledge and Spirit of God within us, learning more about Him every day," she said.

Henry looked at each one and added, "I will never forget how you all helped me grow and change and understand your...I mean our...God. I would miss you greatly if we should not be friends any longer." And then he looked specifically at Bridgett and smiled gently. She returned his smile, staring into his eyes.

"I hope, no, **I know,** we will still see each other," Bridgett said to Henry, then smiled and looked around the room at the others. "All of us must stay friends. I know we will see each other at school, but even more than that, we need to get together often. We've been through too much together to not see each other outside of school."

They all nodded in agreement.

She went on, smiling, "It shouldn't be a surprise to you guys, but I've decided to be an art teacher after High School, so I will be changing my classes. My parents have conceded to my desire to leave the modeling field. Thank God! Of course, I can't really explain to them fully why I want to continue in art; drawing things that really materialize would blow their minds!" She laughed. They all laughed with her. "I've been afraid to see if that gift still works since we've been back. Perhaps I will in the future."

Zoe said, "Well, I'm still going to the Police Academy when I graduate, but I have a different attitude and purpose now. I think before, I just wanted to be tough and get the bad guys! Now, I truly want to help those who need help."

Alex snickered, "And guess what I am going to do?"

"What?" They all asked, looking at each other quizzically.

"I am going to join the military and become a Chaplain!" Alex laughed.

"That's perfect!" Zoe said.

"Great!" Shouted Max and punched Alex gently in the arm.

Bridgett and Henry smiled broadly at him in agreement.

"My parents were mortified when I told them, but said, 'If that's what you want to do with your life dear...'." Alex smiled.

"I think I will still go into Videography," Henry said. "Perhaps I can create documentaries or films that will speak to people's hearts. Zoe has found a couple of places I will apply to for apprenticeships as well." He nodded appreciatively toward Zoe, who returned the look with a warm smile.

Bridgett nodded approvingly at him.

"I'm gonna stick with the technology stuff," Max said as he stood and moved behind his chair and rested his hands on the brightly colored wooden back. "As we have seen, it can be used for good or bad. Maybe I can help in some way, with the Lord's help, to keep things on the good side." He moved behind Alex and put his hand on his shoulder. "Plus, Alex's parents are letting me move into the apartment over their garage in exchange for doing yard work and other odd jobs around their house. They said they could use the help since Mrs. Griffin is no longer there. They are even letting me use an old vehicle they have so I can pick up things for them if they need me to. That is, as soon as I get my driver's license." He smiled warmly at Alex. "I'm so grateful, Alex, for every-thing you've done for me." He looked at Zoe, "You too, Zoe."

Zoe smiled back and nodded at him.

Alex smiled up at him, "No problem, buddy. I'm happy to see you come into your own."

Sparkles – who was back to being a cat, jumped through the win-dow over Zoe's sink and then down onto her sofa. Seeing this little, sleek, black animal look so 'normal,' who they knew to be such a fierce defender, was amazing.

Henry got up, went to Sparkle's side on the couch, and petted him. "What will happen to my friend, Sparkles, here? Can we still call him that?" Henry asked, looking at Alex as he stroked the purring cat.

"Yes, we can still call him Sparkles," Alex said with a laugh.

"Oh, he will have a home here, with me for as long as he wants," Zoe said, smiling at the cat.

They all fell uncomfortably silent again.

"I am really going to miss having adventures with you all," Max said sheepishly. "You are the only real family I have ever known."

Zoe got up and hugged his arm.

"We will still see each other, my friend," she said. "Hey, why don't we get together for bible studies until we have to go our separate ways." She looked down at Alex, who was still sitting. "That would give you some practice, eh?" She smiled at him. With her shortness and him being a bigger guy, they were almost at eye level even though he was sitting and she was standing.

They all agreed.

"And who knows," Alex said with a wink, "we might be given another assignment one day."

They all smiled warmly and laughed, again recounting some of their adventures and remembering their fantastic experiences.

Sparkles lay with one eye open and one closed. It almost looked as if he was smiling.

THE END?